Death's Life

By

B. Latif

For Mothers

Table of Contents

Death's Life

"Humans know a small fact; they are going to die.
But I know a bigger one; it's something they always forget."

Chapter 1

"I was never born but I still exist,

A parlous being swirling in a black mist,

I am where all hopes end,

Before me strutting beings bend,

Here a masquerade on my eyes, Guess

the mundane, who am I?

Beautiful creatures call me 'alone being,'

Well, here's a fact; all souls reside with me.

Disguised as a weapon for a perfidious doll,

Warm as hell for a pious heart.

The nightmare that haunts your dreams,

You might be oblivious, but that's me,

I rule all hearts, a common fear,

And you, just a lamenting tear, Angelic

love for a virtue.

White funeral for a sin.

Excruciation, paroxysm, ecstasy, and pain,

I mock you, your life's in vain.

Sanguinary – you might call,
In my kingdom, everyone shall fall.

Lo and behold, hold your breath,

For this is my realm and I am Death."

I might sound patronizing, and to some, I presume, conceited, but I won't refrain from telling you that I know everything.

I've scared you.

Just for a moment though.

And let me tell you another thing, you've scared me as well. Yes, you.

Who is *you*? You might be wondering. What is the creature, the *thing* Death is afraid of?

Humans.

Yes, humans scare me, but I won't divulge it right now. You'll learn that for yourself.

Let me reintroduce myself, in just one word.

Death.

I wish I could give myself a name. but what would I possibly call myself? And what do *you* possibly call me, huh?

Pain. The end. Destiny. Killer. Cruel. Unpredictable. Fact?

And Lord… you know, it's an amusing little coincidence that I also call you by these names.

You are pain to nature.

You are the end of sanctity.

You are the world's destiny. You

are killers.

You are cruel, barbaric covets.
    You are infinitely unpredictable.

So, I wonder what is the difference between you and me? Even if I asked myself that question a thousand times, and don't get an answer—you might think that's out of order—I have had the question in my mind since life was given to man.

Let's not uncover the clandestine beginning of life just now.

Life.

What a controversy for humans. They call me Death when I am more alive than they are.

I lived to see the first murder on Earth, when Cain killed Abel. I lived to see blood turning against blood, when Joseph's brothers threw him in a well. I lived to see the enigmatic, dark magic of the Pharaohs. I lived to see clouds flooding the world and Noah's Ark with the only survivors in it. I lived to see Jesus being taken alive to the Lord God. I lived to see Abraham ready to sacrifice Isaac. I lived to see Muhammad.

I lived to see revolution.

I lived to see you.

I *live*. And humans *die*.

Does any human know the secret of nature, or the world that I know? The inscrutable times?

I do!

So, why is that you call *me* death and *yourself* life? I just needed to clarify the misconstrued candor in humans' minds that I *don't* exist I do.

Keeping all the beleaguering words aside, I want to tell my story. I just want to tell humans that I know the facts about them that they have forgotten.

And this is what scares me the most.

Observation No. 1

"Humans know they are humans. Humans don't know they have humanity. Something that I would call dead in them."

I must register a complaint as well. Why do humans think I'm a villain? I'm not meant to play that part.

It was meant to be played by Satan, and as I said before, one of the billion facts that scare me is that this part is also being played by humans.

To take souls is a duty bestowed upon me by the Lord, and for this purpose I travel the world with such speed that no one could imagine, faster than the twinkle of your eye.

I'm not bound by time, but man is its prisoner.

There's no time limit for me, however, I can't go into the future or back to what has passed but having traveled the world, I've observed people.

And they bring to me the first human trait, which is *curiosity.*

I'm not reluctant to inform you that I'm curious.

Since the beginning of time, why have I been portrayed as a heinous figure? Incarnated in black robes with a scythe in my bony fingers, two hollow sockets for eyes, bald, a rictus smile, honed nails, in short, a skeleton.

But I tell you what, human.

The skeleton is a part of you humans—not me! When I saw the sketch of Death for the first time in 2000 BC, it made me laugh.

You know why?

Because it's exactly what I think humans are. Again,

what a wonderful coincidence.

Humanity skinned from their bones, their eyes hollow to observe nature, their heads naked from dignity, their nails honed because of resentment and greed that murky, somber gown of helplessness on them with an axe of jealously to kill everyone.
Pity. Pity. Pity.

I wonder, if I were a human would I be like that? Would I also forget I was a human and my purpose on earth? Would I also forge the Lord?

That has made me wonder for ages, since times I can't even remember... and there's a second feeling beside curiosity—*a desire.*

Just to experience what's it like to be human, even once. I've seen flowers. They are buds and then they bloom into ruddy petals, looking beautiful.

I don't know when that desire turned into a bud and then a flower blossomed. It just seemed to attract me.

But of course, it is impossible. Do

you believe in miracles?

I do. Because I saw Moses' rope turning into a giant snake. You'll also believe only if you are able to watch a small flower blooming or a seed growing into a tree. *It's called a miracle.*

Not burgeoning.

But your dictionary will define it still as a process called growth.

Why have I turned the whole conversation to miracles? Because a miracle happened to me. Not that I would become visible to the world. No, not that.

The miracle started in 1923. But first, I'll start with the sketching-my-image thing. So, there I was, roaming around, trying to find the true meaning of the word 'death.'

Humans invented it. I think the one who concocts something must know its meaning as well. Of course, it was ages ago and I had killed many people until then. I use the word killed because that was the meaning of death back then.

It was a cold winter morning. There was a chill in the air and the shrouded bodies searched for a tinge of sunlight.

I felt nothing but saw humans feeling it.

I had to go to a church and unlock the souls of fifteen people there. When I have a soul to free, I usually go beforehand to see the situation. So, I was before time in that basilica on Sunday. The bishop was speaking about me.

Curious, I listened.

"My dear brothers and sisters. My dear children. The path of righteousness isn't a difficult one. You take one step and God moves ten steps toward you. Don't fear death, fear sins. Everyone must die one day, sooner or later. Everyone must face death, but death is cruel. It gives pain…"

And so on.

Death is cruel.

I frowned at that human. How unfair. If I could, I'd appeal in the court. I – am – not – cruel.

And then a blast and fire everywhere.

It was my duty, I had to free the souls from their cages. And, Lord, how do I do that?

As I mentioned earlier… disguised as a weapon for a perfidious doll and warm as hell for a pious heart.

I become a beauty for a spiritual human. For instance, there was a guileless child in the church. His was the first soul I had to free, and in that moment, he could see me.

When the time comes, the person can always see me. He was propped on his elbows, staring strangely at me. I smiled.

I don't give pain to the innocuous. So, I smiled as he contemplated my unexplainable beauty in his mind.

White silk robes undulating in air that was filled with the aroma of jasmine and roses. My eyes pure blue, silver hair flowing down my back, and a crown on my head no less than a queen's. Just infallible.

Seeing my paragon beauty, the child couldn't speak or blink. I have seen that look on the faces of many pious humans when they finally see me.

"I have come to take you," I told him in my most euphonious tone, offering him my serene hand.

"Who are you?" he finally managed to ask.

"Who do you think I am?" I smiled.

Taking a child's soul has always been a delight. After all, the sooner you leave, the less burden of sins on you.

"A… a… dream…"

"If you say so," I shrugged my shoulder, "Come along, boy."

A dream…

And what a haunting nightmare for sinners. I become fear itself when I take a sinner, and then they call me fear.

14

I know human nature more than humans know themselves. Humans ask for evidence and their eyes seek proof. I can't show you the scared faces of sinners but I can tell you about them.

The one who murdered fourteen people in the church in a suicidal bomb attack.

A terrorist, a clean-shaven, pathetic Jew. -

Excuse me, I don't want to sound blasphemous here by discussing religion, neither do I wish to be sardonic on the division of creators, but sometimes I feel a lack of senselessness in humans when they don't have unity in religion.

They can't even agree on one god!

I've seen people praying and prostrating themselves to the stars or the sun. A little sense developed, and they began worshipping statues.

And civilization brought with it the theological existence of God, Allah, Buddha, Brahma, Jesus.

That was much better.

I would like to control myself before I reveal the veils of the Universe or before I slip some aspersions to mankind.

I was talking about death, which is me, of sinners.

The obliterated basilica went black, my eyes turned crimson and my hair black as it snaked above my head, my robes became black too, smoke and ashes rising from them. I could feel my eyes beginning to glow.

But more than that, I could clearly see fear suspended in the terrorist's eyes.

The most silent time is when I take a soul.

As the cracks began to appear on the walls of the forlorn room I had created, a cat-like grin formed on my face as the man began to crawl back like a rat in a trap.

I feel nothing… absolutely nothing. When I take a soul there's no mercy, no fear, no felicity, because I'm not human.

I had to give him pain and fear, so, with a flick of my eyes he slammed into the wall and broke his spine. Even if the suicidal attack had been malevolent and his flesh had been blown to bits, when I take a soul, the person becomes perfectly well.

So, I broke his spine and then his leg.

Then, as if he were a puppet, he tossed and swayed in the room as my long nails danced in the air to the music of my devious cackle. I could almost imagine myself as the most hideous creature.

Thank the Lord, my reflection doesn't appear on water or glass, otherwise, would have been either very envious or full of vanity.

In summary, I've never seen myself. Don't you consider that strange? How can a person live without seeing his own face?

OBSERVATION No. 2

"Humans see their faces a million times in their lifetime and still don't recognize themselves."

Sometimes, I wish I could see myself, but then I remind myself that I shouldn't wish. Wishing is a human trait, remember?

And there is a fact about wishes and desires too. You can't call my words adages, maxims, or dictums because my experiences are from the beginning of life, so I call these my conclusions or observations.

OBSERVATION No. 3

"No bomb, no fire, no bullet can perish a soul. The only thing that truly perishes a man is his desire."

Desire perished me too. So again, I desired. I hadn't desired to be a human. The thing I wanted to experience the most was what I couldn't have, even if I lived to the end of time on Earth.

Feelings.

Human feelings.

Basically, time never ends, it only starts. Doomsday will start a new life and time henceforth.

It is humans who end.

I wonder what it's like to live as a human. Three things about human beings intrigue me, creativity, nature, and religion. Creativity, as it is infinitely and constantly expanding. Nature, as it is diplomatically changing. Religion, as there is monotheism, but confusingly there are innumerable religions.

I just wondered what masterpiece would I create? What kind of nature would I have? What would be my religion?

Tut.

No, that isn't going to happen.

So, I continue doing my duty. As I mentioned, I wander in the world. They say people change their opinions and thoughts with time, but I say they don't.

The same things repeat with little change, because they always have the same opinion about me. I want a difference, I want to ask the question, 'What is death?'

The most different answer I heard was in 1303 BC from some tribal people in a desert in Arabia. Did I mention I can understand languages?

They were destined to die from thirst. I listened as the sweltering and scorching heat of the sun burned their skin. With a black hood on my head and golden eyes, I walked silently with my bare feet on the sand, feeling nothing, and my white skin glowing in the sunshine.

"Oh, this heat is going to kill me..." "If only we had brought some more water..."

"Even if we had, it wouldn't be of much use. It would be boiling and burn your mouth and throat."

"The camels, we should kill one..."

"No, find an oasis."

"But it'll take time, and by then the sandstorm would kill us!"

"Good," one of them stood up with a leather bottle, "Death will give me freedom."

I stared at him. Death is freedom.

I am freedom!

Wonderful!

At least I'm of some use to humans then.

"Oh no, Allah, have mercy!" I didn't listen as they began to discuss their rival: the sandstorm. And soon it came. I have patience. I waited until I had to take the life of that man who had said those words.

He was neither a sinner nor a pious man. So, I took his soul gently, but not without some effort. First, I stared at him and he stared back.

"Who are you?" he spoke, bewildered as he lay there on the sand.

"Freedom." I gave myself a new name.

"Pardon?"

I frowned. He had given me the name himself and now he failed to recognize me.

17

It's hard to believe humans. *Diplomatic.* Without wasting any time, I clenched my hand in a fist and he was gone without excruciation. I moved on.

It is tiring to search for answers, but even more to wait like a helpless, netted bird. I guess I'm not really freedom. Freedom means to have nothing to worry about. Humans have their life in a graveyard and hell to worry about, so I'm not freedom.

Time progressed.

It was 1900, and I was passing a school in India. It was some very illiterate village where Muslims and Hindus lived together.

The school had no gable and was made of mud. The Muslim children were sitting under the shade of a fig tree having a class, narrating their lesson aloud.

A riot was about to break out, and British soldiers were going to murder civilians.

The class was stridently revising their lesson when the docent arrived.

"Children, have you learned the lesson I gave you from the Koran?"

"Yes, master!" they all replied.

"Good. Haider, narrate it for me."

The child began to repeat verses from the holy book.

I noticed a small girl wearing rags, but with a clean face, who was standing behind a wall outside the school, watching the students.

"Okay, good, Haider. Now, who will tell me about death?"

Nobody answered or raised their hand. I became attentive, after all, I was being discussed there.

"Osama? Zainab? Fatima? No one? I told you yesterday!"

The mentor was becoming angry, twisting the stick he was holding in his hands. How cruel of humans to punish others for not knowing something! The Lord didn't punish them for not knowing medical science or anything.

OBSERVATION No. 4

"If something isn't known by somebody, they ought to be told about it, not punished for their lack of knowledge." I remained stoic. I can't feel. It's not my fault.

When the teacher was going to punish the first girl, someone spoke very loudly and clearly.

18

"Master?"

All of them turned their attention to the nine-year-old girl standing outside with her hands on the chest-high mud wall.

"Death is belief," her innocent words touched me.

"What?" the question telepathically transferred from my mind to the docent's mind.

"If you had believed in death, you would've believed in answering Allah one day. And you wouldn't have refused me when I begged you to let me sit in the class as I have so much love for learning. Would you tell Allah that you expelled me for not paying the fees? I'm poor and I believe in death, which is why I'm telling you the right thing. Otherwise, what would I have said to Allah when he asked why I didn't give you the right answer?" I stared.

If I were a human, I could have said my heartbeat stopped. For the first time, after centuries, a human surprised me.

And I learned two facts from this stranger who was being stared at by everyone.

First, death is belief.

Second, no invention or discovery can impress a person as much as words do.

I concluded the second one by the look on their faces.

The riot.

I wanted to see the girl clearer, but she ran away as soon as the British arrived. All I had was a glimpse of her small feet running away down the street.

I took lives in a dazed mood. Her answer was right.

And there was a third fact, if people believed in death more than they did life, this world would be a happier place.

No one would commit a sin. They would believe that they had to answer to the Lord.

So, this was my preliminary introduction. I might have bragged about certain things, but humans do that a lot.

My life had just begun.

Chapter 2

Aisha.

Her name was Aisha, and I had waited for two years before learning her name. Coincidentally, by that time it was no longer concealed from me.

Wait – did I tell you I learnt?

Well, it was the first human attribute I unknowingly did, and at that juncture, I had no idea what I had done. I had learnt.

I noticed that humans learn names first after they begin to talk. Isn't it so? I've seen some toddlers, when I take their soul, they call me by different names. So, they grasp the skill to 'learn names' shortly after birth.

I was also born.

Once again.

I had to take a soul of a Hindu, a slave in the subcontinent and I saw her there. It brought back a memory, a deep-rooted memory in myself, which began to flash in my eyes as I saw her.

Pity. Pity. Pity.

OBSERVATION No. 5

"Death destroys all memories humans collect, even the most precious ones."

Cruel, aren't I?

But I have billions of memories, perhaps trillions, even a greater infinity than the humans' numbers create. And I, unlike humans, don't forget. All these memories are as fresh as the moment they first occurred.

Wearing torn attire, hair in a straight braid, running away from the riot breakers and the hungry British eyes… And I can picture it, even now.

The man's hungry eyes and her wide-eyed gaze, staring in fear, as if in a lost state, there she was that little guileless human, standing like a slave at a side, shoulders shrouded inward.

I wanted her to say something.

I wanted her to say anything about me because every man in that palatial room seemed to have forgotten me.

I know.

OBSERVATION No. 6

"If a man believes in death, he will never look at a woman with hungry eyes."

Also, he will believe he has to answer to the Lord for this.

I know because Aisha was thinking the same thing. Her eyes told me that. The only person in the room who believed in me was her.

And I can't believe it. No, not the quantity of people, but the quality of faith she had in me.

She never even looked at the most handsome man there.

The Hindu was shot in the head due to some indictment of high treason or other.

I had to leave. But after that, I kept an eye on her because a small girl like her had understood life *and* death too early. She had gone to the end without living it and concluded something that even the oldest and most experienced didn't.

I'm not saying that I was a big fan of hers, I'm just trying to convey my message of 'belief in death.'

I won't mention how I took the Hindu's soul because I'll explain later the demise of an oppressor.

Yes, Aisha was made a slave. She did little things, simple chores as she was just a child and lived in the servant's quarters. As she was a lieutenant's slave, she learned English.

That riot cost her a lot. She had run as far as her little feet could carry her, but alas, she was captured and taken to the lieutenant. Her parents had protested, and it was at that time she became an orphan.

I had to take the souls of poor people who had been shot. They were pious so I showed leniency. First, her father and then her mother. I didn't talk to them about their daughter but treated them as I always do.

After all, I was given a life to kill others, right?

And then again, I am the beginning of new life that never ends. What a paradox, I end a life and begin a life.

It is an invidious arrangement as it is all opposite for me and humans. They have a mortal life on Earth, and I have immortality. Once they die, they'll live forever, but once I die, I won't even live again.

I'm not jealous, of course, I can't be that. I can't feel that. Only humans can.

Now, Aisha was mostly silent. She never talked to anyone, so I heard fewer wise words from her, but the wisest words I heard from a human are too simple to convey and yet too difficult to understand:

"You are going to die." Got
it?

All the people with all their dreams of achieving their destiny, listen:

22

all of you have one common destiny and that's me, Death.

So, I ask you, why do you think and walk on Earth as if it'll never turn into dust?

So, why do you pass through the graveyards as if the ones in the graves never lived once? As if you won't be joining them one day?

So why does it surprise you when someone dies? Don't you know it's your fate too?

I think a sensible person would shiver if he heard those words.

He didn't.

The one who heard them first.

Her childhood faded and her skin glowed, her eyes gaining sparkle and her hair beautified, she was in her teens now, but that head cloth never left her body. It stayed there together with her self-respect and silence.

But men noticed her beauty now. She was forced to wear emblazoned garments and dance, but she refused boldly.

Sitting on the floor, leaning against the wall, as the man ordered her to get ready, she listened, gazing downward. I thought she might be afraid now and would obey, becoming the same as other humans, but as soon as the man turned to leave, she looked up and said clearly, "No." Just that.

He turned back.

"How dare you refuse me?" he said calmly in a sonorous tone, "I'll kill you."

For a moment, she stared at the man. Satisfied, he turned to go.

"You're going to die," she whispered, "*Trust me.*" "Great discovery," he laughed sarcastically, "Everyone is going to die. The thing is… you will die at my hands."

I sat on the chair wishing he could hear me mock him. You'll die at *my* hands, just wait, dear.

"I won't do anything for you or your ostentatious guests!" her voice full of fury.

"You wish you had a choice, dear, but you see, you're my slave and I'm the man with the gun."

I saw her grit her teeth so hard I thought they would break. At first, her eyes full of embers stared at the floor, but then she looked at him for her final verdict.

"My mother gave birth to a free human being, who are you to make me a slave? I'm the slave of my Allah and believe me, you're not him!"

I stared at her dry-mouthed, her gaze purely meant to provoke the barbarian, and so it did.

I wished I could slam him to the wall, scare him as I always did when I killed people, as he began to whip her. He whipped her hard, but again…

23

I felt pity for her because she only cried harder and repeated stereotypically like a machine, "I am only my Allah's slave!"

He whipped her harder for that. Her clothes began to tear away in places, her head cloth slipped off and her hair strands escaped the braid as she covered her face with her arms.

"I am only my Allah's slave!"

I can tell with full surety, if it had been any other person, he would have blamed his god for all that was happening. But not her.

No. rather, she still… what should I say? She still loved her god? She still accepted his decisions?

Or maybe she still had patience?

Whatever it was, it was rare. I have seen this kind of faith in Muslims before as well. Hundreds of years ago when they were dragged onto the burning sand in the desert, and they still believed in Allah.

On hearing her cries, the door opened and in came a group of men.

They saw her weeping, wounded, and that inhumane creature standing with a whip, breathing heavily. Thinking she was adamant, he sold her to a man who took her to England.

After that, I saw her often because I wanted to, I needed to. She was in even crueler hands now. His name was Jason and he was a drunkard. Rich but vulgar, obnoxious and despicable. *Ah* – take all such words from your dictionary.

Aisha was extremely upset at having to leave her homeland and live with a man she had never met in her life. He kept her locked away in his house, torturing and abusing her physically and mentally with ways only he could come up with. He wanted her to stay with him without marriage and change her religion, to dress the way he wanted her to.

No matter what he did, Aisha didn't lose the dignity and pride of her religion and remained herself.

Everybody sets certain rules for themselves. For some, going beyond the limit is like the death penalty, and for others it's like a game where you can always start all over again. The weak ones often break their rules and call it compromise, but the strong ones don't.

And I must say, Aisha never compromised. Even if he would slay her, she would *never* live according to his rules. She had her Holy Book, the Koran.

He took it away too, but she had already learned all the principles by heart. Even if he took away her book, he couldn't take away her heart.

Could he?

And for this, I smile. There he was now, totally helpless. And to prove he wasn't, he used to beat her, abuse her, mock her.

But again, I say – *she never compromised herself.*

24

Sticks and stones may break her bones, but she was never tainted by him.

I know it's long gone and that she isn't here anymore, but I want to tell you that I felt sympathy for a human after centuries, and for that, I am grateful to her.

Why?

You see, only humans feel sympathy for each other. Do lions and beasts feel sympathy for their prey? No.

There I was again that night, roaming the world in my leisure time when I came across that wild demon yelling at her again.

"SHUT UP! SHUT UP, YOU BITCH!" he was snatching her hair, "YOU WILL DO AS I SAY!"

"I won't!" her painful voice, accompanied by a slight scream. I stopped at the door.

If I had the option to take whoever's soul I wanted, I bet on my graves I would have taken Jason's first, with pleasure.

My graves. That's an expression for all the graves that humankind possesses.

Those were tears.

I wish I could know what it's like to cry, to have tears on one's face. Of all the expressions I have seen on humans' faces, tears fascinate me most.

They only come out when a person is in deep physical or emotional pain. Smile is ordinary. People smile a hundred times a day, even at strangers! Weird.

And he slapped her and began to kick her with his leather boots. I wanted to tear apart his mustache.

He crouched, taking her hair in his fingers again, "Then believe me, I'll be your death!"

I glowered at him. *Yes, go on, be me, wear a mask and black hood with a scythe.*

You would look like a cartoon to me. Poor
Aisha. She just cried.

I wondered why she didn't want to be his wife. Being so old, I suggest she should have married him on the very first day and saved herself from the whips and the kicks.

But procrastinating over the marriage for no reason was an incomprehensible enigma for me. She grew weak, tired, and sick.

Waiting for me, just me.

But I never come before time. She had to wait and so did I. I couldn't see her for a year but when I did, a shock was waiting for me.

She had given up. She was his wife now. I stayed there for a while to look at the poor girl. Had she changed her religion too? But for the first time in forever… I was wrong.

She was his wife but was never Mrs. Jason. She remained *Aisha*. From head to toe, from heart to soul, she was a Muslim.

Now, he abused her for not changing her religion even when she was his wife. Such is the faith of the pious who are pious human beings, they truly deserve Eden.

And now I realized the answer of 'incomprehensible enigma' as well. When her little girl was born, Aisha wanted her child to be a photocopy of herself, but Jason wanted her to be only his daughter.

Who won?

Cheers. *Nobody.*

I'll explain later. Patience is your weakest point, I know. But have a little here.

A father loves his child and takes good care of her. He didn't. He was the same obscene drunkard, a ribald man who hadn't even visited the church once in his life, not even accidently. His erotic nature never changed, and that is the thing I hate about humans: they are driven by their libidos.

They don't understand each other. They don't even understand themselves. Their life is just enjoyment, and they teach this in schools: life is like a big examination hall.

So, I ask you, what is the role of enjoyment in an examination hall? Do you have a party when you are taking an exam?

When the priest was called from the basilica for the ritual to baptize the baby, Aisha protested.

"She is my daughter! You can do anything to me but leave her alone!"

Wrath on the faces of the baby's parents.

"GET OUT OF MY WAY!" Jason slapped her hard and she fell. He began to take the baby from the carriage when, to my surprise, Aisha pushed him away, grabbing the front of his shirt.

"LEAVE US ALONE! LEAVE US ALONE! WE DON'T NEED YOU! YOU RUINED MY LIFE AND I'LL LET YOU RUIN MY CHILD'S LIFE!"

Jason's eyes widened at his wife's sudden, unexpected reaction, so did mine. *What was it* that made her stand up against her cruel and abusive husband? She hadn't dared to when he had whipped her or almost broken her bones.

There was blood of such indignation and warning in her eyes that I saw even Jason shiver for a second.

But just for a second.

26

Then his satanic nature overwhelmed his mind and he pushed her so that her head hit the corner of table, tearing her skin, blood oozed.

After beating her, he left. As soon as he was gone, Aisha quickly took her daughter in her arms and began to kiss her cheeks.

So. It was love, a mother's love for her child. Oh, how I sighed and wished I could feel for someone the same way she did. But I am alone... How unfortunate.

Two years later, I had to take a soul. As I traveled to that place, I became excited and full of vengeance because it was Jason's soul.

How would he die? I wanted to see that. Would Aisha kill him?

Chapter 3

When I saw the situation, I was extremely annoyed. Following Jason on that cold December's night, I thought about how I would scare him and inflict pain upon him. So, I covered my head with my hood, appearing the way humans like to draw me.

Soft pebbles of snow were falling, and Jason was accompanied by three muscular and barbaric men who were similar in appearance to him.

He unlocked the door of his house and walked inside with the men, unknowingly letting me in too.

Without a word, the three men settled on the couch in the dark sitting room. So much had changed since I had visited it last time. Now it wasn't palatial and looked run down, almost destitute.

As was the whole house.

When Jason went upstairs, I followed him like a shadow, then into the room where Aisha held her daughter so close in her lap she looked as if she was part of her body. "Everything is arranged, you have to go," Jason said calmly.

"Please," she whispered as the silent tears rolled down her cheeks and she sat on the floor, "Please, Jason, don't do this. We can solve this together! *Please…*"

"How?" Jason replied with a frown, "How, huh? I need money and there's no other way. Those men are going to give me enough to pay my loan to those profligates!"

I began to chew my lip, having no idea what was going on. Aisha was pleading continuously.

"Have mercy, Jason," she said with so much helplessness that anyone's heart would have melted for her, "this girl is your blood! I'm your wife!"

"I don't care!" he really didn't. I knew it. "At

least, don't sell your daughter," Aisha cried.

"She would have been my daughter if you had changed your religion, bitch!" he roared, "Now, come with me, I don't have the time to listen to your stupid words!"

When Aisha didn't get up and keep on crying, Jason grabbed her arm, pulling her to her feet and dragging her out of the room.

I felt such immense hatred toward him, more than anyone could imagine. Even now, when I sometimes remember that man, hate is the only thing I feel for him.

Hate.

That was the first time I truly wanted to kill someone. If I were a human, I am certain I would have killed him.

"Jason, please don't! I'll do whatever you say, just don't..." she kept pleading in sobbing whispers.

But he dragged her all the way to the top of the staircase. Throughout this, her daughter was asleep. Aisha broke away and ran, but Jason raced after her, slipped, and fell far too hard on the stairs, injuring his head and hitting every step as he tumbled down.

He lay motionless halfway down the staircase.

I wanted to see Aisha, but she never looked back and locked herself in her room.

Now was the part where I played role of villain, with Jason as the victim.

Slowly, he opened his eyes. I stood in front of that atrocity of a man, looking straight in his eyes. Clearly puzzled, he blinked and looked around because the room had changed. In the darkness, there was a dim red light. His worst nightmare and his worst fear, *me.* He tried to get up.

"Don't bother." I hissed.

I must remind you that I only mentioned once how I take the lives of sinners and pious ones. Here is an example of how I take the lives of perfidious beings.

With a crease between his eyebrows, he looked at me. He couldn't see my face as it was hidden by the shadow of my hood.

Propping himself up on his elbows, he asked, "Who are you?" The same boring old question I have heard too many times.

"I am," I began to laugh sardonically and sharply as I drew my hood back, revealing the face of fear, the form I had taken then. My face thin and long, high cheekbones, clown-like lips with sharp teeth, long nails, a snake's tongue, hair like thorns, and a stooped figure, "*you.* I am you, Jason, the inside of you. I am the figure of your sins!"

The same figure he was for Aisha. The My sly eyes scared him, and he swallowed hard.

"What do you want?" he asked in panic. I grinned again.

"You're going to die," hissing Aisha's words, I smirked, "Sound familiar?"

"HELP! HELP!" he yelled, but there was just darkness.

I laughed louder, "Help, help, help… ahh... pity, pity, pity." I teased him, "Look who has come to help you? *Me!*"

"Who are you? Where am I?" the panic clear in his voice.

I frowned this time. Malice filled me once again. It always does when humans fail to recognize me, and as they reach their end they shout for help.

OBSERVATION No. 7

"No matter how many close friends you have, no matter how deeply you are connected to someone, there is just one truly intimate relationship you have in the end: Death."

Angrily walking towards him, I flared my nostrils, twisting my hair around fingernail, "I am the one you didn't believe in, Jason. I am the one Aisha warned you about. I am… Death."

He turned pale, just like a wingless bird in front of a cat.

"Please… please, have mercy…"

The epitome of my indignation was sky high now. Have mercy? What is that, by the way?

I grabbed the front of his shirt and the tip of my nose almost touched his, *"Have mercy? Did you have mercy when you bought her?"* I slammed him into the wall, breaking his nasal bone.

"DID YOU HAVE MERCY WHEN YOU LOCKED HER AWAY IN THE HOUSE?" I roared as I slammed him again onto the floor, shattering his teeth.

"DID YOU HAVE MERCY WHEN YOU TRIED TO FORCE HER TO CHANGE HER RELIGION?"

The grand whip that belonged to him appeared in my hand and I whipped him with all my strength.

"DID YOU HAVE MERCY WHEN YOU WHIPPED HER?"

As the lash disappeared, I placed him motionless on the embers, his body seared. My roars added to his wild screams.

"DID YOU HAVE MERCY ON YOUR DAUGHTER?"

He was a puppet now. The man who had made his wife a slave was himself a marionette before Death.

He was dangling in the air, slamming into the walls.

"DID YOU HAVE MERCY WHEN YOU WERE GOING TO SELL HER?" I shrieked, *"I WISH YOU WOULD DIE AGAIN AND AGAIN AND BE BORN AGAIN AND AGAIN, BECAUSE SHE USED TO DIE EVERYDAY!"*

He was lying on the floor now, which was scorching like hell itself.

I stepped forwards, staring at him, "Let me give you a demonstration of the hell that has its gates open for you."

I narrowed my eyes, and his body lit up like a wick. I watched him running around in desperation, yelling in pain. It was probably enough pain for the sins he had committed, although I wanted to continue.

As the fire extinguished itself, his skin began to peel off his body like that of a snake, and he screamed when I clasped my hand in a fist and his soul left his body.

He fell.

It was over.

For a moment, I stared at the dead body on the stairs. Then I spit on his face and left. I entered Aisha's room where I found her sweating with fright. After all, a locked door is hardly a barrier for Death.

Hearing the heavy steps of three men ascending the stairs were loud and clear. They were coming to get her. With a gulp, she took her head dress, tied her daughter to her and opened the window.

Climbing outside, she carefully stepped onto the pipes.

Once she jumped on the ground, she ran at full strength, glancing back frequently in that cold night of snowy winter.

As she reached a bridge, she decided to take shelter beneath it in the shadows. Although she was shivering herself, she untied her daughter and wrapped the headdress around the baby, even though she was already covered. Anyone could possibly meet me because of that coldness.

Once again, she kissed her daughter as she took off her socks, covering the baby's feet again although they were protected.

Is mother's love so strong that she forgets herself, becomes selfless and cares only for her child? Is it?

I was watching in amazement as she wrapped her arms around the baby to provide warmth from her body.

I left.

I learned another thing about her. She could've killed herself, committed suicide and ended it. In fact, she could've have done it years ago, as people commit suicide because of small issues, but she didn't.

OBSERVATION No. 8

"When the Lord gives you a reason to die, a human doesn't realize it, but he gives a million others the chance to live."

And her *optimism* was her reason before, and her *daughter* was her purpose now. She was living for another soul.

Of all the loves in the world, the strongest is that of a mother. She sacrifices herself for her child.

But I've seen humans. A child turns into an adult and then that child begins to scold his mother on small things. He forgets that she was the one who taught him how to speak and now he scolds her with the same tongue.

31

Do you scold the mother who taught you how to speak so that she may regret she taught you?

Do you scold the mother who asked a question twice when she used to answer you even if you asked the same question ten times?

If I could, first, I would remove tongues of humans. Why do they need a thing they can't control?

Just think how much euphoria there would be in the world without tongues, because most humans are sinners because of the words they speak.

I watched Aisha pray that her daughter wouldn't be like other humans.

And I prayed that she would be like Aisha and not Jason.

And both of us prayed that she would understand nothing hides from the Lord's eyes.

***

It was morning and Aisha was standing outside a café, very hungry, weak and sick. A man tossed a piece of bread towards her and when she didn't move, he tossed an apple to her.

She didn't eat anything herself. No.

She fed her daughter and saved the rest for the next day. I looked under the bridge wishing there was someone there with an ounce of human compassion to help her.

Even if I'm not human, I still felt something inside me. A desire to help her.

So, why didn't others feel anything when they were humans?

Maybe, because they hadn't seen her life or the way she had lived it.

Even so, why didn't they feel any pity? I couldn't understand why everyone walked around on the street as if she didn't' exist, unaware of the circumstances around them. She never begged anyone, she only sought help from Allah.

And help came. Me.

It was evident from her situation she wouldn't survive. The moment I had anticipated since the first day I saw her, was near.

Under the bridge, trembling in fear and cold, I came to her.

This time, I never changed anything. The place remained the same except there wasn't anybody around, only me, her, and the baby.

The most enchanting face with small glittering stars by her eyes stared at me. Her blonde hair styled in an updo with a royal crown placed on her head and clad in a princess-like dress.

I looked down at her, as she moved her eyes slowly towards me.

I wondered what she was thinking about me and she was probably wondering why all the pain and coldness had suddenly disappeared even though the snow was there, and she was sick.

She didn't shiver anymore. It seemed a long time because she just looked at me, maybe wondering what a beautiful lady was doing there, or who I was.

I wanted *her* to initiate, so I remained stoic.

I knew what the first words would be, 'who are you?' I thought I had surprised her with my uninvited presence, but she surprised me. So much so that I couldn't speak.

With a faint smile appearing on her dry lips, she whispered, "I'm angry with you. You kept me waiting for a long time."

It made me wait. Wait to understand. Was I imagining her erudite words or not? I stepped towards her and sat down beside her. After a long pause, I asked, "Since when?"

"Since the day of the riot when I was captured by the British Army," she said, staring in to midair.

I smiled at the little coincidence, "That was the day when I first saw you. Aisha, you have been very brave."

After years, the shy smile appeared on her face at my kind words, "Is that supposed to make me feel better?"

I laughed at this. Then, to confirm if her thoughts were right about me, I asked curiously, "You know who I am, right?"

Rather than answering my question, she asked me one, "Do you always talk to people like this?"

"No, not normally. In fact, never… just a few, fourteen hundred years ago."

She nodded.

"Listen," I looked at her suddenly, "Why didn't you ask anyone for help?"

"But I did," she replied. When she saw I was unable to understand, she continued, "I asked Allah for help. I only beg from Him. No one can help anyone unless He does."

I changed the topic because I had little patience, "That day you defined me. I liked it, you didn't call me cruel or anything like that."

"Humans are cruel," she cut across me, "Death is a healer."

"Thanks," I smiled, "You know, you didn't deserve this kind of life."

She remained reticent for some time and when she spoke, her grief was audible.

"No one deserves the kind of life they live. It is a test of whether they can live the kind of life they don't deserve and have patience or not."

Our conversation came to a long pause during which she kept staring

33

at her child. I knew she didn't want to leave the baby. But what she asked surprised me.

"Will you write something on my gravestone for me?" She looked at me with hopeful eyes.

"Of course. What do you want me to write?"

"You are going to die."

I stared at her for speaking the greatest truth of life: death.

"Why do you want me to write that?"

"So that..." she hesitated, "if... if a man like Jason looked at these words, he might believe in Death then."

We became silent. I wanted to tell Aisha that it was time to go now, but she had her daughter in her lap and was looking at her with love and the pang of separation/

She breathed heavily. "It's time to go now," I whispered.

Aisha was crying now, caressing the baby's cheek, "She... she doesn't have anyone in the world..."

Silence again. I watched her tears drip on the baby's cheek when she kissed her.

"Can't you take her too?"

"No, I'm sorry. I'm not allowed." I told her it was impossible to take a soul without order, "You gave her your bread, your clothes, and stayed hungry so that your daughter might live. Now, you want her to die too?"

"No," she wept, trying to control herself, "I'm scared."

"You are scared of me?" I was shocked. After so many words, could she still be afraid to die?

"No," she was still weeping, "I'm scared of another Jason who will take her... I told you... humans are cruel... and... she is alone..."

Suddenly, she looked at me with something in her eyes that I couldn't recognize. She licked her lips, tasting her tears.

"I'll die... and rest in peace only if... if... if..."

I frowned. If what? I had an impression that whatever it was, it was probably impossible. She held my hand and squeezed it.

"If... if you would take her and look after her, away from humans, because I only trust *you*." The winter froze me.

Or was it her words?

Chapter 4

"*Please,*" she stressed the word.

I was stuck in something odd that humans are often stuck in. Confusion.

"What?" I stared at her. Almost immediately, she placed her child in my lap.

"Take her," she was trying to control her tears, "keep her safe. Please! For God's sake, take her!"

Her plea began to melt my... what should I say? *Heart?*

I directed my eyes at the baby who was awake now and looking at the sky.

"Don't mind my asking," I asked dubiously, "but are you using me in some way?"

She didn't answer my question, but replied, "Please, take my soul. I can't bear this pain anymore."

So, life had given her pain. I was victorious after all.

I had a chance, for the first and last time, to experience what I wanted: what it would be like to be a human and feel. My chance was lying in my lap and letting go of this opportunity seemed a stupid mistake.

While I was ruminating about it, I realized I had been staring blankly at Aisha. So, I cleared my throat, finally putting my arms around the girl.

"Okay, I will."

Her whisper was so grateful and full of happiness that she had never had before, "Thank you... I'm ready."

I raised my chest, put my hand on hers and... She

flinched for a moment, then she was gone.

Her body lay there, eyes closed, motionless. I sat there with the baby for some time under the bridge, staring at that human.

Thinking has never been my strong suit. I don't think, certainly never about things such as this.

Now I was trying to *think.* Where to keep her? What to name her? What to name myself? How to bring her up? I

scratched my forehead.

"Mama," a small voice said.

It was the only word she knew as it was all Aisha had taught her. I smiled at the poor girl. She began to play, dancing her hands and feet.

"Mama," she said again.

"She is gone." I whispered.

I got up and began to search for an isolated place where there were no humans, where nobody could come, where the girl and I would be alone. Soon, I began to feel pity for myself.

It was a difficult job. She couldn't survive in the sweltering heat of a desert, or the killing coldness of Antarctica. I had promised Aisha I would look after her child and bring her up away from humans, as if she didn't exist.

Her girl was pretty. Her features were different from her parents'. Black hair, white skin, and red lips. I wondered if her persona would be like Jason or Aisha.

While traveling, I thought about her name. What would I call her?

I never asked Aisha about her name, so it became a great mission for me.

Giving a name, why was it a difficult task?

A name could be an identification of religion. Was I to give her a Muslim or a Christian name? Was I to make her a Muslim or a Christian?

I knew Aisha would want her daughter to be a Muslim, but a child inherits the father's religion. She should have bequeathed her religion too.

It was a difficult decision for me, I don't make decisions usually, humans do. I lack the phenomena of proper judgment.

How can I judge anyone?

My duty is just to take life. And the sudden endowment of another duty was a burden on me.

Once or twice, a thought struck me. Why not leave her in an orphanage? But then, I wanted to prove desperately that I could be a better human than humans are.

***

Tropical rainforest.

Our home.

I chose the place because it was full of nature but devoid of humans.

Carrying her through dappled sunlight, I walked to the middle of the forest, the deep place where scarcely any sunrays reached.

The mere sight of it was scary enough to make humans flee. And the most frightening thing was the haunted graveyard, which would give any human a heart attack should they venture there by chance.

With a gesture, endless gravestones appeared with the names and dates of dead people already inscribed on them. A long path through the middle led across a drawbridge to a somber castle made of ancient black stone.

Perfect.

The inside of the castle was tranquil with a bed of grass creating a soft, green pillow, a garden of roses, jasmine, daffodils, and sunflowers, which turned towards the little sunshine that penetrated there, and a cornucopia of fruit trees.

No wild animal could come there, as it was totally isolated from the rest of the forest.

No man-made thing existed there. It was all the Lord's creations. When she fell asleep, I went to Aisha's grave and wrote the words she had willed. I stayed there for some time, although I knew there was nothing in the grave, just a skeleton, her decomposed body, and rotting skin.

Her soul was gone.

OBSERVATION No. 9

"People don't lie in graves. Graves are the memory of humans who existed once because humans fear oblivion and graves are only a reminder of their existence. Oblivion is one of the greatest, inevitable truths."

People come and people go, no one remembers anyone.

Graveyards are like huge museums. Those who make history become a part of history themselves. People play the part of heroes and villains, or simply extras and then they expire.

The difficult task is not to make history, but to make a future.

***

She used to call me mama. I didn't call her by any name, but I used to talk to her for hours, about everything, and she just listened with interest, unable to understand words.

I never taught her another word. I wanted to but I didn't know where to begin. She ate fruits, vegetables, and beans, and never left the castle, even by accident.

When she slept, I went on my duty. My time is different from human time, so it wasn't an issue.

The only problem was she was growing up.

Her clothes didn't fit her anymore. I didn't steal anything, I couldn't. Rather, I gathered the silkworms and made her attire from their silk.

Now I had something to think about. There was her education and her needs as she was growing.

I used to lay down with her sometimes and watch her sleep. Just like a mother performs her duties, now I had another duty aside from taking lives… being a mother.

The most holy and sincere relationship. Humans don't deserve to have such relations. Perhaps it's the Lord's greatest blessing on them.

I played the role of a mother, looking after her when she crawled, feeding her with fruits when she was hungry, playing with her to make her happy, soothing her when she was hurt, and closing my eyes when she was sleeping.

Once, I left her to take the souls of some people in Burma. When I came back, I saw her there by the roses, tearing off the petals and playing.

I sat beside her, taking the rose and tickling her with it. Her laughter gave me pleasure. I promised myself I wouldn't let her become a sinner. Away from humans, she wouldn't even know what a sin was.

"Mama." She held the rose towards me as if asking what it was, because I was lost in my thoughts.

I took it and her toothless grin made me smile.

"Rose," I said. I frowned at the baby and then at the flower. *"Rose!"* I exclaimed, taking her in my arms.

Yes, I would name her Rose. It wasn't a Christian or a Muslim name, it was the name of the Lord's creation.

And from that day onwards, I told her the names of simple things, such as birds and flowers, the things we had in castle.

But most of all, she loved two names, Mama and Rose. Pointing her little finger at me and herself, she used to repeat them. And how I longed for the time she could talk eloquently with me.

When she turned six, I brought some books for her that I had found in the garbage. One was to teach her English. Another was the Bible and the last one was the Koran.

I didn't know what religion she wanted for herself, so I thought it was best if she chose by first studying them.

Now, she was learning avidly as she had nothing else to do.

One day, I was sitting inside, and Rose was outside when I heard her calling me, "Mama! Mama! Mama!"

I quickly went to see if she was hurt. She wasn't, but was standing by the flowers, her long, silky black hair at her back.

"Are you alright, Rose?" I asked her worriedly.

"Yes, Mama?"

She was pointing at something. Whenever she wanted to know the answer to some question, she just asked, "Mama?" and I would answer her.

39

It was a butterfly. I knelt beside her, my white gown covering the grass, and held her arms. "Butterfly." I told her.

"Flutterby?" I
laughed.

"No, Rose," I smiled, "it's a butterfly."

I saw the fascination in her eyes as she stared at it.

"Mama, I want a book."

"You have one already."

"No... I want to write its name in the book so that I can learn it."

"Okay, Rose. The next time I go out I'll bring you one back."

She lovingly kissed me on my cheek, "Oh, look, Mama! It can fly! Can I keep it?"

"Rose," I began, sitting on the grass and taking her in my lap, "Everything here belongs to you because the Lord made it for you, but He made it free. How can you make it your slave?"

There was ignorance in her eyes as I put my chin on her shoulder.

"Slave?" she paused, "Mama, what's a slave?"

I thought hard as she wanted me to define it. Maybe I should get a dictionary soon.

"Err... obeying somebody's rules is a slave." "I
am a slave?" she asked innocently.

"Why are you saying that, Rose?"

"Because I obey you." I
laughed.

"Rose," I said after a while, "You are my daughter and I'm your mama. Just remember that for now."

She looked upset as she had hunger for knowledge, and there were things I couldn't explain, not yet anyway. Her words were as if there was a third companion with us.

"You have to take a bath now." I told her reluctantly, knowing that she hated it. "No." she said firmly.

"See? You're not a slave, you don't obey me," then I added, "but you have to take a bath."

She began to run away from me.

"Rose! Rose! Come back now!" I
chased her.

***

"Ooh! That's my book!" she exclaimed as I held the new book towards her, which had blank pages.

"Yes, it is, now you don't have to write on the walls anymore. It looks dirty, right?"

I loved it. Her, writing on the walls, but I had to organize her. Learning looked fascinating to me. Her small hands scribbled on the walls with chalk, making drawings, writing words. I loved to watch my little girl do it. She hugged me suddenly.

"I won't, Mama," then she sat on the grass at once, opening the book.

The first word she wrote was 'buterfly'.

"That's a double 't'," I corrected.

Nothing. She kept holding the pencil after writing the word. I waited for her to write more, but I could see that she was thinking.

"Mama?" she looked at me, the tip of pencil between her lips.

"Hmm?"

"What is a butterfly?"

"Rose, you just saw one yesterday!" I said incredulously.

"No, in words... what should I write for its meaning?" she looked at me with hopeful eyes. I smiled.

"Beauty."

I defined it as beauty, not as a slender bodied diurnal insect with broad, brightly colored wings. I told her this because humans had forgotten the beauty of nature.

"That's not B-U-T-Y." I laughed, "It's B-E-A-U-T-Y."

There was silence in which Rose stared at the words she had written with the end of the pencil between her teeth now. I knew she was unable to understand it, but I waited for her to ask me. When she didn't, I took her in my lap.

"Rose, beauty is what reminds you of the Lord," I explained in the simplest way I could, "it's what gives pleasure to your heart."

"Mama?" she protested this time, "who is the Lord and what is this heart?"

I placed her on the grass so that she could face me and held her little hands in mine. "Lord is the one who made you and then He made all of this for you.
Heart is what you feel."

She quickly noted it in her book, and I read, **Lord: made me. Heart: what I feel."**

Then she looked at me again, "Mama?"

"Did He also make you?"

"Hmm."

Then she added something that made me smile broadly:

"Lord: made me and Mama."

I began to make a beautiful plait on her hair. They were long and nice and I hadn't cut them.

"I think you are beauty, too," Rose said after some minutes, and my hands stopped midway.

"Why?"

"You said beauty is what gives pleasure to your heart and you give me pleasure."

When I didn't reply, thinking what a hideous figure I was for some humans, Rose looked back at me. To make her happy, I smiled and kissed her cheek.

"Then, Rose, I think you are beauty, too."

***

Let's take another soul.

This time, a suicide case.

I'm going to give details because this one influenced me greatly. The girl was twenty-two years old.

Emily.

Arriving early, I found the girl sitting on her bed, her fists clenching the sheet and her eyes completely red in a valiant attempt not to cry, glowering at the pen and paper on the desk.

Opposing her silence, I could hear voices, yelling at the girl perhaps. I couldn't make out her parents' words as I was too absorbed in the girl's tears leaking slowly from her red eyes.

With her jaw twitching, she sniffed, still staring at the paper and the pen.

Was she going to write a note or will before dying? That is a typical thing humans do, a tradition now.

Abruptly, as if she couldn't take it anymore, she got up, opened the door without touching the pen and paper, and went out on the balcony. She began to climb the ladder placed at one side, going to the third and last floor.

I raised my eyes to see her. I stood behind her on the rooftop as if I would be the one to push her from there.

She didn't jump, she just grasped her scalp with both hands, crinkles at the corners of her eyes as she cried harder.

Then she kneeled and howled.

Taking control of herself, she got up again, took deep breaths, and closed her eyes for a second.

42

"Okay," she whispered. I
frowned.

She looked towards the sky and her nostrils flared as if she were angry with the Lord.

Too angry, and she had no one to complain to. Then she gritted her teeth as if she could crush them right then and there.

If only I could read her thoughts, because I knew she was feeling pain but it's a sensation I can't experience.

I stayed motionless as she closed her eyes. Her parents' yelling grew louder, calling her name and shouting abuses, and then...

She fell straight, like falling into an abyss, flying in the air and then slamming the cage of her body on the stone floor.

Her tears stopped, replaced by blood.

Now it was time, I went to her.

When she opened her eyes, she could only see me, standing over her like the ghost of her past. She looked at me with malevolent eyes. I think she recognized me.

It wasn't her home now. We were in a different place; white, light, but no sun, no floor, no sky. Just nothingness. Emptiness. In between me and life.

"If you would have come yourself, I wouldn't have committed suicide." She said with a tinge of venom in her voice.

I remained silent until I could give an appropriate answer. "You
are blaming *me* for the life you had," I told her calmly.

I wasn't looking too ugly or too scary. She had sins, but she had virtues too. a balanced soul.

She was still crying, "I am blaming God."

I frowned. It wasn't a pleasant response for me. However, I had patience.

She continued, "But how would you know? You're not a human."
How rude.

"Can we talk?" she asked.

"About what?"

"About life, *my life*..."

"Why?"

"Because I need to be heard, at least once. No one has ever listened to me... maybe a catharsis, because I don't want to say these things to God... sit down, please."

Her request was obsequious. I went towards her, my silver robe sweeping behind me and sat beside her.

43

She licked her lips, tasting her own tears. I waited for her to begin the conversation, and when she finally did, I could sense the deep pain in her sobbing, "I was just fourteen when I started writing."

A small hiatus and her trance. I looked at her.

"Will God hear any of this?" she asked, casting her eyes on me. I shrugged, "Don't know... maybe... we are in nothingness."

She nodded in approval, "Good, even if I am angry with God, I don't want to hurt Him with my words."

I wanted to tell her that she had already hurt Him many times in her life, but it was of no use, she was dead now.

"When my sister told me mother that I was writing, she beat me with a stick, ordering me not to write again. She said a poor family can't afford luxuries," I could see the disturbance in her eyes, as she looked at me, "Do you know what I mean, Death? Do you understand?"

It's awkward to be called Death.

She couldn't call me cruel, the grim reaper, or the end because I was just myself to her. I was Death for her, and it had no meaning.

"This was the stick that broke my bones, and she was about to cry again, resisting hard, her words broke me. They broke my soul..."

I couldn't say anything. She must have presumed I was a good listener, but the truth was, I didn't want to talk.

"I had to study hard to be a doctor, and I did. By the age of eighteen, I had secured top grades, but what always gave me pleasure were the {sic} manuscripts I'd written and hidden in the closet. My parents... always... *always* discouraged the idea of being a writer. I had to make money, and how could I do that by not being another Shakespeare? So, I had to stop it."

She paused, not allowing the words to pass through the dry corridor of her throat.

"And *I did*. I did because there was God who wanted me to stop, and I didn't get a single opportunity to get my manuscripts published. I became angry with him for not giving me the chance. So, I tried what my parents wanted me to... as I knew my parents had sacrificed their dreams for me. Then because I couldn't confess the mental torment I was going through, I felt constant pressure on me." She gulped, "besides I failed the test."

There was a long pause, and she kept staring at the white nothingness at her feet.

"They didn't beat me this time." she told me, then raised her eyes, "But they started killing me with their taunts." Silence.

More tears.

Helplessness.

It looked as if humans were only capable of *this* in hatred, pity and desperation.

In this case, I couldn't make out what it was for her. But hatred came to mind first.

"I hate it when parents make children their own personal property and vicariously impose their lives on them, as if they were allowed by God to do this! When young, everyone thinks they know what they want to be in the future. But later, they are held back by a negative force. And that force is…"

She cast her eyes on me, quite suddenly, with a devious expression, "is parents! It makes you do what you are *capable* of rather than what you are *excellent* at!"

Then came her pity:

"God makes us free creatures. But every man is a slave to another man. We spend our lives for others only. All of it. First, unwillingly, and when we can't stand it, then we *willingly* devote ourselves to someone, thinking we are doing it for ourselves, but we aren't! It's just a way of comforting oneself!"

And finally came her desperation.

"I would rather do what I'm excellent at than what I'm capable of. I can become a teacher, a doctor, an artist, or a pilot… but does that mean I will reach the height of that profession? No! because it would be *tiring* work for me and being myself would be a pleasing job for me that I would never get tired of it!"

She wiped away her tears on her sleeve and then, as if she had wiped away all the past as well, she looked at me.

"Will it hurt?" she whispered. "What will happen after this?"

I replied with as much indifference as I could muster, "I'll take your life away. Then the angel will come to take away your soul."

She nodded and it gave me an impression that she didn't want herself to be an open book anymore, "Will it be painful?"

"Yes."

"Not more than I had in life," she said sarcastically. Then she added, "Why? Why will it hurt?"

I smiled. How oblivious the humans are with their doings on Earth. When the end comes, they don't remember the cause of the pain.

Why will it hurt… "For your sins."

She bit the inside of her cheek, "My sins… and what exactly are my sins?"

"Well… according to your religion, Christianity, committing suicide is a sin."

She remained calm at this, "Is this the part where I tell you I didn't kill myself, my parents killed me."

I think from a philosophical point of view, she was right. I'm not a judge, so I remained stoic.

"For hating your parents."

"Wrong, I don't hate them." She was denying the sins she had committed. "I hate the system. Giving birth doesn't actually make you a mother."

I frowned. *Rose.*

I asked her impatiently, "Then what makes you a mother?"

She licked her lips, swallowed, and drew back from me, "Sacrifice and understanding."

For some time, I looked at her.

"For blaming God," I tried to trap her, but that that sly rat of a human kept denying.

"No, wrong use of the word 'blame.' I would say that God is *responsible* for my life and saying this is not a sin." I became angry.

I became angry? I

became angry!

"Okay, for lying. Lying every day. *Lying all the time. What kind of person tells lies and not even thinks once?"*

As I stared at her in anger, tears welled in her eyes. She had been denying all the indictments, but now she was going to surrender.

"A desperate kind." She whispered and closed her eyes.

My frown vanished at her answer. Tears formed beads on her lashes. I narrowed my eyes and she twitched.

A lifeless body lay in front of me. The tears remained suspended in her eyes and she would grieve no more.

I kept sitting there, thinking about Rose and myself.

Will she behave this way when I tell her who I am? Will I be the kind of mother this girl had?

That day, I decided I would never be the kind of mother humans have. *Never.*

Chapter 5

Funeral.

Are they here for the dead or the living? I am still thinking about that one.

Because the girl's death brought many people. Perhaps, more than, she would have expected when she was alive.

OBSERVATION No. 10

"People seem to hate a person when he is alive and never bother to visit them. It seems odd that they would suddenly start loving the person after they are dead! Is it right that they should show up just once at the funeral, bringing flowers for the dead person when they really needed them when they were alive? They say a eulogy when it can't be heard by the person to whom it is addressed. What they needed were kind words and thoughts when they were living a life of hell."

It was the first funeral I ever attended. I wanted to look at her mother, who was crying hard.

I frowned.

Strange creatures, humans.

Why cry now when it was far too late? Whose fault was it that she was no longer here?

Her family had played a part in it all.

I left like a shadow, unnoticed and unseen.

***

It was night

I was lying on the grass in the castle grounds and Rose was by my side, studying her book and I was thinking about the dead girl.

All I know is I was trying to send her a message that she would be punished for disobeying her parents. And the message she conveyed to me through her eyes asked, 'what about the parents who made this child's life hell?'

I vowed I would never make Rose's life hell.

"What are you doing?" Rose asked, turning towards me.

My eyes were on the cloudless sky, illuminated by the stars. "Thinking."

Rose drew closer to me, "Mama... you don't look happy."

"Umm..." I stayed motionless, "Yeah... it's umm... thinking is what's troubling me..."

"I know what will cheer you up!" "What?"

I asked, in a trance.

"You can unthink the thing you are thinking!"

Finally, she made me smile. I turned towards her, facing her twinkling eyes that were just like the stars above.

"Okay," I sighed and changed the topic, "So, how was your day, Rose?"

"It was good."

"Let me see your book."

I took it from her. There were words and their meanings in her dictionary. I had defined all of them for her. It ended with the stars.

"Why haven't you written the meaning of stars?"

"Because I was waiting for you to tell me the meaning of stars."

"No," I teased her, "I won't."

"Mama! Tell me!"

"What if I don't?"

She folded her arms angrily, "I'm not talking to you now." I waited. No, she didn't talk to me.

"Rose?"

No response. I laughed.

"C'mon, Rose!"

"I won't talk, Mama!" she sounded annoyed.

"Oh, you're already are talking, baby. Let's go inside, it's getting cold."

She didn't move. I tickled her but she didn't laugh.

"Rose is going to laugh now, give me your sweet cackle! Give up, baby!"

First, she resisted, but then outbursts of laughter rippled from her, and we laughed until we were tired. In the dark, moonless night, no human heard her. I had never laughed before, and now it felt good to laugh.

Happiness felt good.

We both lay there, watching the stars. For some time, we stayed quiet.

"Mama?"

I knew what she was about to say now, "Hmm?"

"Stars?"

I laughed silently, "Yes, what about them?" "Tell me!"

She embraced me in her little arms, but I held my answer back as I wanted to see her curiosity.

"Sleep now, goodnight, Rose."

I watched her sleep with a feeling of euphoria. I loved to watch her sleeping.

She was growing, inheriting her father's white skin and her mother's beautiful, black hair. She was also learning as she was growing. I taught her about everything except three topics: sin, humans, and materialistic things. I planned to make her strong like the storming sea and as elegant as an eagle's soaring flight.

Rose slept, hugging me, and I witnessed the break of dawn, the chirping of birds awakening her.

"Good morning, flower," I said cheerfully, "Did you sleep well?"

She smiled, yawning, "Yes... I wish it was always like this."

"Like what?"

"Sleeping with you." She said, not letting go of me. "Did you sleep well?"

I had no answer as I couldn't sleep. Stroking her pink cheeks, which gleamed in the early morning sunlight, I answered, "Err... I didn't sleep."

Rose frowned and then asked slyly, "Why? Was I troubling you?" "Yes," I teased, "Can't you control your legs when you're asleep? It seemed as if you were playing football."

"But, "she protested, "there's no ball here!" I

laughed faintly, "As in, *I* was your football."

Rose blushed, I grinned.

"You see that big ball of light, Rose?" I tried to divert her attention by pointing at the sun. "That? No." She blinked, unable to look directly at the sun.

"No, what I mean is... every time that big ball of light brightens the morning."

"So! *That* is the ball!"

I laughed, "That is the Sun."

Rose quickly grappled to find her book in the grass, sat upright and began to write.

"Not S-N. It's S-U-N," I informed her.

"Oh," she uttered quietly, "What's its meaning?"

I sighed seriously now. I looked straight at the sun without blinking. She waited for my answer and looked at me.

"Mama?"

No, this time I wasn't going to tease her. I was just thinking of an appropriate answer to her question.

"Life," I told her, "Sun means life."

"Good," Rose seemed happy with my answer. Then she asked, "And what is life exactly?"

I got up and held out my hand, "Come on, I'll show you."

She held my forefinger and I led her into the forest, for the first time.

I was going to show her life. Until then, she had just seen insects, flowers, sky, Sun, stars, Moon, birds, and some animals.

Now, it was time for her to experience the wonder of nature.

As we passed the graves spread across acres of land, which I had shrouded in a permanent state of total darkness, Rose looked around in amazement.

"Mama," she stopped, "What are these?"

She wasn't afraid. I hadn't taught her to be afraid of anything. She was simply pointing at the graves.

"These are…" I thought. I had created them to terrify any human who accidently stepped in my area or trespassed there, "These are rocks, Rose… but…"

I crouched to say the important thing, "You won't go near them, okay?"

"Okay."

"No, I mean it. Promise me that you won't go near them?" "Okay, Mama, pinky promise."

"Now that's my girl!" I fluffed her hair.

The reason was that I didn't want my daughter to go near any human, dead or alive. I didn't want her to be influenced by them. Not yet.

It was a long way. I had made our home in seclusion and there was a great distance between the forest and the castle.

"I'm tired," Rose looked exhausted.

"Come on," I lifted her, and she put her arm around my neck, her head on my shoulder. I continued the walk.

"Oh, we forgot breakfast." I remembered.

"I'm hungry."

"Well, eat me then." I joked.

"Yuck… now that would taste bad," Rose grimaced.

She kept talking. She talked a lot, she asked a lot of questions, which seemed endless.

"Mama, why didn't you tell me about stars last night?"

"Didn't I?"

"No, you have to tell me now!"

"Do you want to see the stars or see the thing that eats light?"

"Both—wait a minute—*eats light*? Why can't I eat light?"

50

And she opened her mouth and began to chew. I laughed at her little act.

"You can't, Rose..."

"But why can that thing eat light and not me? I thought things can only eat apples, bananas, strawberries..."

"Yeah, I said that, but that thing isn't like you. Hey, are you getting heavy or is it my imagination?" "What is imagination?"

"Thinking about unexpected things, I guess," I told her meditatively, "Oh, no, not now. Don't write it now!"

"But I'll forget it later!"

And she wrote it while I was carrying her, and I never became tired.

We reached the proximity of the forest, finding the lush green trees wet with dew. I placed Rose on her feet on the forest floor.

Her eyes opened wide and she looked at me for permission.

"Run as far as you want!"

Her small feet weren't tired as she ran towards the forest.

"Wow... what is this big thing, Mama?" "This,"

I came towards her, "is a tree."

She began to run around its trunk. I watched that eight-year-old girl circling the tree cheerfully.

"This is so big, big, BIG!" she was laughing, "This is amazing!"

She held my hand in both of hers and pulled me into the forest.

"I guess you have enough space for all of this in your notebook?"

"He-he-he! What is that? Did you see it? Oh, there's a butterfly as well! Apples... wait, why are they on a tree?"

She stumbled while skipping steps, tripping over an outgrown root and fell, looking up at me, "Oops!"

Her frock was covered with mud. She wiped her hands on it.

"I'm sorry," she said, and I knew she was hyper-excited, "But this is so amazing, Mama! Can we take this tree home?" I controlled my amusement.

"If you can lift it," as soon as I said it, she embraced the trunk and tried to pull it. I watched, controlling my laughter.

"This is so heavy. I need six more arms and ten more hands." She said innocently, not giving up.

I laughed loudly, and once I started it was difficult to stop.

"Oh, no... where will we find six arms and ten hands?"

Upon my refusal, Rose looked upset. She brought up an idea and bawled, "We can ask the Lord for extra pairs!" *There*.

I was trapped.

"Err… no, Rose. Trees can't move from their place.

"But…" she stopped and left the tree.

"But I'll show you the flower that is also called rose!" "The tree…"

"And some animals."

"The tree… I want it."

"Okay, you can see this tree every day." "That means?" she raised her eyebrows.

"That means yes. You can visit this forest every day."

Her eyes sparkled brighter than the sun at this and she beamed, hugging my waist, "This is amazing, Mama!"

"Okay, kiddo."

I was very frank with Rose. I didn't want to be the kind of mother who was always very serious with her child so that they never expressed themselves in front of the parent.

"Let's go and see roses!" I said.

We moved deeper into the forest. She was so excited that she let go of my finger and explored everything herself, even the leaves.

OBSERVATION No. 11

Humans are born with a deep-rooted curiosity in their souls. They aren't afraid of anything when they're curious.

Nothing frightened her, not even insects that humans considered nasty or animals humans termed as wild.

Ha. Ha. Ha. Nasty, wild humans.

Excuse my words.

How far her could her little legs carry her? She became tired soon and slowed down, panting. I smiled.

"So, kid, what's your plan?"

"What is a plan?"

I thought. Something humans try to accomplish and mostly fail to achieve. But I didn't tell her that. She would then ask me a hundred questions, which I was in no mood to answer. Such as, 'what is human? What is accomplish?' And the tricky one would be, *'why?'*

Now that why…

Because the Lord had already planned the future, which changes the plans of humans.

Who is the smarter planner? The Lord or humans?

"Plan is something you want to do."

"I want to rest and eat and sleep and play and write the meaning of plan in my book," she slumped at the foot of a willow tree.

"Hmm," I sat beside her," you forgot, you wanted to see the roses as well." "Oh… that too," she said as she scribbled in her book.

And that is how we roamed the forest for a while, searching for roses. Every time she found a flower, she rushed to me and asked if it was rose, the answer was always negative.

But she discovered many things. I was glad that she discovered the things invented by the Creator, not like humans who *become* creators by inventing the things and letting *Him* discover them.

Chapter 6

Just another night, I was staring at the moon, singing a lullaby, and thinking of Rose who was sleeping beside me. I couldn't sleep. After so much work, I still couldn't sleep.

There are some things about humans that I can't appreciate: sleep, taste, see my own reflection in the mirror, smell.

And there are some of my traits that humans can't appreciate either: traveling the world at the speed of light, read minds, freedom, live to see the future becoming history. "Why aren't you sleeping?" Rose asked and I looked at her sideways. She was awake and I hadn't known. I rolled over my side, facing her and curled my elbow beneath my head.

"Because I was imagining what you were dreaming."

I stared at her as she quickly pulled out the book from her pocket and opened it, going through the pages. When she said the next words, I laughed softly.

"Imagine: thinking about unexpected things." She read and bit her lip. Looking at me, she said, "You were thinking about what I was dreaming?"

"Yeah."

"So, Mama?"

"What do you want to hear?"

"What was I dreaming about? "How would I know, Rose? You tell me," I asked and felt curious. "But promise me, if I tell you, you'll answer my question," she imposed her condition.

I agreed, nodding.

"I was dreaming that I was sitting on a giant butterfly and flying through the clouds."

"That is so mean, Rose. Where was your mother in your dream?"

She was taken aback, "I don't know… but don't be upset, Mama. You had gone to your work as always! Yes?"

I nodded, amused. What funny little creatures human children are!

"Okay… so what is your question?" "Stars?"

she said tentatively.

I laughed aloud, facing the stars again. Some things humans never forget. I have never been able to understand if oblivion is positive or negative.

"Come off it, Rose!"

"Mama!" she exclaimed exaggeratedly, "You said you'd tell me!"

"Okay. Stars are lots of glitter. Lots of it..." I made up.

"So, why doesn't the glitter fall down?" she asked with a crease between her eyebrows.

Children always trap you, by treachery, by questions, or by pure innocence. "Because... the Lord has a... glue, which attaches them permanently to the sky."

"So, why does the glitter disappear when the Sun brings morning?"

"Because the Lord says, 'look at the Sun now, the stars are resting'," I told her, thinking fast. Before she could ask me another question, I quickly asked her one.

"Hey, you made up the part in the dream where I had gone to work, didn't you?"

"Err... yes. But Mama, you weren't there, so it *means* you were at work, right?"

"Right." I laughed. "Now, close your eyes and sleep, or I won't let you go to the forest again... and also your mouth." I finished, thinking quickly. She took it as a warning and closed her eyes. I couldn't even manage a yawn.

***

Sometimes, I feel I'm the slave to villains because they keep killing and I take lives.

But as in a game of chess, the time of vengeance comes when I become their master and take their lives instead.

There is a universal disease, tension, which I have a slight touch of. What would I do when the time came to take Rose's life? I was hovering over the world, taking lives when it occurred to me.

How would I do it? How would I take my daughter's life? How could I see my girl dead? How could I dig her grave? How could I live without her? What would I feel?

I wished I had thought about it before I took her from her mother... before I became attached to her... before she became my daughter... But the unnatural thing was already done.

I couldn't give her to humans, or leave my daughter among them... not because she was my responsibility, but because it was the first time I was being a human. Truly and deeply, I was being a better human than humans are.

"Rose? Rose! I'm home!"

I had just come back from work to find the castle empty. Rose was nowhere to be seen. She never asked me what my work was because whenever I came back, I brought her fruit and vegetables in a basket, and so she must have thought that my work was to collect fruit for her.

"Come and find me!"

I heard a very distant voice singing. Looking around, I placed my basket on the ground and wore my hood.

"I'm coming!" I called to her and started searching.

She wasn't in the castle, so I started looking in the garden. Then I thought that maybe she was hiding behind the huge trunk. Yes, she must be heading there. I went out of the castle and into the graveyard.

As I passed through the graveyard in the darkness and mist, I heard her giggling.

What? Rose was hiding behind a gravestone? "Rose? Are you hiding here?" I asked, alarmed.

No response. The giggling stopped. She wouldn't reply and I couldn't look behind every gravestone as they were endless.

The fear was what if she read the *writing* on the gravestones? The names... the dates.... She would ask thousands of questions.

I couldn't lie to her, I would tell her about humans, which I didn't want to do.

"ROSE!"

Nothing. I looked around, and then finally, an idea came to mind. I'm not used to thinking about solutions to problems, but when the idea came into my mind, it seemed natural.

"Rose, I brought a rose for you today.

Nothing.

I started walking towards the castle.

"Okay, I understand you don't want to see it... so... I'll just throw it away..."

"I'm here!"

I looked. She was sneaking towards me from behind a gravestone that was some distance away.

I staggered to her between the creepy graves, my sins, and my virtues. Strange?

Those graves were my sins and my virtues because at some point, I feel virtue when I take the life of a person who has made someone's life hell. And I feel a sin when I take life of someone who had made someone's life like paradise.

Just like a human.

So, this was my heaven.

OBSERVATION No. 12

Heaven of Death: graveyard.

Rose laughed as I approached her.

"Hush up!" I put my index finger to my lips. She seemed unsettled by my act, so I picked her up and carried her quietly, "I told you not to come here." "But they're just stones..." she said, looking at the ancient-looking rocks.

"Yes, but you're not to come here again."

"Why?"

"Because I say so," I was extremely serious.

"But I want to know. You said that I can go to the forest, so why not here? I mean, Mama..."

I halted, put Rose on her feet on the rough path and glowered at her.

"I said you're not to go near those stones! If you do, then you'll stay here always, with these stones. Without Mama!" I snapped indignantly.

She was frightened because I had never behaved so angrily toward her. Now it looked as if I was the ghost of the graveyard, haunting the little girl.

I stomped towards the castle again without looking back and had a sensation as Rose held the hem of my black cloak and began to walk behind me.

Poor girl, I had sacred her.

Now I understood that when human mothers ask their children to stay away from something it's not because the child might be frightened by it. It's because the mother is already afraid of it.

We reached the castle, and I simply began to wash the fruit in the wooden tub I had built. Rose sat down, looking at the grass. I knew that a thousand questions had invaded her mind, but she wasn't daring to ask even one. I just wanted her to forget about it.

But I also knew that now, every time she went to the forest and passed the graveyard, she would wonder why I didn't let her go near the stones. And the suspense would inevitably draw her toward the graves, and she would read the names on them and wonder what they meant.

And what they meant was disaster. I mean, humans are a disaster for nature.

"You didn't ask what I'm feeling, Rose," I tried to divert her attention, bringing the basket of fruit to her.

She didn't reply. Sitting beside her, I continued, "Well, you know I'm angry."

I handed her a banana, but she didn't take it. Mimicking her voice, I said, "And now, tell me, what is angry, Mama?"

I remained quiet, as she continued to stare at the grass.

"Anger means regret," I sighed. Again, I copied her voice, "Now, what is regret, Mama?"

I knew she was listening carefully, but pretending she wasn't.

"Regret means to wish you hadn't done something, and that you could change it."

Then it came out suddenly, "Oh, Lord! I wish I hadn't done it!"

Getting up, I headed towards the bridge, wore my hood and left to take the lives of humans again. At the edge of the bridge, I looked back slowly.

Rose was writing something in her book, I knew what it was.

I smiled and left.

When I came back, I saw Rose was already sleeping with the rose in her hand that I had left in the basket.

It was a beautiful crimson rose, the petals perfectly curved and an amazingly ravishing scent. I took it from her hand, opened her book, placed it inside, and put it back by her side.

But there was something even more beautiful than the rose. I embraced her in my arms, she was my own charming Rose.

***

My life was passing peacefully with Rose discovering things and me watching her grow, just like a flower, which is a bud and suddenly begins to blossom.

And what a beautiful flower she was becoming. I think if there were more people like her in the world, then maybe I would have liked humans. I like a pure soul, without sins. And Rose was a pure soul.

I made her what I wanted every human to be like.

She cared for me when she became tired from exploring the forest, as if I were also tired from my work. She gave me water when I came back, washed fruit for me, and ate after I had eaten something. Even if it was tasteless, I still ate for her satisfaction.

Every time I nibbled anything, I chewed harder expecting to taste something, but nothing was bitter, sweet, or sour for me. I couldn't feel the wind that made her long hair become a lustrous banner, or shiver in the cold when she curled herself into me, nor did I sweat in the scorching sun.

Nothing.

And she would help me with my work by collecting the autumn leaves and sweeping the castle floor. Not only did she help me, but tended every living creature there, even if it was a snake or a wolf.

I asked her to stay away from the animals and watch them from a distance, which she did, only going near them if they were injured, and sometimes, she carried them home to me.

"Mama, look at this poor deer, her leg."

By then, she was ten years old, and she placed the deer in front of me on the grass so I could inspect its broken leg.

It was strange, my work was to take lives and there I was, healing the animals, saving them from dying.

But of course, it wasn't a human.

Rose didn't know what dying was. I didn't tell her or let her see tigers hunting or dying reindeer because then she would know death.

I just wanted her to know I was her mother, not Death.

She turned twelve, and one day when I returned home, I saw her standing, waiting for me. As I approached near, I saw impatience on her face. "Rose, today I brought…"

"My gown is torn!" she said, talking over me. I stopped, looking at her.

The navy-blue gown she was wearing was torn, but where? I couldn't see anything.

"You are joking, right?"

Can you sense my fright at that? It was because I didn't want to weave a new one for her! Lord… it took time, and it was an extremely boring thing for Death to do.

"No, Mama, really, it's torn!" She seemed very happy about it. I placed the basket on the ground and stared at her in alarm.

"Where?"

"At the back!" She said excitedly.

I quickly pushed away her black hair and saw it. Yes, it was torn and her white skin was visible,

"See?"

"Okay, I'll sew it up from here…"

"No! I mean… it's so dirty and old and… just smell it, oh dear, it smells like dung, see?" She sniffed it.

I eyed her dubiously. I didn't bother to sniff because no matter how pungent it might be, I still couldn't smell it.

"Don't worry, Rose. We'll wash it." Rose was taken aback.

"Wash it?" She gulped, "I bet it won't go away by washing. And anyway, Mama, what will I wear when you're washing it? Do you want me to sit here, *naked?*"

"Why not, who will see you?"

"You will!"

"But that's okay, I'm your mother."

"No, that is *not* okay. Totally not okay."

"Rose," I stopped her at once, "what is it that you really want?"

"I was hoping, you know… that maybe you would… you know… make a new gown for me?"

"Oh no, Rose!" I shielded my eyes from the sun with my hand, like a salute. "Oh no… did you tear it on purpose?"

Rose hesitated, "Err… kind of…"

"Why?"

"Because I wanted a new gown! I don't want blue anymore. I want a beautiful gown like yours!"

"White?"

"No… I mean… what was that word you used last week? Yes— clamorous—" "Glamorous."

"Whatever! I don't want to wear a plain gown. I want shiny, silk, glittering like stars, and I want my hair like yours too. And a silver crown like yours and to look beautiful like you!"

For a moment, I looked mournfully at her. Then I smiled. I smiled because this was the only human who wanted to be a miniature version of her parent. *Only.*

Most humans hate to be like their parents.

I appeared beautiful to Rose because she was free of sins. I knew she had a direct ticket to paradise as she was as sinless as a wee baby.

She was looking at me with inquisitive eyes. As I exhaled, the words flowed with it, "Okay, you could have just asked instead of tearing your gown."

I couldn't produce a dress like mine out of thin air because I didn't have that kind of magic. And for the first time, I realized I needed to buy it from humans.

How?

It took me three days to figure out what I was supposed to do. I didn't have a paper with a stamp on it regarded as money. Until then, Rose wore her torn attire.

When she asked me about it, I simply teased her, "Now, this is your punishment, Rose."

For the first time, as I traveled the world taking lives, I also visited dress shops. Oh, Lord… and what kinds of dresses there were! I could barely call them clothes when most of them left the females half naked.

OBSERVATION No. 13

Humans have forgotten the meaning of clothes.

When Rose asked me the meaning of clothes for the first time, I told her:

Clothes: hide yourself.

And she had asked me why? I had told her exactly what I'm going to tell you: precious things are always hidden.

I found Rose a school in America where the students were going to perform a play by Shakespeare.

It was10 March 1933. There would be an earthquake in California. The characters would die when the building fell on them. I knew the dress would be buried there.

So, I played the part of the hero and rescued the dress.

It all happened before the play could even start. I stared at the girl who owned the dress. She was about the same age as Rose.

"Am I going to die?"

I rolled my tongue, apparently lost in thought, "Yes, I suppose you are." "Okay," she seemed terrified, but didn't fight me.

I looked at the dress lying at her side. Should I or shouldn't I?

It was the second time I had to make a decision and only the Lord knows how difficult it was.

To beg from a human? No way.

But Rose would be happy then.

It would damage my self-respect. Rose

would be happy.

My ego…

Rose would be happy.

A war was happening in my mind. The stupid part was convincing my egoistic part.

"What are you waiting for?"

The girl asked me in astonishment. I cleared my throat.

"Can I have your dress, please?"

I was surprised by the request I made. I could have ordered her. I could have stolen the thing from the dead girl.

But humans steal. So, I asked directly.

"Yeah, sure," she said, looking at me on the floor in the sunshine I had created. There was no building around. Just me, the girl and the dress in the sunshine, on the marble floor.

"Why do you want it?" she asked curiously.

Oh, humans, they don't let go of curiosity even if they are dying. Wait… sometimes they die *because* of curiosity.

I smiled as I thought about Rose, "I want it for my daughter."

The girl, propping herself up on her elbows, was bewildered by my answer.

"I didn't know Death could have a daughter." She said, almost to herself. "It means there are more of you. How many Deaths are there exactly?"

I stared back at the girl who had inquisitive eyes. How did I look to her? Not as beautiful as I appeared to Rose.

I couldn't say it was a human daughter. I had no interest in narrating my story.

It was my ugly little secret and no human would be involved, dead or alive.

I frightened her by my gaze, as I took her life, saying darkly, "Just one."

It was pretty rude of me not even to thank her, but I returned home.

It was a black, glittering gown that looked perfect on Rose. She was very happy that day and I told her not to tear that one.

I found the leftovers of perished places that humans call junk, I picked up the valuable things: pencils and paper and gave them to Rose.

It was delightful when she made her first drawing of a tree. It wasn't exactly the tree she was looking at and copying, but it brought a smile to my face.

I gradually learned that she wasn't only interested in writing her own dictionary, but she had an interest in art as well.

I helped her with it. we would sit by the trees in afternoons and I would tell her the areas to shade. First the trees, then the birds. That is how she saw things.

First Rose, then the roses. That is how I saw things.

Whenever she woke up and I had already left to carry out my duties, she always found a red rose by her side, placed on her book. It meant a lot to her as it gave her the message that I had been there.

And it meant a lot to me too.

She was nothing like other humans at all. She seemed to be human but a version from another planet where there was no concept of sin and only me, nature, and the Lord existed with her.

In winter, when it became too cold for the first time, I asked her to collect wood with me, but not to break any branches from the trees, just to look on the ground for some. I didn't want her to harm any living thing, even if it was a tree. She asked me why, but I didn't tell her.

When we had collected enough, we took it to the castle where I stacked it in a pyramid and asked her to sit at some distance.

Then I set fire to it.

I sat down on the opposite side with the fire between us. and I could see her fascination.

"Whoa! What is this, Mama?" she asked as fire flashed in her eyes. It was the first time she had seen fire, and she was so mesmerized by it that she forgot her 'customary move.'

"Fire."

"What does it mean?" She asked, reaching out for it.

"No— *don't touch it*! It'll burn you!" She leaned back at my warning, "Remember all those animals I told you to stay away from? The dangerous ones? This is also dangerous, like them."

"It's an animal? But I can't see its mouth or claws... or eyes... or..."

"It's not an animal, Rose!" I laughed. "You see, this thing is the opposite to water. Water flows, but this dances. Water does nothing to your skin"

"It does! Wrinkles appear on my fingertips if I stay in the river for too long!"

"But that's temporary. After you have been out for a little while, like now, your fingertips are normal. But if you try to touch the fire, it will permanently harm you."

"Why?"

"Because... umm... it just doesn't like to be touched."

"Okay. But it is beautiful, isn't it?" She laughed slightly, staring into the fire. "That is why it should stay alone." I said to myself in a whisper.

"Did you say something?" she looked at me and I shook my head.

OBSERVATION No. 14

Beauty might seem the most important thing at the time, but it should be left alone because it can ruin everything in the fulness of time. Like a sweet poison.

After some time, she took her book out. This was her customary move.

"What are you writing, Rose?"

"F-Y-A-R-E."

"No, it's F-I-R-E."

"And what is its meaning?" she looked at me.

To give her the meaning of fire was a difficult task. It took me a while to construct something.

Beauty? Warmth? Danger? Hell? A hunger that consumed wood?

"It's..." there were many meanings, but still I had nothing to tell her. "It's... obliterating beauty."

63

I concluded finally. I didn't want her to think fire was a negative thing. She wrote it down. It must have confused her though.

And she sat there, sleepless, and I sat there, staring at the fire, wondering how it felt to be burned.

What were the feelings of those humans burning in hell, with their skin reborn every time it was burnt?

There thing about our castle was that, even if Rose was alone there and it seemed haunted, she loved it.

And when she slept, I left the rose on her book, leaving her alone.

***

Rose turned fifteen the day she carried a wounded toucan in the castle. The bird's wing was cut, I had no idea how, but it was dying. I didn't want the toucan to die because Rose had never seen dying birds or animals.

I didn't know how she would perceive it. If she would question me *about me*. How would I tell her about myself? I just couldn't. I was her mother and I knew it would horrify her to know Death existed in the world.

So... I played the part of nurse. I treated the toucan with the best herbal plants while Rose held its colorful beak and stroked it.

Colors.

Two colorful images make me smile, the bright sunset hues, when the layers of clouds have a golden glitter on them, and the second is the full moon in darkness giving a silver shimmer to the scudding, clouds as they cross its path.

What a contradiction. I hadn't noticed all this until Rose explained her fondness of those shades to me.

So, Rose and I smiled at the same time when we saw them, even when we weren't together, I would stop my work for several minutes and smile at the shade, knowing that Rose would be holding a rose and doing the same thing, both missing each other.

I didn't let her see death as I cured the toucan and Rose's tears were saved.

The realization of unrealistic things. How does that sound? Should I have told her that one dies and then there is nothing. "What is nothing, Mama?" she would have asked. I imagined the unrealistic in my mind as I wondered nothingness.

Some people want to be nothing. They don't want to be human, so they wish for nothingness.

And what if there was something in that nothingness too? Maybe, up in the castle of clouds, there was a place where nothingness existed, looking down on Earth, watching the privilege of being a human. And their names would be nothing number one, nothing number two, leading to infinity.

That nothingness, my dear friends, exists. And that nothingness, is in a grave.

When you die with a belief, you are something. But when you die without a belief, you are nothing.

That was when I realized Rose needed a belief. She needed a faith.

I couldn't choose between her parents' religions, I had thought she should make that decision herself, so I got two books for her.

"Hi, Mama! What are you doing?"

Rose was sitting by the rose plants, digging. She was interested in gardening these days, trying to make an orchard in that desolate place. And with some fluke, roses along with jasmine and daisies had taken birth in my kingdom.

"Uh—nothing. Any luck with the new flowers?"

"No," she got up, brushing her hands on her gown and looking at me, "sunflowers are pretty hard work. Do you know what happened to Macaw today?"

Macaw was her pet. She chose the parrot because it was red, and the roses were red too. She thought everything red belonged to her. "No, got injured?" I shrugged.

"No!" She said cheerfully, "You always give me wrong answers about Macaw, you know?

"Well, there is one thing I do know about Macaw," I told her, looking at her disheveled appearance, "It'll soon make a nest on your head." Rose exhaled heavily, "That wooden comb you gave me broke." "Yeah, why wouldn't it with all these tangles in your hair?

Even though she was fifteen, she needed more care than a baby.

"And what about taking a bath?" I asked, "Let me guess, all the water evaporated from heat."

Rose giggled, "No. A river can't evaporate just like that. It's just that, I didn't get time to take a bath."

I raised my eyebrows in surprise. Of all the humans in the world who didn't have time to spend on themselves, it wasn't this girl. She was alone in the forest with nothing but herself to worry about. It was impossible.

"Fine." I said, wondering how I would tell her about religion. As I sat on the grass, staring at her. she sensed my uneasiness.

"What is it?" she asked, coming towards me. I didn't answer straight away, "What is it, Mama?"

I kept looking at her. What should I do now? She was fifteen... she had to choose.

"Mama?" she seemed concerned. "Go, wash your hands, Rose."

She didn't ask me the reason, she always obeyed me without question because she knew I always told her the right thing to do. She trusted me blindly.

She came back a minute later and stood in front of me. By then, I had something wrapped in my cloak, in my lap.

"Sit down, Rose."

She sat down in front of me with her legs crossed and a worried expression.

"I have something for you."

"Really?" she brightened up, "Let me guess. Umm… a pencil?"

I shook my head. "Pages?"

I shook it again. "I've got it… a dress!"

When I shook my head this time, she seemed disappointed.

"Some new words to write in my book?" She asked with hope.

Slowly, but carefully, I unwrapped the cloak and there lay the books.

"A book!" She exclaimed.

"The book, or should I say, the books."

Rose reached out for the first of the two books.

"Where did you get these?" she asked, looking pleased.

Scratching my cheek, I wished I had prepared myself for her questions. "From… the Lord."

Her jaw dropped in amazement, then she asked in a whisper, as if her Macaw would hear and somehow translate the language, "Did you meet Him?"

"No." I broke her fantasy, "Rose, save your questions, okay? You'll get your answers later."

Rose looked at the book cover but seemed disappointed. I knew why. Immediately, she took the other book and seemed even more disappointed. I laughed slightly.

"Mama! Am I supposed to laugh?"

"No…" I replied. "Okay, okay – I won't laugh again. Now, you can't read them yet because they are in a foreign language. I'll teach you and then you'll understand the meaning."

"Can't you get them in English?"

"I'm afraid not, Rose." I held her hands tightly in mine. "Listen to me very carefully. These books are for you to read and understand, and then…"

"And then what, Mama?"

"And then you'll have to choose one of them only."

66

"What do you mean?"

I knew she wanted to ask why she couldn't have both.

"That means… you have to be a Muslim or a Christian."

There were many religions, studying them would take up her whole life. So, it was better to only study those of her parents.

"Well then, it's obvious, isn't it? I'll choose what you have chosen!" "No." I said abruptly. "You see… I can't tell you what I have chosen. The decision is yours to make. You have to think very carefully." "I don't understand a single thing, Mama. Can't we leave it." She wanted to go, but I still held her hands. "No, it's very important, Rose. You can't leave it."

"Okay, Mama. So, let's begin. What are the names of these books?"

I let go of her hands. Holding one book in my right and the other in my left hand.

"The Koran and The Bible."

Chapter 7

Henry Cavills.

No, I'm not going to take his life. I'm going to introduce him.

That son of a bitch.

For me, he was a sinner and for Rose, he was the most pious man. For me, he was a thief, and for her, he was a rescuer.

Age twenty-three, height five foot five inches, religion Christianity, country Brazil, occupation tourist, blue eyes, fair complexion, black hair, perfect jaw line with a touch of unshaven beard.

Damn it.

Some humans don't deserve to be beautiful. I often wish what they are inside should show on their face and be perfectly reflected in their eyes.

OBSERVATION No. 15

Beautiful things often lead to sin.

I suppose I have made myself clear.

Now, let me reintroduce that son of a bitch.

It was the year that Rose turned nineteen. And what a beautiful young lady she was becoming. I was proud of my daughter. Nineteen years old and not a tinge of sin in her records. It sounds impossible.

But as I said, she had no human influence.

Rose was so desperate to get a new gown that I had figure out a way to get her one. I entered the crowded shop with no money, just a gold piece in my hand.

Rose was getting older, but I wasn't. My face was the same as it had been nineteen years ago. I was still young. Soon Rose would become old and I would look like her daughter rather than her mother.

It made me laugh.

Back to the shop. I chose a gown and placed the gold piece in the cashier's drawer. Too much for a gown, right? Consider it a token of my generosity.

When I came back, the sun was setting.

"Rose?" No

response.

"Rose!"

I called aloud, getting a sensation that something wasn't right. Maybe she had gone to the forest to complete her sketch of the spider monkey she was drawing. But soon it would be nighttime, and to me, forest, solitude, and darkness didn't feel like a good combination.

I left the gown inside the castle, covered my crown with the hood of the cloak and headed towards the forest.

I had told her to return before sunset, so why wasn't she back yet?

My furrow deepened. Something was most definitely wrong. I started looking for her in the forest, neglecting the negativity that had entered my mind.

It was obvious that I wouldn't tire from searching for her, but the thing was, the longer it took, the more dangerous it became for her to be in the forest. After searching for half an hour, I found her, but the scene wasn't pleasant.

She was lying on the undergrowth and outgrowing tree roots and a ten-foot-long bushmaster snake was coiled beside her inert body.

Rose's face was pale, and she was gasping for air with all her might. It wasn't her moment to die, as I knew, but to see your own daughter in such a condition was disturbing.

Like all mothers, I panicked as if I were human. Before I could reach out to her, I heard footsteps and laughing.

And again, like humans, I hid behind the tree even though they couldn't see me. The voices became clearer, and soon they were in sight: Henry and his friend, Daniel.

Rose was losing her battle, and I had to do something. Popping up there and saving her wasn't an option because only Rose could see me, and it would seem like magic to them.

How unfair. I am Death and I don't have the power to kill someone. If I had, I would have killed those two men immediately.

"JESUS!" Daniel, the Englishman, cried.

Henry also looked at the girl he assumed was going to die. And just like me, they panicked.

In a second, Henry drew out his arrow, notched it in the bow and let it fly, straight in the snake's eye. The snake hissed in pain, but Henry didn't stop. Firing another arrow into the snake's body and drawing his dagger, he stabbed it into the snake's neck, severed its head, and tossed it away on the ground.

Breathing heavily, he looked back at Daniel who was frozen in place, wide-eyed, staring at the scene.

"Get a medic from tent," Henry said, but Daniel didn't move, *"NOW!"*

"Okay! Okay!" Daniel ran off clearly shaken.

69

Henry began to determine whether she was still alive by checking the pulse in her wrist, breathing a sigh of relief when he found that she was.

Casting one anxious glance in the direction Daniel had gone, he scooped Rose up in his arms and began to walk hurriedly in Daniels's wake.

I followed, wondering when Rose would wake up. I knew the poison was spreading in her body but had no worries as I knew she wouldn't die. The thing that did bother me was what her reaction would be when she saw another human.

Henry reached a clearing where there were two tents set up. Daniel was holding the first aid kit and another three men were standing there. I watched as Henry placed Rose on the grass and Daniel brought the kit to him. *"A girl?"* a man from his team asked, "What is she doing here?"

Henry didn't reply as he was urgently searching for something in the box. He lifted a syringe and a bottle of serum from the kit, and carefully filled it. Tearing her sleeve, he swiftly injected it in her arm. After that, he took another and did the same. In all, three injections were inserted in her upper arm.

Again, Henry checked her pulse and then let out his breath, relaxing. Sitting down, he started re-packing the box.

Daniel, the poor guy, was so frightened that it took him several minutes before he could even manage to kneel on the grass.

"Will anyone tell us what's going on?" The red-haired man asked.

Henry looked at him, "There was a bushmaster. It was just waiting for her to die."

"But what the hell was *she* doing in the forest?"

Henry frowned, "Maybe she was lost. Maybe there is some other tourist group here."

There was a pause, nobody moved. All had their eyes on her. Five separate thoughts in the minds of five people:

Who is she?

What is she doing here?

What is her name?

Is she going to die?

The last thought was in Henry's mind, but I couldn't tell that from reading his face. Most of all, I didn't like the look on Henry's face because he wasn't frowning as he was looking at her face. Unlike the others, he didn't have his arms folded, nor did he have the same questioning look in his eyes.

He was smiling slightly at Rose.

I immediately knew he was trouble.

After five minutes, the others dispersed; two went back to tent, and two started cooking, but Henry kept sitting there, looking at her.

I hid behind a tree as Rose would soon wake up and I didn't want her to know that I was there, I hadn't come to take her away.

An hour passed, and Henry unexpectedly left his duty of watching her with a frown and went to have his meal. By then it was completely dark and the fire they had lit would probably attract animals. Rose was still unconscious. Maybe there was something in the injection…

It is devastating to see your daughter and not be able to go to her aid.

The group was cheering and talking when I saw Rose begin to stir. I became alert, so did the men. They came and stood over her, watching with curiosity.

I knew that they expected Rose to ask them for help, shelter, and company. But Rose began to blink and propped herself up on her elbows.

Silence.

Her eyes went to Daniel first and she began to breathe rapidly. One by one, she looked at each of the men standing over her. I knew she was scared.

In a spur of the moment decision, before anyone could speak, Rose leapt to her feet and ran towards the forest again, never looking back.

But I stayed there to make sure no one followed her. The men stood there, all taken aback. Henry unfolded his arms, narrowed his eyes, and took hold of his bow. For a moment, I thought he was going to follow her, but he didn't.

"That was weird." Daniel uttered and they all began to busy themselves.

Henry shook his head and walked toward the tent.

I followed Rose. It was dark and I didn't want her to fall and hurt herself.

"ROSE!"

"MAMA!" The reply was coming from nearby.

"Stop! I'm coming to get you!"

"Okay!"

I soon found her. She was still extremely frightened. The moment she saw me, she hugged me. "Are you alright?" I asked. 'Yeah… I'm fine. Let's just go home," she was shivering with fright.

"Okay, okay, calm down. Hold my hand, we're going home."

We didn't talk to each other on our way back through the forest because I didn't want to attract any animals, but as we reached the graveyard, Rose began to explain everything to me.

"I'm so sorry, Mama. It was that bushmaster. It was hurt, I wanted to help, but… it… it attacked me! It was going to harm me! I don't know what happened, but when I woke up, I saw… I saw…"

"What? What did you see?"

71

"I don't know! They were some new kind of animal! Tall... standing on two legs... Surrounding me, and I thought they too were going to harm me, so I ran away."

I laughed faintly, thankful that it had been dark, and she hadn't seen properly.

"Okay... that teaches you that you don't have to stay out late, no matter what. And you don't have to help every dangerous..."

"Mama!" Rose almost bellowed, stopping in the middle of the graveyard.

"What?" I turned to look at her.

"My gown! It's torn!" She was holding her sleeve.

"Don't worry, Rose. I have a new one for you. And look at your hair. I bet tomorrow you'll find your parrot resting in your head."

***

The Koran and the Bible.

Rose had read them several times, but without translation. She had asked me the meaning many times, but I always refused, saying that I would explain when it was the right time. It involved humans. I didn't want her to know yet.

Meanwhile, after a day's break, Rose decided to go to the forest again.

"Mama?"

I was combing her hair, "Hmm?"

"I was thinking..." She began reluctantly, "Will it be okay for me to go in the forest again?"

When I stopped combing. Rose looked back at me.

I know humans would expect me to imprison her in a tower just like in fairytales and a prince would come to rescue her.

Sorry to disappoint you: wrong.

I'm not a human, I don't create fairytales. I am Death, and I have my own reasons to let things happen.

"Of course, Rose! It's your home, why wouldn't you go there?"

"But I'm scared."

"Oh... that bushmaster, it won't bother you again."

"No," she held my knees, "I'm scared of those new animals, Mama. They were strong and... and..."

I smiled and held her hand.

"Trust me, Rose. You trust your mama, right? I'm always with you. *Always.*"

72

Curling her lips, she turned her face away, and I began to comb her hair again.

"And you'll finish the sketch of the spider monkey too."

Rose laughed, "Mama, did you know I can climb trees like one too?"

"Really? Since when?"

"Some days ago. It's more fascinating to see the forest from up there. You know, I can teach you. It's not that hard."

"Shut up, spider monkey!" I laughed, "I'll ask you when you fall and break your leg!"

And it happened.

I couldn't leave her alone until I was sure those men had left the forest, so I spied on Rose. First, she searched for the spider monkey and completed its sketch in two hours. Then she placed the folded paper in her book and put it in her pocket. Purple was so her color.

There was an anteater with an injured leg. She spread a paste of herbs on the wound. After a general promenade, Rose chose a huge tree with abundant branches and began to climb it. And how she managed to climb it wearing a gown, only I saw, and it made me laugh. It was hard to control my laughter!

But I appreciated her effort. Soon, she wasn't visible.

After a while, I heard voices. *Oh no, not again. That Henry couldn't stay away, could he?*

"I think we need to rest," a man's voice. They were speaking Portuguese.

"Paulo, you look as if you've run a marathon!"

I looked up at the tree, wishing that she would either stay or come down that instant.

Neither happened.

"Did you call your father?" It was Daniel's voice. The steps were growing loud, crunching the leaves beneath boots.

"No," it was Henry, "I didn't bring my mobile with me."

Now they were under the tree. Maybe Rose was up there and couldn't hear their voices? She must have reached the top by now... what if she slipped?

"Okay guys," Paulo said, putting his bag down, "I'm stopping here... why? I didn't even have a decent breakfast!"

"You should have thought about it before agreeing to come on the trip, Doctor," Daniel smiled.

Henry also placed his bag on the ground along with his bow and cornucopia of arrows, "We should get some rest."

While the other men began to chat, he remained silent, looking perturbed. Standing akimbo, staring at the trunk, he was lost somewhere.

"Henry, your mother called yesterday. She said your dad is still upset about you leaving…" THUD.

Rose fell right on top of Henry. The other two jumped to their feet suddenly, looking at the unexpected visitor. Henry lay with his back pressed to the forest floor and Rose lying on his chest.

Placing her palms on the soil, she propped herself up and stared straight at Henry's face. He looked back, frowning.

Terrified, she swiftly sprang up to run away, but this time, Henry was faster. He clambered up just in time and chased her.

The men stood frozen in place.

Rose was running fast in a panic and Henry was following her with his frown deeper than usual, his jaws shut tightly and hands in fists.

He won. He grabbed her arm, twirled her around and held her to his body, her back against his chest, face at his side, and a dagger pointing at her throat.

Rose seemed as if she could hardly breathe.

"Para de lutar ou eu vou te matar." Henry whispered in her ear. *Stop fighting or I will kill you.*

She didn't understand, but his whisper was enough to terrify her.

"MAMA!" Rose screeched, "MAMA!"

Henry placed the dagger in his belt and covered her mouth with his palm to silence her.

"Ande, ou eu vou cortar o teu pescoço assim como eu fiz à cobra." *Walk, or I will cut your throat just like I did with the snake.*

He began to walk with his arms around her, imprisoning her. They reached the tree like that. As soon as they did, Daniel whispered.

"Que… diabos?"

What the… hell?

Henry whispered ominously in her ear again, "Eu vou te deixar ir, mas se chorares para a tua mae eu vou te matar."

I'm gonna let you go. But if you cry for your mother, I am going to kill you.

Rose didn't respond.

Very slowly, he let go of her and then, holding her arms still, he led her to the tree and made her sit by the trunk.

With his jaw twitching, Henry stood over the poor girl with his arms folded like a military officer, staring down at her.

Tentatively, Rose looked up once, then twice and held her gaze on his face.

"O que estas a fazer arvore?" *What were you doing in the tree?*

"Henry! Es maluco?" Paulo asked.

Henry! Are you crazy?

"Cala te!" Asking Paulo to shut up, he didn't take his eyes off Rose, and repeated his question, "O que estas a fazer arvore?" Rose was looking incredulously at him.

"O Kellerman mandou-te para nos espionar?"

Henry said and this time the other men also became alert.

Did Kellerman send you to spy on us? No answer.

"Okay... you have found us a mute," Daniel told the others, this time in English.

Rose understood and shook her head.

They got it. She couldn't speak Portuguese. Henry didn't reply. She looked at them, one by one, lastly at Henry.

"Recognize us?" He asked, "I saved your life a night ago when I thought you needed help. But now I get it, you're a spy." No answer, just a blank and scared stare.

Henry sniffed and then crouched in front of her.

This time, he asked softly, bringing his face close to hers, "Why did you run away that night?"

Rose looked straight at his face and then, after a long pause, she croaked a whisper, "You animals... can talk..."

"Huh! She talks!"

Henry didn't pay any attention to the others. He stared stoically at her, perhaps expecting something but she simply stared back into his eyes.

"Excuse me, ma'am. First of all, you are insulting such notable people. Do you have any idea who are you talking to?"

"Of course, she does." Henry was talking to Rose instead of Eloy. "Don't you? Tell me if Kellerman has sent you and I'll let you walk away on your own two feet or... these animals you see are going to do some nasty work on you." Tears filled her eyes.

"Mama," she whispered, "I want to go home."

Henry frowned. As he continued to stare at her, an argument broke out between the other men.

"Let her go. She's just a girl lost in the forest."

"Shut up, Paulo! She is Kellerman's spy and if we let her go, she'll tell him we're here and he'll kill us!"

Henry and Rose were still sitting there, face to face, staring at each other.

"Let's go to the tent."

"Henry?"

Without turning away his gaze, he said, "Give me rope."

Eloy handed him the rope straight away. Henry held it up in front of Rose's eyes and said, "I'm going to tie you up. You have thirty minutes to tell me your plan and if you don't, there's going to be a lot of trouble here." He wasn't loud.

He tied her wrists at her back and then tied her to the trunk.

"You are scaring her, let her just go." Daniel challenged him.

Nobody dared say anything. Ignoring Daniel's plea, he took off his watch and stood in front of her again. Then he admonished her, placing the watch in her lap, *"Thirty minutes."*

The four men sat at a distance, keeping watch, while Henry sat beside her, looking at her.

She was sobbing silently to herself. Fifteen minutes passed.

"I'm going to ask you two questions," Henry said, placing his arms on his knees and scratching the soil with his dagger, "What are you doing in the forest?"

Her lips trembled, "I... I... made a sketch and then... I climbed the tree to... to see the forest from up there."

"Okay, can I see your sketch?"

"My pocket," Rose whimpered, "in my pocket."

Henry frowned. He pulled out the book from the pocket on her waist, "A book. Wow. You study."

As he opened it, the sketch of the monkey fell at his feet. He took it and studied it for a moment.

"A monkey? You really are convincing, girl." His tone was sarcastic, "I'm keeping this book. There must be codes in it. Next question, why are you always in the forest?"

"My... my... home is here." Rose said in a whisper and looked at him with pleading eyes, "My mama is waiting for me... if you let me go,

76

I'll never tell her, and she won't scold you. Please... I have helped all the animals and..." Henry was laughing under his breath, "Unbelievable... Kellerman has really trained you, hasn't he? Once I let you go, I guess you are going to use your kung fu on us and overpower us. Do you think I'm stupid?"

"No!" Rose was getting angry now, "Give me my book!"

"You still care about your damned book?" Henry cast his eyes on the watch. Seven minutes were left, "Your life is at stake. Seven minutes and... you are going to die."

"I don't understand. What you are saying?"

Rose was irritated, but Henry was infuriated. He clenched her upper arm and squeezed it, bringing her closer to him. She had gained the attention of the other men too.

"Keep. Your. Voice. Down." He warned her, "Or I'll take away these seven minutes too."

He opened the book and said, "Let's see what is so important about it..."

He began to scrutinize it, and Rose looked at the weird thing in her lap, the watch.

The more he read, the deeper his frown became. He looked at her, discombobulated now.

Again, he read the words and their meanings.

"What's your name?"

"Rose."

"How old are you?"

"Nineteen."

There was change in his eyes and his gaze. There was a pause then, "I'm Henry. Twenty-three. Do you know Kellerman?"

Rose shook her head. It had seemed at first that she was following him, but the book said something else. He brought his hand to her face, but Rose said suddenly in fright, which froze him, "Are you going to eat me?"

Henry drew back his hand. Before he could answer, there was a noise nearby, the breaking of a branch and chirping as many birds flew off.

The men became alert. They got up and Henry put the book in his pocket.

"What about her?" Daniel asked.

"She'll be safe here. Let's go and see what it is... there must be jaguar or something..."

The men walked away, Henry in the lead.

I was glad they left. It would only be seconds before they would find it was just a broken branch. I had done it to create a distraction.

Hurrying towards Rose, I grabbed the dagger and began to cut the rope.

"Mama!"

"Come on! Be quick, go home, I'm coming. I'll make sure no one follows you."

She nodded and was gone.

I stood in the open now, knowing she wasn't there, and the men wouldn't be able to see me.

"Where did she go?" Daniel asked, looking around.

But Henry stayed there as the others searched the area. The wristwatch was gone, and his eyes were on the dagger by the rope.

He smiled, drawing out Rose's book from his pocket, "No need, fellows. She'll come back."

I left.

Did I mention before, apart from being the son of a bitch, Henry was the son of the president of Brazil?

Chapter 8

"He wasn't an animal, he was a human and so are you, Rose."

It was the second day. She had composed herself and now she was asking me questions. I sat down beside her, watching the waterfall. I asked her to keep quiet and listen carefully.

"First answer my question. I gave a book to read."

"But how can I understand it, Mama. You said you'd translate it into English."

"I have brought the translation. If you accept what's written in the Koran, you'll be a Muslim."

"Okay," she nodded. I opened the book of translation and read:

"The day of noise and clamor. What is the day of noise and clamor? And what will explain to thee what the day of noise and clamor is? It is a day whereon mankind will be like moths scattered about and mountains will be carded wool." (1-5 of 101)

I looked at her. She was staring at the translation. After a long pause, she said, "I'll read it."

She began reading that very day. She read continuously without pausing. I tried to coax her to come inside the castle and have lunch, but she skipped her meals.

I left to do my job, I had to take the soul of a Christian who had never touched his holy book more than once or twice in his life.

Before unlocking his soul from his body, I asked the old man a question.

He was dying in an accident. The scene of the devastated truck changed, instead, there was emptiness all around. He looked at me with fear in his eyes.

"How old are you?" I asked.

"Seventy-five," he said simply, sitting next to me on the bench.

"How many books have you read in your lifetime?" I asked politely. even if a man of his age made me, his Death, look horrible to him.

The more years a person lived, the more horrifying I appeared to him because he had had more opportunities to commit sins. "Two hundred, approximately," he did the math.

I stared at him, "How many times have you read your favorite book?"

He must have thought the discussion was a distraction. It wasn't.

"Ten times, maybe."

I continued, "And how many times have you read the Bible?"

No answer. His mouth remained open. Not even once, and there was regret on his face.

I smiled. He fell on the floor on the embers, roaring like a tiger.

His soul was stuck in his body, I closed my fist.

OBSERVATION No. 16

It's a shame you read the books of human writers several times and forget to read the book of the master of all writers: God.

This was the first time I had taken a soul with a smile playing on my lips, but still, it was a sarcastic smile. I only have one chance to mock humans and I avail it.

When I came back, I was glad Rose was asleep with the book open in her hand. I didn't want to answer her questions until she had read it all.

The next day, I left before she woke up and left a rose by her side. At least she would know I had come home.

Actually, I was afraid.

Afraid that I might fail to answer her questions. Assault with words is stronger compared to assault with the hands.

Rose didn't even go to the forest. She was obsessed with the book. The shocking thing was she never asked me about it. I didn't know what she was waiting for as I watched her pronouncing the words quite wrong. She seemed impetuous about it, forgetting everything.

Even me.

Yes, there were no more roars of mama. The castle was soundless. I didn't disturb her peaceful reading.

Meanwhile, I found the elusive Henry Cavills and recovered Rose's book. Henry would never know who took it.

He had left forest with his mates three days after the incident with Rose and was in Brasilia with his father with no intentions of coming back.

I didn't return her book. First, I made sure there was nothing written on it, there was no page torn from it and then at night, when she slept, I quietly placed the book at her side with a rose on it.

She would find it in the morning and then she would ask me where I found it.

But when I came back, I was astonished as Rose asked me no questions. She kept reading the Koran with the book in her lap.

I wondered what was going on in her mind. She hadn't said a single word to me after our last chat. Was she upset with me for not helping her?

**

It was the seventh day and I was beginning to get worried about her. She was sitting on the grass when I picked up my gray cloak to go to work.

Her words paralyzed me because what she asked was totally different from what I had expected. My list of expected questions:

1. What is a human? 2.

Why didn't you tell me?

3. Where can I see humans.

But her questions didn't involve humans. It was something I had told her days before.

Something deeply related to me.

"Mama," she called and asked before I could turn to face her, "What is the day of noise and clamor?" The

day of my victory.

The day when every human will be able to see me.

The day when I will rule.

My last day on Earth. The

death I will die.

I didn't say any of the words above. No. I simply turned around and stood, looking at her with the Koran closed in her lap.

She had finished it.

And what a question she had asked among the zillions that must have been stirring in her mind.

"Doomsday," I replied seriously. I knew her eyes demanded an explanation. For me to go and sit there with her. And so, I did.

Her eyes fell on me as I sat beside her, not uttering a word. The thing she loved most in the world: words.

"Once upon a time," I began my story, "God decided that He should create something. Something that wouldn't completely be as obsequious as angels. Something that would have the power to disobey Him. So, He might test his creation. And for that, he made man. You remember Henry and his fellows? They are men. And you are a woman. But when God sent man on earth, the devil didn't want man to obey God because he thought his worship was enough for God. So, he made man stray from the right path and men started hurting God by disobeying Him. God wanted His creation to be good and created paradise for the good ones and hell for the evil ones. They would enter either one, depending on their acts on earth. God promised man that one day he must come back and tell Him what he did on the earth. That day, everything will turn to dust. You see those distant blue mountains? They will turn to dust. The earth will shake, and the sky will split in two. The sun will be blazing hot and man will return to his God.... and that day is doomsday."

Silence.

Rose not only looked interested but fearful as well.

She whispered, "Is it now?"

I smiled, putting my arm around her shoulders, "No... nobody knows when it will happen."

She didn't say anything, just kept looking at the wristwatch that Henry had tossed towards her. I knew she was worried.

"I returned your book, Rose. Do you want to give him his thing back?"

"No," she said without looking at me, "No need."

"You want to keep it?" She

nodded.

"Why?"

Rose looked at me, "He will come back for it."

I didn't reply. Obviously, he wasn't coming back for a cheap watch.

"Won't he, Mama?"

"Why do you want him to come back?"

"I want to warn him about doomsday. I want him to obey God. Right?"

"Hmm."

I kissed her cheek and she put her arms around me.

"So how was the Koran?"

"It was the best of all books!"

I laughed, "How many books have you read?"

"I haven't... but I know it's the best of them all. I'll never get tired of reading it. Thank you, Mama."

"For what?"

She beamed, "For being with me."

Most of the time, I was at my duty and we met only at night. By morning, I would leave a rose at her chest. At night, we would lay down on the grass and look at the stars for a while. The cosmos was incredibly beautiful. She would ask me small things and I would explain it to her. Except one.

"Mama, what is death?"

I became serious. How rude. Couldn't she ask *who* is Death?

"Rose, please don't ask me that question ever again. It's the only question I won't be able to answer."

I tried so hard not to appear inscrutable.

"But..."

"Please."

She buried her head in my neck and wrapped me in her arms. She understood it. She never asked me again.

"Okay, I won't." Nothing
that night.

But in the days to come, I understood Rose well, and the she was constructing something in her mind. One meets God after dying and she was creating a link between death, man, doomsday, and God.

Thank the Lord that she didn't know how to kill herself or she would have done it in an instant because of her desire to meet God.

After reading the Koran once, she started it again, carrying it to the forest and standing on a hilltop or sitting on a tree branch, narrating it aloud to the nature that surrounded her.

And it was such music to my ears, the like of which is unknown to mankind.

When a shooting star would run away from our sight, we would both join hands and pray to God and then afterwards guess each other's wish.

One night, as we lay down, Rose quoted the Koran to me.

"Have they not observed the sky above them, how We constructed it, and beautified it, and how there are no rifts therein?" And we stared at the stars in silence.

"Rose?"

"Hmm?"

"Thank you."

"For what?"

I smiled, "For being with me."

***

Before we knew it, a year was gone, and Henry Cavills was back.

I don't remember what she was saving that day, pink river dolphin, I guess, when out of nowhere the piranhas attacked her. She yelped for help and I heard her, and followed her screams, "MAMA! MAMA!"

I hadn't even reached the river when I heard voices and discovered we weren't alone in the forest. There were humans there as well, and Rose had drawn their attention too. The poor girl was being bitten by sharp teeth and the water was turning claret. I had to reach her before them, but then the yelling faded.

She was drowning.

Oh, Lord, I had never felt so helpless and instead of helping, I shouted back, "ROSE! I'M COMING!"

If I had a heart, I know it would have been racing as fast as my feet were. Rose didn't reply and it made me more anxious.

The humans had already reached the river. So, I just stood beside them knowing that if I were to save her, they would know something preternatural was around. So, I looked for the buffoons to help her.

Henry made me look like a loser. It was a shame for me to see my daughter drowning and being rescued by someone else.

I watched in horror as the water turned crimson pink. It was Henry whose instincts made him take off his jacket and shirt, and with a dagger in his hand, he jumped into the water.

After a minute or two of my impatient waiting, he emerged with the unconscious Rose in his arms. There were four or five bites on his muscular arm, but he seemed all right.

He carried Rose towards everyone and gently placed her on the ground.

Oh, Lord, it was dreadful. Rose had turned the color of a rose. There was blood everywhere on her body, only her face was safe.

Henry checked her pulse and Daniel brought his first aid kit, meanwhile, Henry pressed her chest with the heels of his hands.

I knew she wasn't going to die but that stupid idiot didn't. How could he? He was being human.

He only stopped when she coughed, exhaling, as if she had been holding it in forever.

Sometimes... I feel envy when humans breathe. Is life defined by sucking in air and letting it out? Is life that simple?

I often try to breathe, to feel life, but then again, I can't even feel the air!

Rose stirred. She blinked several times and then... it was the first time she had felt pain. Physical pain.

Wincing, she slowly sat upright in front of Henry, not noticing him at all. I knew she wasn't sure what to do with the unpleasant feeling of pain and how to get rid of it.

She looked straight at him.

What was it? The human figure? His naked upper body? Or the blood erupting from his arms? Or his face that made her shiver with panic feeling scared and wanting to run. Run.

Henry stood up and muttered, "Stupid girl."

He didn't chase her, and I knew why. Rose's legs were wounded, and Henry knew she wouldn't be able to make but a few yards. He just strutted behind her as the other three men watched.

Rose fell, giving up, and began to cry.

OBSERVATION No. 17

Tears are instinctive to pain, either physical, mental, or emotional. Sometimes... humans are unable to see them.

In her case, it was physical. This was the first time ever Rose had cried. International discovery day for her. Pain and tears. Lying on her back, she rolled over, curling her legs up and clutching them tightly. Pitiable.

She was crying harder now. I was standing on the tree branch where I was well hidden from Rose and could also view everything.

Henry sat beside her and gave her a strange look. It wasn't only the look of surprise that masked his face but also a tinge of recognition in his eyes.

"Rose?" he muttered tentatively. It's weird the way humans remember a name after one meeting and a gap of a year.

Hearing her name, Rose looked at him while crying, trying to remember the face that had saved her life a year before as well.

She gripped the grass and began to yell, crying in pain. Henry scooped her up in his arms and she put hers around his neck, clutching him tightly and buried her head in his chest, weeping unstoppably.

"It's..." Paulo uttered, "a girl..."

I guess he didn't expect a girl in the wild.

Daniel and Paulo urgently attended to Rose, cleaning and bandaging her wounds, while Alex turned to Henry who kept looking at Rose. She had been given a sedative and had now passed out.

"Glad we have a doctor with us on our trip," Alex acknowledged, referring to Paulo.

Henry didn't respond. He was the kind of man who was reserved and the one whom his friends treated like their teacher.

He put on his shirt and jacket and dried his hair. I kept sitting on the branch, watching.

"We can't spend the night here, let's go back," said Daniel.

"Yeah." Alex was about to move but was interrupted by Paulo.

"What about her? We can't just leave her."

Unlike me, Paulo was all about saving lives as he was a doctor.

"Yeah, we can't take her with us, right? Our tent is far away..." Alex kept saying, "Besides, who knows, maybe she is convicted criminal or something."

"Yeah, she might stab you in the back and take your diamonds?" Paulo mocked.

"You want to spend night here? Good. Then stay!" Alex said in frustration.

The argument was heating up. Daniel was packing the kit while Henry was staring at Rose, his hands buried in his pants' pockets. Daniel was neutral while Henry looked phlegmatic. "Henry?" Daniel picked up his stuff.

Carrying his bow and arrows on his shoulder, Henry turned to go, "Let's move."

"What?" Daniel muttered in disappointment as everyone was ready to leave. Relief took over me, they were going to leave.

Vain hope.

They had not gone far when Henry's eyes moved towards Alex's hand.

A silver thing dangled from his hand. He frowned.

"What's that?" Henry asked with a high degree of friendliness in his voice.

"Oh this," Alex held it up, "found it in her pocket. Looks like it's precious... she surely doesn't need it here... So, I took it as payment for our services."

"Payment for help?"

"Of course."

Henry stopped dead in his tracks, staring at Alex and then dropped his bow and arrows.

"When will she wake up, Paulo?"

"In six or seven hours," Paulo looked confused.

"By midnight?"

"Yeah. Why do you ask? Hey, where are you going?"

"To get her," he didn't bother to look at his fellows as he walked back, taking the silver thing from Alex's fingers, 'By the way, this belongs to me."

Alex looked bewildered while Daniel looked concerned, "Should we wait?"

"Suit yourself."

By the time he got to Rose, she was just as he had left her. He stared at her with a frown, studying her, then picked her up and carried her away.

If I were human, I would have said, 'Holy shit.'

Excuse my language but that's how humans express anger.

Daniel and the others were still waiting by the time Henry returned. He didn't stop or even glance at them as they stood with astonished looks on their faces. Daniel picked up Henry's bow and arrows and they all followed dutifully.

The tents were a long way off and I knew even a strong man like Henry would tire from carrying Rose. He couldn't ask anyone else to carry her as he had accepted her as his own responsibility. They didn't know I was the sixth traveler in their group.

As they reached the tents, Henry took her to his own tent and came out quickly to join the others. Together, they lit the fire and sat around it, eating a cooked deer Henry had shot.

"This is the same girl..." Paulo didn't finish.

"Same?" Alex questioned.

"Last year, we met her. Remember? The one we thought was Kellerman's agent."

"Oh."

Henry didn't participate.

"What's she doing here?" Daniel seemed curious, "It means we're not alone here..."

"Yeah, maybe some tourist party is still out in the forest, looking for her." Alex told them.

Paulo grinned, "Whatever. She is pretty, right? If only we had met in Brazil..."

"Talk about something else." Henry ordered. Nobody spoke.

After four hours, they went to their own tents to sleep, but Henry looked uncomfortable. There was an unknown girl in his tent and Daniel hadn't bothered to pack an extra one.

He changed his clothes and examined his wounds. *Pretty nice bites from the piranha, I must say.*

It wasn't as if I was anti-Henry because I wasn't only his foe. I'm everyone's foe, even Rose's.

Humans accuse me of separating them from their loved ones and that's what foes do.

After that, Henry sat down, looking at Rose with the silver object still in his hand, the bow and arrows at his side.

I was surprised that he kept sitting there, despite how much he wanted to sleep. He accidently closed his eyes and fell asleep by her side.

Rose woke up at midnight. First, she kept laying there feeling the pain and probably believing that she was with her mother.

Until she rolled over on her side and came face to face with Henry. She sat upright immediately and stared at the slumbering man.

She didn't even run this time. Then she stooped and looked closely at his face. A flash of familiarity passed in her eyes and then they went on the silver thing in his hand.

Carefully and quietly, she slipped the silver from his hand, as if it belonged to her and got up to leave.

"Going somewhere?" Henry held her wrist.

She seemed startled as she looked back, sitting down again with dilated pupils.

Henry opened his eyes wide and looked at her seriously. He didn't let go of her wrist and just kept laying there. And Rose was now frozen in her place.

"Running away, are we?"

Rose blinked as if she had seen one of the wonders of the world, "You can…"

"I can talk and I'm not going to eat you, if that's what you were going to say."

Silence.

"And I'm not an animal." He added.

"Where did you find me?" she whispered.

"Are you scared of me?"

Oh, she is terrified, I said to myself. Even though I was standing outside the tent, I could see behind the wall. Lucky me.

"No," she gulped and sat up, releasing her wrist but flinched and squealed, "Please don't hurt me!"

"You are scared of me," Henry nodded.

Rose stared back at the human and then exploded in questions she occasionally asked me, "What is this place? Where am I? Who are you? What is this on my body? Why am I feeling so unpleasant? How long have I been here?"

Followed by a long stare at him for answers. Henry was already watching her, studying her with his eyes.

Rose gasped, "Where is Mama? Did she come? Has she gone back to work? Was she here?"

"Shut up," Henry said reticently, and Rose shut her mouth, "*Answer,* why do you still have my watch?"

Rose looked at it, the silver thing in her hand, and then back at him.

"I demand an explanation," Henry ordered calmly.

"I..." she began reluctantly, "I wanted... to give it back!"

For a moment, he stared at her and then held out his hand toward her, "Well, give it back then."

I knew she loved that watch. It was the only human invention she had, but now she must return it. She was staring at his palm.

Hastily, Rose put it there and locked her fingers in her lap. Henry kept holding it.

"What are you doing here in the forest?" he asked cynically.

Taking her eyes off the watch, she replied, "I live here."

"Alone?" he raised his eyebrows.

"No, with my mother."

Perhaps he thought she had fabricated the story, so he asked sarcastically, "Since when did your mother decide to abandon Brasilia and live here?"

Rose remained silent.

"Well?"

"I don't know."

Henry frowned, "How old are you?"

"Twenty."

"Tell me about yourself."

"I..." Rose began innocuously and it was as if she was thinking, Lord, who am I?

90

There was a long pause.

"Why do you want to know?" she asked finally.

Henry shrugged, "Just curious. Tell me from the beginning."

"My name is Rose. I live…"

"Surname?"

"Just Rose," she replied as I had never told her about surnames, "I live with my mother. I'm twenty… I sketch… write words in my book… and… and help animals."

He waited for more but seemed utterly disappointed at this hiatus, "And?"

"And…" she thought hard, "And… I read the Koran"

"Really?"

"Yes. Didn't you?"

"No, I'm a Christian."

"Did you read the Bible?" she asked excitedly.

"Once. When I was ten. Now I'm twenty-four and never touch it."

There was an awkward silence. Henry kept staring at the wristwatch in his hand and so did Rose.

The disturbing silence lasted for five minutes but seemed like a lifetime.

Chapter 9

OBSERVATION No. 18

When two people are silent, it means they are thinking about each other and they go to the second level of intimacy.

"Who are you?" Rose blurted out.

"Henry cast his eyes at her, "The son of the president of Brazil, Fernando Cavills."

Rose stayed silent, her eyes on the ground, unable to understand the terms in his answer.

"Is that good?" she asked quietly. "Horrible as hell if you ask me. Chased by guards all the time. No time for family... I live among friends. Dictatorship and all that.

That's why I became a tourist, to find peace in nature." She

was just able to understand the last line.

"Okay. What was your name?"

"You don't remember?"

"No... it was difficult." "Henry Cavills." He told her again, "Sorry, I lost your book. The one I took from you last year."

She smiled mischievously at him, "No I have it. Mama got it back. Here."

She took it out and showed it to him. As he moved closer to take it Rose drew it back. He halted.

"You're still afraid of me," he told her and then smiled for the first time, "And God knows I'm loving it."

Rose remained stoic as the word love wasn't in her dictionary. "Did you write some new words in your book?" he asked, changing the topic as he judged her expressions.

"Yes. I did." And then she cried out in fear, "You'll let me go in the morning, right?"

Henry frowned and then intentionally terrified her, "I'll never let you go."

The color faded from her face, "What do you intend to do with me?"

"I haven't thought about it yet," he joked but realized the seriousness of the situation, so he added, "Don't worry. I won't bite you."

There was an awkward silence again.

That was the longest night of my life. I don't like it when humans stare at someone. It means there is something going on in their mind... if only I could read minds. Maybe they were judging each other.

"I want to see the stars." Rose said suddenly. I knew what she really wanted was to secure herself a way to escape

"I won't let you leave this tent," Henry said straight forwardly.

"But the stars! I want to see the stars!"

"Consider it to be a cloudy night," Henry said, staring at her.

That was one rare occasion when I saw no hunger or lust in his eyes as he stared. But I saw something I didn't recognize.

There was silence again. Rose had surrendered without a fight. She looked at him.

"Why are you staring at me?" she finally asked.

"I just like to," Henry didn't smile, which wasn't unusual as it was something he rarely did. Since the meeting with Rose, he had only smiled once.

"I'm looking... oh, God! Is this blood?" Rose freaked out as she looked at herself. She touched it and winced. She had never had a wound before.

"Yes."

"What is this?" she was still confused.

"You're injured. Why are you asking?"

"Because... I don't know!"

"Well..." Henry got the idea that she didn't know anything about wounds, "You know... you get hurt then you get a wound... and there is pain."

"What is pain?"

Henry looked at her with incredulity, "Pain... the thing that defines humans. Without which no one will be called a human."

93

"Why?"

"Because..." Henry's forehead creased. She was giving him a tough time, "How can you feel joy without tasting sorrow?" Rose frowned.

"You can't." Henry explained. 'Human life is based on this."

"Henry?"

"Hmm?"

"I'm hungry."

"You want me to go out and get something for you?"

Henry was astonished, having never taken an order from anyone before.

Rose nodded. He got up and Rose's eyes trailed on him as he went out. When he returned, Rose was slumbering so he didn't wake her up.

It was a golden morning when she woke up by Henry. He held her upper arm, crouched over her, and moved her slightly.

"Rose?" he said gently, "Rose, wake up. It's morning."

She blinked, and when she saw him, she sat up quickly, flinching away, still afraid of him.

Henry sat upright, "Still scared. Am I a monster?"

"What's a monster?" It
made him smile.

"Nothing. Come on, have breakfast."

As Henry moved towards the entrance to the tent, Rose stopped him.

"Did my mama come?"

Did your mama leave you, Rose? Not even for a second.

"No," Henry broke her heart, "She didn't."

"She must be looking for me," Rose told him sadly.

"Come on."

Henry opened the entrance for her, and the sunshine poured in. Rose got up and went out with Henry following behind her.

As soon as she saw the two men sitting on a log, and one standing to one side, she turned around in a rush and crashed into Henry's chest.

He held her upper arms, looking in her eyes. The three men stared at Rose.

"They won't hurt you," he whispered so that no one could hear him, "I won't let them."

Rose wasn't sure but Henry tried to boost her self-confidence, "Turn around."

Rose shook her head, "No."

Henry's frown deepened, "Turn around, Rose."

"No."

"Rose!" he pressed, "Turn around."

His anger scared her, and she complied, swallowing hard. Henry walked toward the men with Rose by his side.

"The girl is still here?" Alex said in surprise.

"Her name is Rose," Henry minded the way he spoke about her with disrespect. Then he addressed Rose, "This is Alex, that's Dr. Paulo and my best friend, Daniel."

Paulo, standing nearest, held out his hand to shake, but Rose grabbed Henry's arm instantly and attached herself to his side.

Both stared at her, Paulo in astonishment and Henry with an expression I didn't recognize. When Rose didn't leave him, Paulo drew his hand back.

"She is," Henry's eyes were still on her, "a little shy."

"I... I... need to go."

Saying this, she walked away. Nobody stopped her, not even Henry.

***

"Hi, Mama," Rose sounded exhausted.

"What happened to you?" I got up from the rock and looked at her torn attire, tangled hair. She was totally disheveled.

"Long story," she walked towards me, "he took that silver thing."

"Who?" I asked. Was she just upset about the watch? "Henry," she hugged me, "He saved me. I was drowning."

She kept her arms around my waist as if she were meeting me after a long time. "What did he tell you?" I asked, trying to sound normal. I... couldn't understand what he was saying... and I didn't ask him… I had to leave him. I don't want to talk about him. Let's talk about us."

I smiled.

She hadn't changed after her first conversation with another human. "What about us?" "I missed you," she acted like a child even now, kissing my chin.

"Damn it, Rose. I thought you had left me and were off enjoying yourself somewhere."

Arm-in-arm, we entered the castle.

"Enjoying? I was stuck there. Henry wouldn't let me leave at night. He said it was too dangerous."

"I think he was right. Did you go to the river on purpose so that you'd ruin your dress and I would have to get you a new one?"

Rose halted and gasped at me, "How did you know?" "I am your mother, who would know you better than me?"

Her mouth hung open at the divulgence of the new fact about her. I continued as we sat, "Why?"

There was silence for several seconds. Then Rose got up quickly, went inside, leaving me on the rock, and came back with a rose in her hand.

"You still have this one?" I asked, remembering it as the last one I had placed on her book before going to work.

"Look at this!" Rose complained, "This is so beautiful!" "Yes," I agreed, not getting her point at all.

"And look at me now."

Looking at her, I raised my eyebrows, "What?"

"Mama!" She seemed annoyed, "*I am Rose.* I should be look like a rose. Beautiful and… wearing a red gown!"

"Oh!" I realized, "That's the point." She grimaced.

"Well, you could have just asked me! If you'll drown yourself or do something equally as horrid simply to get a dress, I won't get it for you Rose."

It cheered her up, "Okay… this is going to be the last dress. "Thank the Lord."

"Mama!" She nudged me. I laughed.

***

Henry was walking on some boggy ground with his bow and quiver, ready to shoot. The splendid colors of sunset were fading, and he was alone, but alert. He made his way to the dark cave carefully and steadily, and entered it, the small torch on his belt illuminating the interior.

Water dripped on him, and there were silhouettes of bats hanging upside down as he made his way toward the faint sound

He turned the corner, about to shoot, but stopped as he came face to face with a pair of rosy cheeks and cherry lips. "You?" there was surprise in his voice as he lowered his bow.

"Henry!"

He frowned at her, "What are you doing here?"

Her answer was unsure, "Umm… exploring."

"Exploring what?"

"Bats?" she replied hesitantly. Henry looked at the stalactites and the bats hanging by them.

His jaw twitched as he looked back at her, "Do you know they suck blood?"

"They do?" Her answer carried innocence.

Henry smiled, "They are vampire bats. And yes… they do."

Rose was standing on a rock, looking down at him, while he had his arms folded, looking up at her.

"But they are sleeping," she said calmly and then her eyes popped open, "Oh, no… they are going to wake up, Henry! It's getting dark!"

"We need to leave," saying this, he put his arrow back in the quiver, shouldered his bow, and held up his hands. Rose stared at him.

"I won't bite you," he promised. As she leaned towards him, he reached under her arms and hoisted her down.

Holding her close, he looked at her just for a moment, then he released her.

They made their way out quickly and saw the colors of the sunset taking the light away with them. Once they were out, Henry turned to her and said, "Okay, Rose. Goodbye."

97

He had just taken a step when he stopped.

"Err... Henry?"

He didn't look back.

"Err... I'm lost... I think..." her reluctance came out. He turned around at the words.

"So?" he asked rudely.

OBSERVATION No. 19

The problem with people in authority is that they think they are kings.

"So... err... will you guide me home?"

"Seriously?" he frowned, "Rose, I don't even know where you live!"

"I meant you home. From there, I'll be able to find my way home."

At first, it seemed he didn't understand, and then he laughed suddenly. What an interesting girl Rose might be for him.

"Okay, come on," he said, offering his hand to her. Rose didn't take it, so he quipped, "I told you, I won't bite you!"

She still stared at his hand, refraining from holding it, so he withdrew it.

"Good," he uttered, turning away, "just walk alone then."

First, both were silent on their journey. Then, as the darkness prevailed, Rose walked closer to him.

"So." Henry began, "What happened when you got home?"

"Mama got me this new dress!" Rose said cheerily.

He halted, looking at her dress, "New dress? Pretty cool Mama I suppose..."

As Rose couldn't construe his words, she remained silent. He stared at her, his eyes moving from head to toe, studying. With his same reserved, elusive tone, he admitted, "You look ravishing, Rose. I thought you deserved a compliment."

Rose didn't have the words ravishing and compliment in her dictionary. She didn't ask him either. Shrugging, she said, "Okay."

With a smile playing on his face, he led the way again. They remained silent until they reached the waterfall where the path was comprised of slippery rocks amidst the stream.

Eyeing the dangerous way, he asked Rose, "Sure you don't need to hold my hand to cross the stream?"

She shook her head even though the tension was evident on her face.

Henry smirked, and cautiously hopped on the flat rocks. Rose followed him with outstretched arms to balance herself. Henry was jumping like a rabbit and she was the turtle following him.

The damp rocks weren't easy to cross, but poor Rose managed to cross without incident. Henry only looked back when he was on the bank.

Rose seemed confident now, after skipping on three rocks successfully, but Henry was there to comment on it, "Oh... how can we forget Rose lives here."

She was too far away to hear that.

When they got closer to the tent, Henry turned around and grabbed her upper arm, telling her in a serious tone, "Stay close to me. Don't listen to them. If anyone tries to harm you, just run to me. Okay?"

They locked eyes as if it was the most crucial moment in their life. He was demanding an answer and Rose appeared ignorant.

"Why would they do that?" She wasn't even whispering, though he was.

"Because," Henry paused, he bit his lip, deciding what to tell her, "Because... you look ravishing, Rose."

"But... isn't that good?" she asked innocently.

"Rose," his eyes smiled and gained a sparkle, "it's a bit too good for the bad world. Just don't get too friendly with them, okay?"

Not waiting for her answer, he released his grip on her and walked towards the tents.

"Hi, dude, where on..." Daniel's voice trailed away as his eyes went to Rose, "Oh, hi, Rose."

Rose didn't smile back. She frowned.

Paul and Alex also directed their attention to them, appearing surprised.

"We ran into each other," Henry told them in an undertone, removing his bow and quiver.

"You guys keep running into each other a little too often," Alex got up and came towards Rose, holding out his hand, "Hi, again, Rose."

Rose looked at his hand, ignoring it before frowning and folding her arms across her chest as if annoyed, "I don't shake hands."

The four men stared at her. Alex jerked his hand back in embarrassment.

"Would you like some vodka?" Paul broke the awkward silence.
"I don't talk to strangers," Rose said indignantly. Paul looked hurt and Rose seemed not to care.

The silence lasted an uncomfortably long time until Henry sat down on a log, eating from the cans his friends had packed.

The others busied themselves lighting the fire.

"Sit down, Rose," Daniel's voice quivered with fright in case she embarrassed him too.

"No, thank you, I'm good," she replied as if taunting him, far from her usual sweet and innocent tone.

"Sit down, Rose," Henry ordered. Rose sat down on the log at once, opposite the one Henry was sitting on.

The other three men exchanged looks of astonishment.

"So…" Daniel began, followed by another uneasy silence.

"Don't you *so* me!" Rose snapped, and Daniel stared at her, insulted in front of his friends.

Henry looked at Rose who had her eyes cast down now. When she looked up, their eyes met, and she smiled faintly.

With his eyes full of understanding, Henry got up and walked towards her with her eyes trailing him.

He crouched and whispered, "Don't be so hard and fake. Just be yourself, only tell me if they trouble you." Rose nodded, "Okay."

Henry went inside the tent and Rose decided to apologize immediately.

"I'm sorry. Hello. I'm Rose."

"Err… we know," Daniel said awkwardly. Rose cheered up, "So what are your names?" Silence, and her eyes seemed impatient.

"But Henry told you last time," Paul said.

"I don't remember."

"I am Dr. Paul, that's Daniel and over there is Alex."

100

Henry came out of the tent and began to clean his tall boots, crouching as he placed them on another log.

"Oh, such difficult names… you could have named yourself like… Jasmine or Lotus or… Lily! Easy to remember!" Henry halted.

The other three stared at her and then burst out laughing. Rose looked confused about what they found so funny and looked at Henry.

He raised his eyebrows encouragingly and Rose looked at the men.

Henry smiled to himself.

"Nice one!"

"Good joke, Rose…"

Rose waited, her mouth dry, until they were silent again. Her puzzlement about the matter was still clear on her face.

"So, Rose," Paul began again, "That day… we took… I mean, Henry carried you here…"

"He did?"

"Yes," Rose looked at Henry who pretended he was deaf, whereas Paul continued, "And you were in his tent…"

"Were you two in the bed together?" Alex asked suddenly.

"Yes," Rose answered, looking at Alex now.

The three friends grinned mischievously, until Henry eyed them with anger and said, "No, we didn't."

"But, Henry, we were together." Rose argued.

The men narrowed their eyes at Henry as if he had committed a crime and was hiding it now.

"Rose, just let me handle this," Henry walked over to Paul with his boot in his hand. He stood by him and growled under his breath, "Shut up, she doesn't know anything."

"Anything?" Daniel was bewildered.

Henry's expression was enough for him. They all stared at Rose and she shrugged.

"See?" Henry corroborated, "She's as ignorant about everything as a wee baby."

"How long have you been here?" Alex asked her.

"As long as I can remember… both me and Mama."

101

Henry made himself busy wiping his boots again and Rose remained silent. When the silence and men's stares became uncomfortable, Rose looked at the tents.

'Nice homes," Rose praised, "but very small. My home is big. Very big…. Thousands of yours combined."

They started laughing again and Rose blushed.

Henry dropped the boot and said to Rose, "Come on, Rose. I think you should go home. Your mother will be getting worried."

"What?" Rose was lost for a second, she seemed hurt from their behavior, "Oh, yes."

"I'll see her off," he told the others who giggled in response like teenagers.

"Shut up," his admonishing whisper quieted them.

As soon as Rose and Henry were out of earshot, she asked hesitantly, "Why did they laugh at me?"

"No. They weren't laughing at you. Actually, Rose, they're not our homes. Our homes are far away from here. We're just visiting here." "Oh, and why did they laugh when I talked about names?" "Well," Henry chuckled, "The names you suggested are given to girls. We are men. By the way, what name would you suggest for me?"

He stopped, looking at her. Rose had no color on her face except her cheeks had begun to turn red.

Her rumination didn't last long, "I think Henry is the best name." He smiled slightly and started walking again.

"You slept with me that night, why did you say we didn't?" Rose asked as he followed him.

Henry stopped again.

He didn't look back at her this time, but was in deep thought, trying to justify his answer… As if he were procrastinating the inevitable.

"Umm, Rose." He paused and looked back with a slight frown. "Yes?"

"You don't know what he meant?" Henry dared tentatively.

Rose laughed slightly, "Of course I do! He asked if we were in bed together, right? Weren't we? What is there to hide about it? Mama and I also sleep together. Always. She kisses me goodnight on my forehead, right here."

102

She touched the middle of Henry's forehead with her forefinger and looked in his eyes, her smile fading.

His eyes reflected nothing.

Rose kept staring at him while Henry, with his arms folded against his chest, kept staring at her.

"I've decided you don't need to know anything," he finally spoke in a reserved tone, "At least there will be one twenty-year-old girl oblivious to the shame humans have created in this world. And please remove your finger, Rose."

"Oh." She muttered, realizing suddenly she had her finger and eyes on Henry Cavills.

"And stop staring at me or I'll eat you up."

She popped her eyes wide open and said after some seconds, "I'll go now…"

She walked away, and after she had gone several steps, she stopped and looked back once. Henry was marching away too, in his high, brown leather boots, the dagger tucked in his belt at his back and muscular arms at both sides of his body.

Rose watched his gait, which was as handsome as he was. He was far away when something made him stop and glance back.

He scrutinized the look Rose had in her eyes. The stare.

"Do you want me to come back and eat you?" he asked, loud and clear.

Hearing this, Rose opened her mouth to argue, but then digested the words and walked as fast as she could to her home.

***

"What took you so long?" I asked, as soon as she was back, pretending I was unaware of their conversation.

As was her tradition, Rose hugged me tightly.

"I got lost, Mama!"

"How many times do I have to tell you, don't go wandering deep in the forest?" I said, trying to reprimand her.

"But," she released me and said excitedly, "Henry found me in a cave and now I'm back!"

There was silence. I didn't want to talk about Henry or humans, so I changed the topic.

"Are you hungry?"

"I'm starving," she replied, talking an apple from the basket and nibbling on it, "aren't you going to work tonight?"

"No." I smiled, as we laid down to sleep on the best bed that the Lord created: a bed of grass.

Rose put her head on my outstretched arm, and we watched the constellations.

I kissed her forehead right on the spot she had mapped on Henry's forehead and she said, "Do it again."

I kissed her again and she embraced me, falling into a deep sleep like a child.

***

Sometimes, I encounter humans who are almost impossible to forget.

Because I learn lessons from them. Lessons they haven't learnt from their own lives.

I call them wise, because they spend their entire lives chasing their dreams, all wise humans do that and never give up. It is a myth among them that you get there in the end. You don't.

You might get there, but not at the end. Actually, you leave behind in the end because I meet you then and make you leave everything. I make you leave the world.

Eric Scofield was one of those wise men. Beaten by old age, he was eighty-five when I met him. I can remember him drinking champagne in his grand room, his whole body mapped with veins, his hair white as snow, and the beauty of his face long gone.

Director, producer, internationally famous, and one of the most highly-paid actors.

He was pouring wine in his glass when I appeared in his room. As he turned around, taking a sip, his eyes fell on me. I noticed his eyes had no color and weren't reflecting anything. He smiled at me for a second. I remained quiet.

"I'm not signing up for any film for now," Eric's hand shivered, Parkinson's I presumed. He sat on his rocking chair, drinking.

I walked towards him.

"Eric Scofield," I said, not trying to terrify the old man, "You are going to sign up to the last film of your life."

His face didn't turn up, only his eyes did. He was about to take a sip when he changed his mind and spoke.

"Sit down," he said seriously. Despite the fact I didn't want to, I still did.

It was Norway and the snow that cloaked every gable reminded me of that snowy day when I had adopted Rose.

"Would you like to have some?"

I turned my eyes away from the window and looked at him. he was offering me wine.

"I *only* drink the sweetest wine," I replied.

"Oh yes, and what is that, young lady?" he was very polite.

I locked my eyes on his old ones, "Water."

My word made him leave the sip he was going to take and brush his chin on his shoulder as he lowered the glass. He remained silent. "You are an old fellow, Eric," I broke in after a long pause, "and alone. Your eyes tell me nothing except you are traveling in the past, which is futile."

I don't know why I was talking to him on this occasion when I should be thinking about his funeral.

Eric smiled.

It was a sad smile.

"Am I not allowed to travel in the past before dying?"

I was surprised, "So you have figured out that I have come to take you?"

He looked at me, "Dear Death, why are you surprised? Eightyfive years of living makes you read faces with a single look."

Silence again. our conversation was more silent than audible. Dear Death, was an odd salutation for me.

a) First time a human called me dear.

b) First time a human called me Death.

c) First time a human looked completely normal before dying.

Mostly, humans turn psycho, tempered, angry, terrified and in suicide cases, happy.

But this man, this old face, the satisfaction on his face, he was so calm, rocking back and forth while drinking wine with a wisp of the past in his colorless, glass-like eyes.

"It's strange, Eric," I began to elucidate, "I'm going to take you in the middle of your 'nowhere near dying' healthy life." No response. He was ignoring me.

Humans must respond, isn't it in their nature? So, I continued, "Your fans will die to see you die. It will be a shock that you were found dead in the house, no disease, no heart attack or stroke, not poisoned, not in an accident, and not an injury on your body to lead you to me." The rocking stopped.

Eric looked at me, his eyes still transparent as the glass in the window and his skin turning white as the snow outside.

"If people could see the scars of words and taunts, I would be the most wounded person in the world," he told me in a reserved voice, "and that, I think, led me to you, dear Death."

He had led his life in pain, all amazing people do. I could sense it.

The muscle in his jaw twitched and then he took a sip again.

"I can see," I told him, "despite all you have, you are still in pain."

Eric sighed.

'Oh…yes." He confessed. "The thing more painful than starvation, disease, or death is to chase your dreams and never fulfill them."

I didn't understand. He had finished his wine and he got up slowly to get some more.

"But," I began, "that was your past. Now you have everything."

As he poured more in his glass, he said melodiously, "It is the past, dear Death… *it is the past…*"

He turned around and looked at me. he was in his night robes, having prepared himself for sleep. I wondered I he had imagined that night he was going to sleep forever.

"It is the past," he sighed again, "while you chase your dreams, the past starts chasing you. If you find it, it is the past that haunts you and grins at you deviously at night… in loneliness…"

"Well," I suggested, "you can just forget it then."

It was simple, wasn't it? Escape. Forget. Oblivion. Closing one's eyes.

Eric walked slowly towards me. As he reached me, he stood with the glass in his hand and said in a haunted voice, 'A human forgives, dear Death.

A hiatus, he stooped over me, his eyes fixed on mine and said the words as if they were the biggest lesson he had learnt, a secret he would only divulge to me.

"But a human *never* forgets."

He nodded slightly and walked back to his rocking chair, relaxing on it once again. Was it so difficult to forget? I wondered. And then I didn't know what to ask but it just came out.

"Would you like to share some memories?"

Eric closed his eyes at this and said after a moment of anticipation, "I have a memory… of pain."

I licked my lips slightly, then boldly asked, "Well. When does it hurt the most?"

He didn't open his eyes as if feeling that memory again.

He opened his mouth as if to speak and shivered before proceeding, "When the light of hope begins to blind your eyes…"

I waited for him to continue, although his words were enough, I wanted more. More and more until I was satiated.

"You attempt to see the sun and dare to reach it. You look at it at dawn, the beginning of your journey and it seems beautiful. As morning approaches, you follow its trail. You are hopeful that you'll reach it.

"But by noon, you get tired from the time it is taking, and by afternoon…"

The silvery tears began to glitter on his cheeks.

"By afternoon, the sunlight burns your eyes if you look at it directly… so that… you're unable to see anything for some time… in the same way, the light of hope burns your eyes... after you get tired of waiting, for some time you're unable to see anything around you. You become carefree.

"By sunset, you know your dream is leaving you, but you also know it is inevitable. You don't stop looking at it because sunset appears beautiful too…. likewise, when hope starts to give you pain, you let go of your dream and become careless about what will happen when darkness prevails. And the departing dream… how beautiful it looks again at that time… to know how beautiful it would have been if you had achieved it… if only…"

The wine in his hand was long forgotten. Yes, humans are marvelous creatures of the Lord. To be a human meant to enter a pain zone without warning.

For the first time in my immortal life, I felt pity for humans. I tried to make him happy in the last moments of life, "Eric… look at you. You are successful…"

But my voice trailed off at his sardonic chuckle. I stared at him as he looked at me, and realized he wasn't crying any more. He gestured with his hand, the one holding the glass, towards the room.

"This? This is not success."

"Why?"

He smiled, "Because I earned it only to lose it to *you.*"

I construed it in my mind as the greatest failure of mankind. He continued in a whimpering voice that could make the children, teens, and young realize that life and all its luxuries were in vain.

"All this fame, these riches, this charm. I have earned it to lose it to you, dear Death."

I smiled at my victory, "Old man… you are saying what humans earn is worthless. After all, he sells it to me. Loses it to me. He fails. Every human fails eventually."

I was becoming wildly happy. I was victorious after all. Eventually, all men lose everything to me. How did it feel to let go of life?

"But, dear Death, you also don't win."

That made my expression change. Albeit, this man and his words were simple, yet rhetorical, my opinion was going to be changed by what he was about to say.

"Why?" I asked with a frown.

The rocking stopped, his face turned towards me, and his colorless, glassy eyes significantly implied something mocking.

"Don't you lose it all to God?" I
was driven speechless.

Until now, it had always been an insult when humans drive me
into a conversation in which I eventually lose the power of speech. Of
course, these are rare occasions.

His head rested against the back of his chair, his glass still in his
hand, as he began to watch the snow outside the window, which was
falling like cotton balls.

In a deep, lamenting tone, which only I could hear, he began to
hum. The chair started to rock back and forth, and his last words kept
echoing in my ears. My glacial blue eyes remained fixed on the old man
who had earned everything in life… and yet had nothing.

He sighed at the snow and then remained silent for a long time,
without taking a sip or moving his eyes away.

You know why?

When the snow gets too cold, it begins to burn.

I knew he couldn't see the snow outside. He was watching hell
fire. The world should have shivered with fright at his words and his
fate.

Chapter 10

OBSERVATION No. 20

The best things humans ever create comes from the worst kind of pain.

With a clench of my fist, the glass of wine fell, and it began to flow on the floor as if his wounds had started bleeding. His eyes remained fixed on the snow, and the rocking stopped, so did the dulcet tone.

> What is this life, led in pain?
> In the end, you realize it's all in vain,
> Wealth and health, you have earned,
> One day in hell they will be burned,
> Proud you are of your fame,
> In hell it will turn into just another flame,
> All the people who are godless,
> Consider yourself just a body: heartless
> Pretty is the girl, you are chasing lust,
> Beauty of nature, you should have learned as a must What
> is life: it is a game,
> Pity, dear human, you should have shame.
> I sang it that night in the forest.

***

"Tell me," Henry looked sternly at Rose, "Were you following me?"
Rose swallowed hard. She blinked and her thick eyelashes fluttered.
"No," she replied innocently.
Henry took off his quiver and bow as if he were fed up with her.
"Then why do I come across you every time?" Henry asked derisively.
Rose shrugged, her book open in her hands, as she wrote something down. When she didn't reply, Henry began to walk below the canopy, the dappled sunlight decorating the forest's soil.

He put on his bow and quiver again, his chocolate brown leather boots leaving footprints in the moist soil, killing the leaves and saplings beneath them. After he pulled up his hood, he slipped his fist inside his pocket. It was getting cold and the hunt had been poor that day.

Henry stopped by the willow and slumped down, pulled out the berries from his pocket and started chewing them one by one.

There was a rustling and his ears caught it. Stopping his nibbling, he looked around cautiously.

Nothing.

He began to nibble again. This time, he heard the sound and his hand went to his bow. Nothing again.

When he heard the noise for the third time, he didn't ignore it.

He sniffed, spit the chewed berry carelessly, and made his weapon ready. First, he looked right, then left, and then without making a sound he stepped cautiously toward the willow trunk again. His back brushed against it and as his feet sidled past it, he whirled around – and came face to face with Rose.

Rose's jewel eyes were terrified, and Henry's serious ones were angry. They stared at each other, this time, Henry's jaw clenched.

"Following me?" he asked sternly.

Rose nodded quickly, sensing that she was in danger.

"Why?"

"I…" she couldn't babble anything because the dangerous thing, the arrow, was still pointing at her, "I… I took you as my…"

Henry raised his brow for her to speak. It seemed like encouragement.

"Err… hobby."

For a moment, Henry's eyes remained firm. Then as if she had cracked a joke, he chuckled.

"Hobby?" he lowered his bow slowly and stopped laughing, "How so?"

Rose bit her lip, "You are the first human I have seen, and you are… fascinating."

Henry arched his brows as if he had taken it as a compliment. He slumped down against the willow again.

He took the berries out of his pocket and began to chew them again. He looked at her and then moved a little to make room for her.

Rose sat down beside him, and he generously offered the berries to her, but she looked at them with reluctance.

"If they were poisoned, I wouldn't be eating them," Henry assured her.

Rose took a berry and stuffed it in her mouth, savoring the tangy flavor.

"What is that?" Rose asked after some time. Henry saw her gesticulating towards the bow and the quiver.

"Those are my darlings, I guess," he answered with a sparkle in his eyes as he looked at them.

"What do you mean?"

"I mean," he cast her eyes at her, "this is called a weapon."

"What does a weapon do?"

"Kill."

There was silence after that. Rose kept staring at them as Henry had pointed them at her twice, both now and in the cave.

"What is *kill?*" she asked finally, forgetting the berries, while Henry kept chewing them.

"Dead," he replied.

Rose hesitated. Death was one question in her mind that her mama hadn't answered. The only way to get an answer was by asking Henry.

"Henry?" she licked her lips tentatively.

"Hmm?"

"If…" she stopped as if her conscious was stalking her, 'If… I asked you something, would you tell me?"

"Of course." He was still busy with the berries, appearing to be very hungry.

"What is *dead?*" she dared ask.

Henry looked at her suddenly. He wore a frown and Rose seemed to regret she had asked him that. He seemed upset.

"I'm sorry, I didn't…"

"You don't know?" Henry sounded taken aback. Rose shook her head slowly.

For a moment, Henry kept looking at her closely without blinking. Then he dropped the berries as if they were worthless and got up with his bow.

112

"Let me show you, since explanation will be futile," he offered her his hand. Rose held it and he led her away from the willow, neither of them uttering another word.

Rose seemed happy as she anticipated finally getting the answer to the question she had formulated from the Koran.

Henry stopped at the place where the chirping was loudest. He let go of her hand and prepared his bow and arrow. He directed it up toward the canopy.

"Ready?" he looked at her from the corner of his eye. Rose nodded excitedly but looking studious.

The arrow flew through the air like a shooting star.

The clamor rose among the birds as a toucan fell on the forest floor.

Henry lowered his bow as he watched Rose hurrying toward the bird. The blood was oozing, and the arrow was straight in the belly.

"Oh, my God!" Rose squealed. She dropped to her knees beside it and her hands trembled as she gently tried to pull the arrow out, "Oh, my God! What should I do? It's hurt…!"

She held the bird in her hands. The girl who used to help creatures was looking at the bird with two silvery streaks running down her cheeks.

She had no idea what to do with the motionless toucan, as her hands began to turn crimson with its blood.

"Blood!" she whispered, holding out her hands, "Blood! What should I do! God! And as if she remembered Henry was there too, she turned her head, "What did you do to it? help me now! It isn't moving!"

Crying and shrieking, she was panicking. Henry squatted beside her and looked at the bird in her blood-stained hands.

"Wake up!" she shook the toucan, but its yellow and black beak remained still.

"We have to help it now," she continued hysterically, but Henry remained still and silent, looking at the weeping Rose as if studying the depth of her soul.

"We can't," he said, "it won't move or wake up ever again."

Rose looked at him, shocked, and whispered, "Why?"

"Because it is dead," Henry said without any note of sympathy in his voice, "and I killed it."

Rose's nose flared in anger and hurt. She pushed Henry with her blood-stained hands on his chest, toppling him to the ground.

"You heartless, mean human!" she taunted, got up and marched away with the toucan in her hands.

"You asked me, Rose!" Henry justified loudly. Hearing this, she turned to face him and licked her lips, tasting the tears.

"I wish I hadn't," she said mournfully, turning back and walking away, staggering among the trees. Henry sat there for a long time.

***

"Mama!" Rose bellowed the moment she entered the castle's grounds, "MAMA!"

I came out and saw her carrying the toucan, rushing towards me helplessly.

"It's dead!" she told me, "Can you do something?"

I kept staring at the toucan and Rose kept looking at me impatiently. There was nothing I could do. Who could bring a dead toucan back to life?

"Yes," I replied after a while. This gave her some hope. I was supposed to take lives, not save them.

She watched me dig in the ground. I knew she expected the bird would fly if I would help it. I took the toucan from her and put it in the hole I had dug, then covered it with soil.

I looked at Rose as I finished my work, her swollen eyes fixed on me, demanding an explanation.

"Rose, when something dies, you bury it... it can't come back."

She seemed broken-hearted, badly shocked and hurt. She stared at the spot where the toucan was buried, and with her face full of anger, she strutted back toward the forest.

"Where are you going?"

"I'm going to kill Henry!"

Hearing this, I rushed behind her, "ROSE! DON'T!" She just kept walking.

I stopped dead in my tracks, "Do you want to be like him? Do you want to be a killer? A heartless, mean human?" She came to an abrupt halt.

114

At a snail's pace, I reached her. She had her face covered with her palms and was sobbing uncontrollably.

She didn't even ask me how I happened to know about *heartless, mean human.* I knew what to do and put my arm around her and walked back with her at the same slow pace.

"See? That was why I didn't tell you," I said softly.

Rose cried over its dead body as no human had ever cried for another dead human. She sat by the buried toucan and all I could do to console her was to sit beside her silently.

For a week, Rose remained silent, and I tried my best to bring a smile to her face.

Sitting by the toucan's grave, she was lamenting again when I took her by surprise.

"Smile for once!" I sang as I sat beside her, "Look, Rose! I found a perfect rose for you!"

She remained stoic and the rose dropped in my lap slowly.

"If you smile, I'll get you a new dress!"

The offer was associated with greed, but I didn't care. No response. She stayed there like a statue and I started thinking of some other way to please her.

"Please smile for once…" I pleaded, holding her hand. She just blinked at the grave.

"Okay, tell me what you want. A new book? The Koran? A sketchbook?" Nothing. She had lost interest. I didn't get up and sat by her side for a long time.

The sun began to sink behind the veil of clouds, turning them orange as if it were already doomsday. That was the time when Rose and I would stare directly at the sun without blinking until it disappeared.

The moon was already dominating the sky, surrounded by puffy white clouds. What a controversy, sun and moon together in the sky.

What a controversy, Death and life together by a grave.

I had decided to stay quiet, but Rose murmured something in a trance.

"Why is this rose pink?"

"First, smile," I said, suppressing my own smile at her words.

"Answer me first."

115

"Uh-huh. Not like that, lady."

She put a fake smile on her lips and asked, "Now?" "A real smile," I emphasized the 'real'.

"Mama!" she complained, "If you just tell me, maybe I would!" "Okay," I put the rose in her lap, "roses aren't just red. There are pink, white, yellow, and many other colors."

"Like a rainbow?"

"Kind of."

This was the smile I was yearning. A real happy smile. Holding the pink rose, she smiled at it, "Lovely."

"So, do you want me to drop a pink rose on your book every time I leave?"

She was generally indecisive when she was little, now, making decisions was an easy task for her, "But you named me after a red one, so I think I'll go with red."

"Okay," I laughed.

"Mirror mirror on the wall
Who is the fairest of them all?" No.

I didn't ask myself this. I am quite perplexed because at some point in their life, sooner or later, humans always ask themselves this question.

Why?

I am perplexed because to humans, beauty of the body matters most. It is controversial because to the Lord, beauty of the heart matters most.

Nobody, no matter how much humans try to focus on their inner beauty, no one falls in love with that. It's always the face.

Souls are doomed because of the mirror, it makes one proud, overconfident, and jealous. I have never seen a thing that humans have created as useless as a mirror.

Being Death, why I am saying this?

Because the mirror doesn't reflect me.

***

Rose hugged the willow and was weeping loudly, away from me. Embracing it as if it were a person, just as she embraced me, her eyes were closed, and tears washed her cheeks.

"Why are you crying?"

In her solitude, she had forgotten to listen for the alerting sounds of the forest. Abruptly, she turned around to face the man behind her. "Why are you even concerned?" she wept. Henry shrugged, "Why shouldn't I be?"

Hearing his calmness, Rose stepped closer to him hastily and glowered at him.

"You killed a bird. How can you live with that?"

Henry stared back at her bizarrely. *How can you live with that? Killing a bird? Lord... people killed humans and live with that.*

"You are weeping because of this?" Henry held his expression of astonishment, "It's been two weeks, Rose!"

She turned around violently and marched away on her heels, never looking back. but this time, Henry followed her. "I don't care! You killed a toucan!" she said scornfully.

"Well," Henry began to justify himself, snaking his way through the trees behind her, "You asked me to."

Rose didn't look back, she kept stomping with her arms swaying at her sides.

"You shouldn't have! I didn't know what it meant!"

That was the first furious argument Rose had ever had and she was really good at it.

117

Chapter 11

OBSERVATION No. 21

Humans seem to have an aptitude for self-defense even if they aren't taught it.

"What…" Henry pulled his foot free from the root tangling it, "What could I have done?"

Rose turned around so violently to Henry that he halted. "Explained!" she bellowed, "Just… explained!"

His jaw clenched and the groove between his eyebrows deepened. He couldn't think of anything to say because Rose's cheeks were completely wet with tears.

"Okay," he said calmly, "I'm sorry, alright? Next time, I'll just explain."

Rose kept staring in his eyes darkly, then her look softened from Henry's invitation.

"Would you like to have lunch with me?" "Why?" she asked politely.

He thought for a second before answering, as if he had no reason but needed one to convince her, "Because I'm sorry."

Rose stared at him. Then the realization of the level of closeness made her step back. she nodded, "Okay."

She wiped her face on her scarlet sleeve before following him along the speckled floor of the forest.

It wasn't a long journey and soon they reached the tents, without saying a word to each other during the journey.

Paulo spotted them first, "Rose, what a pleasant surprise!" "Salam," Rose uttered nervously.

Paulo exchange a glance with Henry at Rose's salutation. Henry looked at her sideways. "You're a Muslim?" he asked in surprise. Rose nodded.

Before they could discuss religions or start on blasphemy, Daniel came out of the tent with a guidebook in his hand. His glasses had slipped to the tip of his nose and was scrutinizing the book.

"Oh, you're back," then his eyes went to Rose, "And Rose too. Did you save her life again?"

Henry buried his hands in his pockets, eyed Rose, and said in a reserved tone, "Kind of."

He walked away and as he passed Rose, he stopped and leaned toward her, whispering in her ear, "Or you would have cried for the rest of your life."

Rose didn't giggle and kept her eyes on him as he went in the tent, announcing loudly, "She's staying for lunch!"

As he disappeared inside the tent, Rose looked at Daniel who had closed his book, pushing back his glasses with his forefinger.

"Don't mind Henry's tone," Daniel was trying to cover up for him, "He is... he is..."

As he groped for something appropriate to say, Paulo carried the log in front of Rose and stopped, answering Daniel's incomplete sentence in a genuine whisper, "A bulldog."

Daniel smiled as Paulo smirked. Rose remained stoic as she had never seen a bull or a dog or a bulldog.

The fire was lit on the damp forest floor, the food was cooked and served while the four men and Rose sat on the logs around the soaring flames.

Sometimes, they ate silently, but when it became disturbing, one of them broke it. Alex always cracked a joke, which would make Paulo and Daniel grin, but Henry remained indifferent, so did Rose because she couldn't understand them.

After lunch, the men scattered toward one side while Rose sat where she was until Henry joined her.

"So..." the acquaintance was changing into friendship, "How is your mother?"

Rose smiled, "Best as ever," she didn't stop there. She began to describe briefly in literal terms how I was, "She is so beautiful that you can't even imagine."

Henry's jaw twitched and he looked sideways at her as she arched her knees and tucked her chin between them.

"Well, I can imagine," he replied, his eyes on her, "I bet she is as beautiful as you are."

Rose sighed hopelessly.

"Mama says I am, but how can I tell? I've never seen myself." Henry scowled at her words, "What?"

"What?" she looked at him, alarmed that she might have said something vile.

"You have never seen yourself?" he was astounded.

"Of course," Rose replied in a matter-of-fact way, "How can one see oneself?"

He moved his eyes away from her for some time and then looked at her again, "Of course."

Then he smiled, utilizing muscles he seldom used, and asked, "Of course… so would you tell me how I look?"

Rose was avid, "Yes!"

"Then describe me," Henry said, quelling his smile.

Rose eyed him from head to toe without hesitation and jumped to the conclusion without any waste of time, "You are beautiful!"

Henry plucked the grass and cast his eyes on it for a second. Twisting it in his fingers, he wove a plan to trick her.

"But I still don't know what I look like. My eyes, my hair… describe them for me."

Licking her lips, Rose began in a critical tone, her eyes moving on his every feature as she tried her best to describe them.

"Your hair is black, just like the moonless night," she touched his hair and her fingers made their way to his ear, so did her eyes, "You ears are like… like your friend's ears…" her fingers went on his neck and her thumb traced the scar there, "Your neck has a line just like… a line on a leaf."

With her left hand against the ground, her right hand was tracing Henry's skin, making his hair rise, "And your cheeks have short hair, like thorns… but they don't hurt as I touch them… they aren't ugly, they are beautiful, they line your upper lip too."

Her fingers went on the bridge of his nose, moving down, "You nose is perfectly shaped."

And her fingers traveled down to his lips, and she hesitated for the first time as she touched his lips, but only for a second, "And… and your lips are pink…"

Gulping, she moved her fingers to his eyebrows, tracing them with her finger, "Your eyebrows always wear a frown, but it looks good on your face and they are thick… and your eyes…" Nothing came out.

As her eyes met Henry's, she became speechless. Because he had locked his eyes on her face the moment, she had started describing him. He

120

had fixed his eyes on hers and she was unable to blink away that magnetic look.

She had cupped her hand on his cheek and forgotten to remove it

"Well," he asked without changing the intimidating look, "What about my eyes? Ugly?"

She swallowed but didn't unlock their gaze, "No… your eyes are…"

Her hand slowly moved down from his cheek and dropped in her lap. Henry didn't say anything, neither did Rose.

The silence lengthened and her eyes remained locked on his. His lips moved.

"Your eyes are like the most enchanting jewels," he paused his gaze frozen on Rose, "Your hair shines like the golden rays from the sun.

His eyes didn't move to any of her facial features as he described them, "You are blushing right now."

He didn't smile, "Your lips are redder than any rose in the world."

He didn't move his gaze and Rose was wonderstruck already. And the next words came from the things he loved most in the world, "And your brows are like the arcs of my bow… and the sight of you strikes me like an arrow. You are more colorful than any rainbow and more beautiful than any butterfly. You are the rose blooming in the orchard of my home." He stopped.

Finally, Rose blinked, and her lips moved. Her eyes only moved away when Paulo said from a distance, "Uh oh. Henry's in trouble, guys."

Daniel and Alex stopped in their tracks and looked at the couple. Hearing that, Henry got up and started polishing his knee-high boots, ignoring them.

Daniel started reading his book and Paulo sat by Rose, while Alex was wiping his pistol.

"Henry isn't your typical guy," Paulo explained to Rose.

"What do you mean?"

"He means nothing, Rose," Henry answered. He had his back towards them, but it seemed that he was aware of the conversation.

"I meant," Paulo dropped his eyes, "You are the first girl he has dated." "What?" her face was still blank.

"Yes!" Paulo opened the Pandora box, "Everyone thought that being the son of the president, he would beat all records. He did indeed, in *not* dating."

Rose blinked innocently, "Is that bad?"

"Shut up, Paulo," Henry said in an undertone without turning around.

"For me, it would be bad," Paulo sneered, "But for Henry, it is a kind of prestige, I suppose."

"Shut it."

"He is kind of an anti-romantic man. I never thought he would fall for someone younger than himself."

Henry's hands stopped moving, his shoulders rose for a second and hunched again as he relaxed them, "Don't involve Rose in this. It's not what you're thinking."

Paulo addressed Henry directly this time, "Everybody falls in love sooner or later in their life. The ones who deny it are just delaying the inevitable."

Rose blinked ignorantly when Paulo stopped speaking and looked to Henry for an answer.

"Henry?" she said politely when he remained silent, "What is he saying?"

He turned around, his frown deeper than before and his hands clenched in fists, he said indignantly to Paulo.

"He is talking bullshit!" Silence.

Daniel stopped reading and was looking at Henry incredulously. Rose regarded him with innocence in her eyes. The atmosphere seemed fragile as if the friendship would break at any moment, but it was saved by Rose.

"Henry?" she began tentatively and sweetly. His posture didn't change as he kept his infuriated eyes on Paulo. Rose continued in her usual innocent manner, "What is bullshit?"

Daniel was the first one to burst out laughing, then Alex, and finally Paulo. Henry smiled at her question and busied himself again.

"Tell her, Henry!" Daniel said, amused.

Rose was puzzled at the sudden change in the situation.

Henry walked to her and said, "Come on, let's go back... and forget that word, it is a bad one. Just don't tell your mother that I used it, otherwise she will get a bad impression of me. I'm going to see her off, guys, don't bother to follow us."

Rose and Henry began to walk side by side. Their pace wasn't fast, and they didn't talk either. Soon, Rose began to look up at the tall trees, which seemed to go on forever. With her neck craned, she was too interested in the trees, while Henry had his eyes on the track.

Rose seemed to be searching for something, perhaps she wanted to steal a glimpse of the sky. Henry began to play with his dagger, tossing it in the air and catching it with one hand.

After some time of his playing, his dagger fell among the twigs and leaves. He crouched to pick it up, and as he straightened, Rose ran straight into his back. Jerking forward, he managed to keep his balance, as Rose tumbled to the ground.

She just lay there as Henry frowned down at her, as if deciding something, with the dagger twisting in his fingers.

"What?" she stared at him, her palms pinned to the ground.

With the frown still ruling his face, the corners of his lips curved, and a smile appeared, "I have something for you."

Bringing out something reflective from his pocket, he crouched in front of her. Rose held it and looked at her reflection.

"Who is this?" then she saw the movement of her own lips in the mirror and whispered, "I can't hear her." Henry smiled broadly.

"This girl," he pointed at the reflection, "is you, Rose."

She stared at the girl and then clapped her palm to her mouth, "This is *me?*"

She held her hair and kept staring at herself for a long time. It was the kind of impression one got after gaining eyesight after a lifetime of blindness.

Henry observed her very carefully and then after a long time, he asked, "You don't like yourself?"

Rose frowned in a trance and then blinked at herself, "I... I do... but..." she was sounding disappointed, "I... I don't... look like my mother." "You want to look like her?"

Rose nodded without casting away her eyes. Henry raised his eyebrows, "Why?"

"Because she is the most beautiful!" Rose answered in an obviously manner.

Henry kept his eyes on her face as his tongue rolled in his mouth and he bit the inside of his cheek. Tucking his hand beneath her chin, he turned her face toward him.

"You are beautiful, Rose," he told her sincerely, "To me, you are the most beautiful thing I've ever seen."

Her eyes sparkled and the corner of her mouth turned up.

"But how can this happen? How can one look at oneself?"

Henry began to explain the physics, and she listened carefully. *I assume we can see it clearly. I mean, what is coming.*

***

"Mama!"

I didn't reply because I was feeling the weakest human emotion, which is fear.

"Mama!"

My lips trembled. I kept watering the roses without even thinking why I was doing it as I had watered them some hours ago.

"Mama! There you are!" Rose came in. I still didn't know how to avoid it as I didn't have a plan.

"What are you doing?" Rose asked happily, but continued without waiting for my answer, "I've got something for you!"

"Hmm…"

Think. Think. Think.

Thinking has always been a major issue for me. I'm not capable of thinking. I'm only capable of obeying.

I quickly started walking toward the castle with Rose following me, waiting for me to pay her some attention.

When I didn't, she took my hand and stood still, looking at me.

"I've got something for you," she repeated with the same enthusiasm.

I blinked and licked my dry lips, "Okay."

With this, she brought out her hand with the mirror. I stared at it as if I had never seen a mirror before.

"What is this?" I asked.

"A mirror. Mama, we can see ourselves in it! Henry gave it to me!"

The first materialistic thing she received from the world and the deadliest as well.

"Look…"

"No." I pushed it away.

"No, look, Mama, how beautiful you are!"

"No," I repeated, "Keep it away from me."

"Mama," Rose tried to calm me down, "seriously, it won't hurt you."

"It's not that, Rose," I told her evasively.

"Then why don't you look at yourself?" her tone gave me the impression that she was annoyed, but so was I.

"Because…" I couldn't tell her. But somewhere within me, I knew that a mother could trust her daughter with her secret, "Because my reflection doesn't appear in the mirror." Rose was silent.

Was she scared? No… more like sympathetic. Very sympathetic. She just knew Henry's and her reflection had appeared in the mirror, maybe she would assume not everyone's did.

It seemed normal for her to accept what I said. "Oh no," she moaned.

"Rose?"

"Mama, you won't be able to see yourself."

I frowned and thought about what I could do to satisfy her. I wanted to see myself. I knew my face changed according to the lives people led, their sins and virtues created my physical appearance and I appeared beautiful to Rose because she had no sin.

Our discussion came to an end, but my thoughts didn't.

I closed my eyes to see the blackness humans see when they sleep, my back against the trunk of a willow. It was noon when I heard her steps approaching me.

"Mama! Mama!"

I didn't open my eyes. She had found me anyway. When I looked at her, she seemed joyous about something.

"Rose?"

"Guess what have I have for you?" she was extremely excited. "The mirror," I said airily.

"Oh, no. Something better than that!"

Being Death, I had already condemned the mirror and didn't feel it worthwhile to consider the matter a second time. As far as I was concerned the subject had been forgotten.

"I don't know, Rose," I kept sitting there as she stepped toward me and slumped down, holding out a paper in front of my eyes. *Wow.*

I couldn't stop smiling. How could she even compare an evil thing like a mirror to this?

"I knew it would make you happy!" she beamed.

"Is this…?"

In wonderment, I looked at the perfectly shaded visage with a lovely smile, those almond-shaped eyes with long, sweeping lashes, the hair flowing down like a calm and gentle river.

"Yes!"

A sketch.

A sketch of me.

I was speechless. I was far more beautiful than the word. The word was too small for me, even the world was too small for me.

"This is wonderful, Rose," I finally complimented her.

"Sure, it is, Mama. Now you can see yourself." I

smiled, "I meant, your drawing is wonderful."

Her aptitude was rare.

Rose nudged me, "Oh come on, Mama. We're talking about you here."

I laughed, "I'm glad you see me like this."

No, she didn't understand what I meant, but still it was something worth saying.

"Thanks, by the way, I'm flattered," Rose said graciously. Just so you know, I have the sketch. Even now.

***

"Tremendous," Henry uttered.

"Right?" Rose beamed, "She is beautiful."

Henry's stare at the sketch wasn't annoying at all. I have seen hunger and lust in men's eyes when they look at a beautiful woman. But there was respect in his eyes, respect for me, Rose's mother.

"She certainly is," he replied.

He was the first person who saw Death before dying. But it was good that he didn't know what he had just seen.

Henry licked his lips, hesitating. He was going to ask something, and I knew what. I have lived for thousands of years. I know what humans are going to say by their actions.

Sorry, I used the word 'live' for myself. Did it annoy you?

Oh, please, excuse me but you don't live either. You all survive.

"Do you want to come with me to the ball?"

Rose sat beside him on the jagged forest floor, and asked him curiously," What's a ball?"

"It's a dance," he began reluctantly, "Rose. I want you to meet my people, see my world. Will you come with me for a day?"

Rose thought. Half about what she couldn't understand and half of about what she was unsure of.

"Of course!"

Oh, no. Oh, no. Oh, no. Trouble.

"I'll ask Mama."

"You need permission from your mother?" Henry sounded bewildered.

"Obviously, Henry," she said in a matter of fact tone, "Don't you ask your mother?"

"Uh, no," Henry replied honestly. His honesty wasn't limited to himself, he referred to all the humans, "I generally just tell her. It doesn't matter anyway. People don't have time for each other in my world." He was breaking the ice while she was an open book.

"Come on, Henry!" Rose said, "Let's go and ask her now!"

Henry stared at Rose, as did I. Was she out of her mind? She was bringing an unknown man to my territory? Death's territory? "Now?" Henry raised his eyebrow.

"I understand if you don't want to come," Rose replied.

"No, I do. But... look at me, Rose." Rose looked at his face, or rather stared.

"I mean my clothes. They are messy and I haven't shaved, I don't want to make a notorious impression on her."

Rose was silent. He was waiting for her reply, and when she did, he laughed aloud.

"Henry, what does notorious mean?"

He looked at her, laughing at her as if she were an innocent and ignorant child. Then he got up and said, "Let's meet your mother."

Rose led the way cheerfully. I had no plan. The only thing I could think of was to leave or sneak behind them. The latter was the better.

Without saying a word, they reached the river. The waterfall was building pressure against the rocks. He shouldered his bow and jumped on the rock, looked back at her, offering his hand.

Rose looked at his hand, "I can do this." The frown grew on his face, "Seriously?" She nodded.

"You'll fall, Rose," Henry warned. Rose glanced at the flowing stream and the rocks.

"I can do it," she assured him.

With a cunning smile, Henry shrugged and moved on, "Suit yourself."

Skipping steps on the jagged rocks, Henry crossed the stream and went to the other side of the bank. when he reached there and looked back, Rose was still on her spot.

"I don't have all day!" Henry said aloud.

Tentatively, she stepped on the first rock after a gulp. Henry watched her progress as she hopped on the second one at a turtle's pace.

"You'll fall," Henry warned her again.

Rose ignored him and stepped on the third one. Her foot slipped, but she maintained her balance. Stretching out her arms, her eyes fell on Henry and remained on him as he unbuttoned his shirt.

"What are you doing?" Rose asked, taken aback.

He took off his shirt and placed it at his feet, casting his playful eyes upon her.

"Distracting you," he replied slyly.

"Why?"

He moved his naked shoulders, shrugging, and unfolded his arms, "Because I want you to fall."

Rose frowned, "You want me to get hurt?"

Henry smirked, as he knew he was handsome as hell and his plan would work, "No. I want you to obey me."

Rose gulped and jumped on the next rock. She didn't look at him as it was the only strategy to avoid distraction. She never looked up from the stream.

When she jumped again, Henry started whistling a slow tune.

Rose looked at him. Now he wasn't even wearing his vest.

As she stared at him, he kept whistling. Perhaps she was awed by him as she had never seen a male body before, and I thanked the Lord he didn't take off his pants. His torso was enough to cause havoc.

She shook her head and as she stepped again, lost balance, and fell. A smile spread across his face as she splashed in the water. However, it didn't last long as his prediction was fulfilled, and Rose was moaning with her eyes closed.

Henry hurried toward her, skipping across the rocks.

"Hey," he frowned.

"I'm fine, I'm fine." She tried to get up, but it turned into a wince, "Happy now? I'm hurt!"

"You just fell, Rose. Be strong, get up," Henry defended himself as if he were teaching her to be strong.

As the water spoiled her dress, some of it also filled her eyes. Her hands were deep in the water, holding her sprained ankle.

Henry reacted to the situation and crouched to take her in his arms.

"What are you doing?" Rose cringed away.

Henry halted, his frown deepening again, "I'm," he paused, "trying to help you."

Rose still seemed unsure.

"Come on, Rose!" Henry affirmed for the tenth time, "I don't bite, alright?"

She held up her arms hesitatingly, and in a second, Henry was carrying her back. His eyes were on the path, looking sympathetic as Rose locked her fingers at the back of his neck and pressed her face to his shoulder.

"You'll fall, Henry," she told him, "You'll fall."

"Uh-huh," his eyes were still analyzing the way back to the other side, *"We* will fall, Rose."

He hopped, lost balance, maintained it. Rose's nails scratching his neck in panic and he winced, "Ah!"

"What happened?" She looked innocently at his unshaven face.

His eyes went to her face and he told her in disbelief, "Don't scratch me."

Rose nodded, curling her fingers on his neck, "Are we going to fall?"

Henry attempted another jump to the next rock and another wince escaped his mouth.

"I didn't scratch," Rose protested immediately.

Henry looked at her, "You pulled my hair."

"I did?"

But Henry ignored the question and reached the last step. The land was at some distance and there were slippery pebbles on it, making it the riskiest jump.

Henry's chest rose and fell heavily, and Rose closed her eyes, burying her face in his chest. His fingers enclosed tightly around her waist and thigh and he jumped.

There, he landed on his feet.

"Ah! Why are you pulling my hair, Rose?"

He seemed offended but after hearing her answer, he smiled faintly.

"Because my foot is hurting me!"

Henry placed her in the lap of the tree and said, "Stay."

He went away without telling her where he was going, still shirtless, and Rose's face glistened in the sunshine as the tears fell on her cheeks. Holding her ankle, she was trying hard not to scream.

After a while, he came back with a paste of leaves and herbs. Kneeling by her, he held her foot. After rubbing the paste on her ankle, he tore apart the hem of his shirt and knotted it around her ankle. After washing his hands, he sat beside her, exhausted.

"You okay now?" he broke the silence.

Rose nodded as a heavy tear fell from her eye.

"Then why are you crying?"

She didn't hesitate in answering him. she had looked at his face all the time as he played the role of a homeopath, without raising her eyes at her or talking.

"You won't be able to meet my mama now."

"No big deal, I'll meet her later."

There was silence. He kept looking at her as if waiting for her to stop crying. But she didn't. he licked his lips and asked again, "Why are you still crying?"

Rose sniffed and looked at him as if he had made the greatest sacrifice of the century, "What will you wear now? How will you tell your mama that you need a new shirt?"

129

Poor girl, she must have thought everyone asked their mothers for new clothes the way she had to.

Henry resisted laughing. Rose continued, "Now your mama will scold you because of me," she sniffed again, "You can take my dress and make yourself a shirt from it."

The response was strange.

Henry leaned forward and kissed Rose on her forehead. His lips stayed there for a long time, his hands cupped around her wet cheeks.

Everything was silent. Even the birds.

It seemed as if he would stay like that forever, but his lips moved away, placing his forehead against hers. Looking into her eyes, he whispered, "I love you, Rose."

The incredulity on her face was visible. The only thing that moved was her eyes when she blinked. Henry said nothing after that. It looked as if he had taken days to decide, but had failed, and now every word had come into existence without thinking.

"Henry?" Rose said tentatively.

"Hmm?" he gulped but didn't let go of her face.

"What is love?"

Henry smiled. The look on her face was so full of candor that he couldn't consider her question to be a form of trickery.

He moved his head away, dropped his hands down in his lap and smiled.

"Love is…" he stopped. Rose had taken out her book and was going to note down every word he said.

"How do you spell it?" she asked, looking at him.

Henry frowned.

For a second, it seemed he was going to tell her. but then the furrow between his eyebrows deepened and he became indecisive again.

OBSERVATION No. 22

Man is not capable of making decisions. The more options he gets, the more confused he becomes.

Suddenly, he shouldered his quiver and bow, scooped up Rose in his arms, and started walking again.

Rose kept looking at his face, but he was stern now.

"Guide me," was all he said.

When Henry reached the dark and deep parts, he dropped her on her feet.

"Won't you come with me?" she asked.

He just shook his head. Maybe he was ashamed of his confession. He turned to leave, but again Rose called him.

130

"Henry!"

He didn't look back, just stopped on his way. "Why didn't you tell me what is love?"

There was silence at first, then he looked back at her and explained the reason for his capricious behavior.

"Because… I don't know." He left.

Chapter 12

"Mama?"

Rose had her head in my lap, watching the crescent moon and the stars with great interest.

"Hmm?" I asked, brushing her hair with my fingers. I thought the question would be about the night, but I was wrong.

"What is the meaning of love?"

My fingers came to a halt and my smile faded. I had the impression that she had forgotten the question, even the word after two days but here she was, asking me about it. She waited.

I waited too. I waited to make up a meaning, but I couldn't. I didn't know the meaning of love. What can I love? Whom can I love? I have no competition, no companion. I'm alone, yet I have souls with me.

I've lived for ages. I've seen things. I have experience. I know there's no such thing as love, but the name of attraction between opposite genders. Love is nothing, it has no existence.

OBSERVATION No. 23

After years of experience I have realized there is only one *he* who loves you, and it's not he. It's He.

"I don't know, Rose," I told her finally. At once, Rose sat upright, and I knew why. This was the first question I had failed to answer.

"You don't know?" she asked incredulously.

"No."

"Really?"

"Yes."

Silence. It was hard for her to digest that her mother couldn't answer her question. Feeling let down, she dropped her head in my lap again, blinking at the twinkling stars.

"Mama," she said after a while and there was hesitation in her tone, "Henry says he loves me."

I didn't reply as I didn't know what to say to her. Then there was another question. "Is love good?" Good?

It is hell. It is heaven. It is paradise. The answers to the questions in your mind:

1.   If you love a person more than you love the Lord, it leads you to hell.

2.   If you love a person moderately, it leads to heaven.

3.   If you love someone so much that the separation makes you closer to the Lord, it leads to paradise.

But still, my answer for Rose was the same, "I don't know, Rose."

Perhaps she had no other question, or she realized I had no other answer because that was the end of our conversation.

***

"Mama?"

"Hmm?"

We were watering the roses in our gloomy orchard.

"Henry asked me to visit his home."

There you go: Henry, Henry, Henry.

I frowned. Couldn't this man leave my Rose alone?

"So?" I didn't want to sound cold. "Can we go with him?"

I stood up and looked at her, We?

"Rose, I can't go," refusing was easy.

"Why not?" she started following me.

"Because," I replied without stopping, "Because… I have to go to work!" It worked!

"Oh, no… it means I can't go either." She turned around to leave.

Should Rose see the world? Or shouldn't she? I was still deciding when I saw how upset she was. I couldn't stand to see a single tear in my daughter's eyes.

With a heavy heart, I said, "Of course, you can go, Rose!" "Really?" her face lit up once again.

"Yes," I put my arm around her and walked, "But be sure you follow our rules to protect yourself."

"What rules?"

Rules… humans always forget rules. The humans who set rules for themselves and rare, as are those who don't cross the boundaries of their rules.

OBSERVATION No. 24

Following the rules set for your soul is the most difficult goal for humans.

I sighed.

"Listen to me very carefully," holding her shoulders, I turned her to face me, "Rose. The world you will see is a deception and will misguide you. The glare of the greed of the world destroys humans. But remember that world, no matter how beautiful it is, will turn into dust but you will return where you belong."

"Where I belong?"

I looked deep into her eyes. My child was growing up, this was the first time I had realized it. but her guileless nature wasn't suitable for the world.

"To the Lord."

Rose nodded. She understood me very well.

***

"How do I look?" Rose asked me excitedly.

"Like my butterfly," I smiled at her.

I had brought a new dress for her, as she couldn't go with Henry in untidy clothes. It was again her favorite red gown. She thought red was her personal color and never wore anything else. Rose smiled.

"But, Rose, how can a butterfly live without flowers?"

"You mean you are coming with me?" she walked to me looking happy.

"No," I took out a beautiful, ruddy crown of roses I had made for her, "It means my flowers are going with my butterfly."

I placed the crown on her head, and she laughed faintly.

"Why do you always give me roses?"

"Because you, my child, are my rose, and every rose belongs to you." As we walked, the shadow of fear made a home in my heart. Wow… quite a human statement.

I wanted her to protect herself, so again, I reminded her of the rules.

"Rose, stay away from men. If you find yourself alone in a man's company, leave immediately. If someone harasses you, call for help. If you call me, I'll come to help you and don't talk too much, and don't get overexcited, okay?"

To my surprise, she was noting the things in her diary! I stared at her.

"Got it!" she replied.

I didn't know if she really understood because she had never told me about Henry's kiss. There could be three reasons.

1. She didn't understand its significance.
2. She didn't understand what it might mean to me.
3. She was indecisive.

But I never asked her about it. Had I done so, she would have asked me how I knew about it, and then there was no answer to that question, was there?

I stopped as we crossed the graveyard, but Rose walked on.

"Won't you come to meet Henry?" she asked as she noticed my absence beside her.

"I have to go to work," I replied without hesitation.

OBSERVATION No. 25

Some humans hesitate before lying and some hesitate after lying.

She stood for a moment, then turned around and walked on. *Goodbye, Rose.*

I stared at her as she left me alone. Then her steps slowed down, and she stopped. In a moment, she came back hurriedly with tears in her eyes and hugged me without warning, "I'll miss you, Mama, I'll miss you!"

I didn't embrace her because of my sadness. At that moment, I really wished I were a human and could go with her. When she didn't leave me, I wrapped my arms around her, and she kissed me on my cheek.

"I'll be back soon."

"Be a good girl," I smiled at her as we broke apart, "You always have to be."

I was afraid. Being in the human world meant being in a world full of opportunities to sin.

***

Henry was waiting for her, and a slight smile appeared on his face when he saw her. Rose was also excited and giggling.

"Let's go," Henry told her. It was strange to see him without his bow. This was the first time he was without it and he looked bare.

Rose must have thought they would walk as she knew nothing about transport and followed Henry. "Is it far away?" Rose asked.

"Yes."

She was silent, thinking, and then she asked again, "Where will we stay at night? I'm so tired of walking."

Henry stopped and looked at her with an astonished frown, "We're not walking."

Rose stared at him, "I can't run, Henry." The noise grew in the forest.

"Who says? We are flying," Henry turned his face up, looking at the clear blue sky.

Rose also looked up. The immense sound echoed around them, as the rotating wings disturbed the calm air, like a gale out of nowhere.

Rose was in awe of the mechanical beast as it landed in front of them. Henry looked at her shocked face.

"Where did you find such a huge butterfly?"

Henry smiled, "Want to have a ride in the butterfly?"

Rose was wildly excited like the wind, but she looked at him tentatively as he stepped closer, and she gingerly took a step back.

"Come on, Rose," he moved forward amused, holding her waist, "I won't hurt you."

He lifted her into the flying machine and climbed in beside her.

"Sit down please," he asked her as he gestured to the pilot, and the helicopter left the forest floor.

Looking out the window, Rose laughed, "Once I had a dream that I was flying on a butterfly!"

Henry smiled and moved towards her, "Well, it looks as if not all dreams remain just a dream."

"Oh look! Everything is so small!" She looked at Henry and then her eyes scrutinized the inside of the helicopter, "Henry… this butterfly is very different…"

There was a moment of indecision, "That's because this isn't a butterfly. This is my helicopter, Rose."

Rose opened her book immediately and started writing. Henry cast his eyes on the words, stopping on love as she hadn't written its meaning.

"No, no. it is spelled H-E-L-I-C-O-P-T-E-R," Henry told her, and her fingers froze after writing it, "It is a flying machine."

"Henry, what's a *machine?*"

He bit his lip, raised his eyebrow and murmured, "Human replica of God's creations."

Rose understood, and as they flew over the vales, mountains, and buildings, Henry kept answering her never-ending questions.

When they landed, Rose was thrilled by the cars waiting for them. She was very enthusiastic and wanted to learn about everything and write it all down in her book. But Henry told her they had plenty of time for that.

136

"Your home is wonderful!" Rose exclaimed, looking at the buildings from inside the car.

"No, it's not my home," Henry told her, "You see, you live in the forest, but the whole forest isn't your home. I live in a small part of this huge city."

As she looked through the window, Henry kept staring at her with a wrinkled brow. He didn't say a word after that. It seemed that she wanted to observe every minute detail, as she seldom blinked, not wishing to miss a thing.

The three cars stopped. Henry got out of the middle one and opened the door for Rose. He held his hand out for her, and she took it reluctantly.

He walked toward the wooden door and stopped, looking sideways at Rose who was gazing at the palatial house, wide-eyed.

He didn't smile as he hailed, "Welcome to my world, Rose." "Wow," Rose uttered.

Henry walked inside, gesturing to the security guards to stay out. The house was glamorous, after all it was the president's house. The modern furniture, Persian carpets, classical paintings, antique ornamental pieces, there was perfection in everything.

Rose didn't dare to touch anything but admired everything.

"When I met you in the forest, I thought you lived in trees."

Henry smiled at that. Rose looked at him suddenly, "There are no animals and no birds. How can humans live without nature?"

Henry sighed, "They... we are used to it. Are you hungry?"

"Yes, but how will we eat? There are no trees, no fruit," she seemed rather worried about it.

Henry gave a faint hint of smile, "My house, my rules."

He walked toward the dining room where the table was already set. It seemed he had planned lunch for her.

"Come on, sit down, Rose." He pulled out a chair for her and sat at the far end of the table.

Rose seemed nervous as the servants looked at her strangely. She wasn't dressed like the women in Brazil and there was a ring of roses on her head. The servant left after talking to Henry about something she couldn't interpret in her mind.

When he was gone, Rose stared at Henry, who was eating his roast dinner now, and reading a newspaper. She got up and settled on the chair next to his.

"Why have you come here?" he asked, turning his attention to her.

"I'm... I'm scared... stay with me," her timid reply came.

"Okay, now please eat something, you must be hungry."

He offered her fruit, the thing she was used to. She was very surprised when she heard they cooked food, and even more to see the number of dishes there were. Henry asked her to eat as much as she wanted. There were endless questions about everything. After lunch, Henry showed her the house.

"Henry?"

"Hmm?"

"Where is your mama?"

Henry's steps slowed down at the question and he sighed, "Mother's don't have time for their sons here, Rose. You must make an appointment to see your own mother. You're lucky to have such an exquisite mother." Rose bit her lip, and there was silence.

"Come on, let's go out," Henry proposed, and she nodded.

They visited many places with the security lurking behind them. Rose gawked at every human she saw. She wanted to write the meaning of everything in her book, but Henry told her there were so many things that they wouldn't fit in it.

She was impressed by the shoes, dresses, and the jewelry, but what attracted her most was a teddy bear. It was a cute, white, fluffy teddy bear. She smiled at it, the way a girl smiles at a boy, beguilingly. After a while, Henry said they should go home as it was getting dark.

When they left the shop, Henry busied himself with his phone and only looked up when he heard a noise.

"STOP! STOP, THIEF!"

Henry froze on the spot and looked back. The shopkeeper was rushing toward them.

"You must pay for what you took, sir."

"Excuse me? I didn't take anything."

"Exactly," the shopkeeper looked at Rose, "she stole it."

Henry looked sideways at Rose, who had the teddy cuddled in her arms. Licking his lips, he took out his wallet and paid the man more than it cost. He walked off after casting a look of disapproval at Rose.

Henry glared at her, but the innocence on her face told him that she knew nothing about the concept of payment. "Just," Henry fought hard to control his laughter, "don't take anything, absolutely nothing without my permission."

Rose nodded tentatively. She kept looking at him, unable to understand what had just happened. Henry's eyes seemed thoughtful, he leaned forward, held her hand, and kissed her on her forehead.

"You are looking beautiful," he said, his lips brushing her hair, "it took me a long time to say that."

He winked, put his arm around her shoulder and walked to the car. He loved her. he really did.

***

It was 2 am and Rose was still awake, staring wide-eyed in the dark, lying on a huge bed. The teddy was in her arms, the crown of roses beside her on the table.

There was a moment of indecision, but she sat up and put on her shoes. Walking timidly, she reached Henry's room in the illuminated passageway. Poor girl, she didn't know she had to knock.

"Henry?" she called slowly in a scared voice, her heart thumping in her chest. No reply, the sound of crickets her only company.

She turned the handle and walked inside the room, creeping in like a thief. Her eyes searched him in the darkness as she stood by his bed.

"Henry." Rose whispered.

With his torso against the bed, his cheek pressed on the pillow, one arm hanging down from the bed, he didn't response.

"Henry!" Rose whispered eagerly.

He stayed still. The third time, she didn't refrain from touching him. "Henry…" she shook his upper arm. After a moment, he opened his eyes and blinked., unable to recognize who was there.

"Wake up, Henry."

She let go of his arm as his hand went to the lamp and turned it on.

"Rose?" There was utter surprise on his face as he saw her in his room with the teddy in her arms, "What are you doing here?"

He propped himself up on his elbows when she didn't reply and stared at her.

"What happened?" He asked with a frown.

"I'm scared."

Henry frowned at her, "You weren't scared in a dark and dangerous forest, and now you're scared among other humans?"

Rose's lips trembled, and in the next moment, tears filled her eyes, "I want to go home."

At first, he was so astonished that he didn't reply. Then he got up and held her shoulders gently.

"Why do you want to go home?" he asked politely.

The streaks of tears flowed down her cheeks and wet her lips. She couldn't even speak, and her condition was becoming worse. Henry realized it, he made her sit on the bed and she screwed her eyes shut.

139

"I slept with Mama on grass, my head in her lap and she sang me a lullaby…" she sniffed, "and stroked my hair… I can't sleep, I can't sleep without Mama!"

There was silence. He sat on the bed beside her and snaked his arm around her.

"So, you miss your mother?" Rose nodded slowly.

Henry bit the inside of his cheek, "Look at me." She shook her head.

"Why won't you look at me?"

She shook her head again, not willing to open her eyes. Curiosity was etched on his face, puzzled by her attitude.

"Hey, at least tell me why you aren't looking at me," he gently prompted, leaning toward her.

"You'll distract me."

His frown deepened, "How?"

She swallowed hard, her grip on the bear tightening, "You're shirtless."

First, Henry stared at her, then he began to chuckle, then held her and kissed her temple. After smiling at her, he left her with her eyes still closed. Wearing his shirt now, he stood in front of her and spoke gently. "Get up, Rose."

"Are we going home?" she looked at him happily and forgot she had shut her eyes earlier.

"No," he told her, "but some place like home."

When she got up, Henry locked his fingers with hers and they left the room. Soundlessly but confidently, they descended the stairs and reached the garden. Henry sat on the grass in the darkness, but Rose stared at him.

"What are you doing?" she asked, as if Henry was mad.

"Well," Henry gestured around, "Plants, trees, grass, and my lap. This is the best I can offer."

He was being serious. Smiling broadly, Rose lay down on the bed of grass and put her head in his lap. Henry was wide awake now. He sighed. The night would be long for him. "Henry?" Rose asked in a sleepy voice.

"Hmm?" he was stroking her hair.

"What about a lullaby?"

He frowned, "I don't sing, and the mosquitoes are already buzzing in my ear."

"Henry?" Rose asked again after a moment's silence.

"Hmm?"

"Why don't you sing?"

140

His hands stopped moving and he replied darkly, "I just don't. Now, will you please close your eyes?"

"Okay."

***

Henry was awakened by a warm hand on his shoulder. He had fallen asleep with Rose in his arms, his head on the wet grass, and his arm under Rose's head. How his posture had changed during the night he couldn't recall.

Blinking in the dawning light, he propped himself up on his elbow, blocking the light with his arm, shielding his eyes.

"Wha'? Who is this?"

"Henry," said a reserved voice.

He sat up immediately, "Dad!"

There were three men at his side. Now fully awake, Henry stared at the men.

"This is my son," Fernando Cavills, being the president, looked embarrassed, "Henry, meet Mr. Howard, our new interior minister."

"Oh," Henry held up his hand, shaking it with Mr. Howard's.

"What are you doing here?" His father's tone still tinged with embarrassment, "With a girl?"

Henry looked at Rose lying next to him with the teddy still in her arms.

"Oh…" he too seemed embarrassed now, "This is Rose… err… we just came here… and… we were talking…umm…. I don't know when we fell asleep."

Henry was pathetic at lying. There was awkward silence.

"Well," Fernando said before leaving, "You had better go to your room now."

Henry kept sitting there for some seconds, perhaps thinking how badly he had embarrassed his father.

"Shit!" he muttered through gritted teeth.

He shook Rose's arm, but she was slumbering, so he carried her back into her room.

***

Hearing the argument, Henry stepped toward Rose's bedroom and went in with a knock. He halted when he found Rose standing on the bed with the teddy in her arms and the maid by the bed, standing akimbo.

"What's going on?" he asked, puzzled.

141

"She isn't wearing her dress, sir," the maid answered in an annoyed voice. Henry glanced at the royal blue gown placed there for the ball.

He looked at Rose, hands in pockets, walking in, wearing a tuxedo, a white dress shirt, and his hair neatly combed. He wasn't looking himself. Rose stared at him, she was used to the Henry who had disheveled hair, knee-high boots, dirty clothes, and a bow.

"Come down, Rose," he asked politely.

Rose shook her head like a truculent child.

"See?" the maid added scathingly.

Henry turned up his face by the bed, and held up his hands, "Come on."

His encouragement was enough. Tentatively, she moved forward. Henry put his hands under her arms and lifted her down, not taking his eyes off her.

"Why won't you wear it?"

"Because it's blue," she sounded upset. The maid remained quiet now. Both stared at each other.

"Why are you staring at me?" he asked gently.

"Because you're distracting me.

Controlling his smile, he gestured the maid to leave. His eyes trailed on the maid and fixed on Rose again when she closed the door.

"But I'm wearing my shirt."

"No… you look different."

"You mean," he stepped closer, "handsome."

Rose nodded. He slowly smiled his reserved smile.

"So, I guess you want a red dress?" "Mmm."

She kept staring at him.

"Well, we can manage that. I'm sure we'll find one."

"But Henry," Rose asked abruptly, "why are we getting ready?"

"For the dance of course. You'll meet my parents there."

"But why should I meet them?"

He gave an elusive answer, "Because… I'll tell you later."

He finally let go of her hands and gestured to the bear she had dropped, "Don't bring him to the ball."

He was about to leave when Rose called him back abruptly, "Henry! I… don't know how to dance."

"What?" he was surprised, turning back, he walked to her again. Rose shrugged innocently.

"I should have known." He admonished himself, "Okay, okay…"

It wasn't a problem. Henry swiftly arranged a tutor for her and left them together. He seemed worried. Rose was going to meet his parents and he

142

wanted the meeting to be flawless. Being astute, he appointed the task of sorting out her dress to a designer.

It was a busy day, and Henry didn't have time to meet with her. What if she couldn't learn to dance in time? What if she refused to wear the new dress too? He would coax her, she had to, she *must* wear it.

At night, the villa was bright like the sun, looking magnificent. There were mayors, dukes, and ladies arriving to celebrate Henry's parents' thirtieth wedding anniversary.

Henry was busy greeting the guests. During the conversations with the guests, his eyes were always searching for Rose in the crowd. It was getting late and she wasn't there yet, whereas his doubts were changing to panic now.

The orchestra began to play a waltz and Henry excused himself from the ministers. There were couples around and as he looked toward the stairs, he came face to face with his father.

"Henry, son, it looks as if you're waiting for someone," Mr. Cavills said, placing his hand on his back.

"Yes," he tried not to look anxious.

Fernando stood, his hands down in front of himself with curiosity in his eyes, "And who might that be?"

Henry was reluctant but he had to tell him, he had to take the plunge and face the results.

"Dad," he paused, his jaw clenching, "I want you to meet someone."

"Who?" and then he laughed, "Oh…" he must have got an idea from Henry's nervousness.

"I got it, son. Is she the one you want to marry?"

Henry nodded, seriously, "Yes."

Fernando became reserved again, "Then make sure she's eligible to become the daughter-in-law of Mr. President."

With a smile, he moved away. Henry kept looking at the gilded curtains, parted. When he turned to leave, he was stunned as his eyes fell on Rose.

He was overwhelmed by the beautiful sight. Rose walked down the stairs like a lady, wearing a red gown blooming like a flower, her golden hair pinned up, and a few curls hanging loose, red lips and rosy cheeks, it seemed as if a rose had been incarnated in human form.

Her eyes met his, and when she smiled, he held his breath.

"Henry?" she whispered, and he realized she was standing in front of him.

"Hmm?" he could hardly speak as his heartbeat accelerated.

"I'm scared."

He stayed silent and then he assured her, "I swear, you have no reason to be frightened of me… "

143

"No, I'm scared of them," she spoke over him, and for the first time, he realized he wasn't alone with her. There were people around, all staring at Rose.

She was so beautiful that nobody could possibly be jealous of her. Has anyone been jealous of nature? And she was nature. She was Rose. To divert their attention, Henry gestured to the orchestra and waltz music filled the hall once again like an aroma.

The couples started dancing, but Henry lost his courage. The silence lasted a long time, and Rose stood looking around as if waiting for someone.

"What are you looking for?" he asked.

"My tutor."

Henry frowned, "For what?"

She stared at him and told him in a direct manner, "To dance of course! I danced with him all the time, and you said I had to dance at the ball. I can't find him... why are you laughing?"

He couldn't stop laughing, and she couldn't take her eyes off him. He looked at her, licked his lips, and informed her, "He just taught you to dance, he isn't going to be here."

Rose looked really worried now, "Oh, no... now who will dance with me?"

"Oh, no," Henry was still controlling his laugh, his chest heaving, "You've got a real problem."

Rose sighed, hastily looking at the other couples, "Yes. I think so..." "But I can help you," he raised his eyebrow.

"How?"

Taking his hands out of his pockets, he slipped one on her waist and took her hand in the other, "I'll dance with you."

The moment he touched her, Rose held her breath. He waited, finally, she placed her hand on his shoulder and he took the lead. It took them a while before began to dance.

Rose didn't look at him, her eyes were fixed on her feet. Whereas, Henry couldn't take his eyes off her. The silence between them wasn't comfortable, but they lost themselves in the music. Rose was a good dancer.

"Why are you panting?" he finally asked her.

She didn't avert her gaze at his question and answered slowly, "I don't know... I'm feeling... something... something I've never felt before."

Henry smiled. He knew what feeling that was, the same one he had for her. It seemed she was uncomfortable with it, so, he tried to calm her.

"You are a quick learner, Rose."

She smiled, Henry felt safe and held her waist in both hands, lifting her. When her feet touched the floor again, she was grinning.

"And you are a good dancer," she complimented him.

Henry was right, Rose was a fast learner and she danced very well.

"Henry?"

"Yes?"

"Umm… can we go out to the garden again?"

He could sense that she was uncomfortable, letting go of her waist, and locking hands with her. Quietly, he led her outside into the garden, glad nobody was there. The music played on in the distance as Henry looked at her under the star-gilded sky.

They stood silently for a long time, Rose staring at the stars and Henry looking at her.

"I miss Mama," she told him, her eyes still fixed on nature's marvel.

Henry didn't reply as if he didn't know how to make conversation. But then, without wasting time, he said, "You owe me a dance, Rose."

A slight crease appeared between her eyebrows, which was clear in the moonlight.

She looked at him, "How so?"

It seemed he excelled in trickery, "Your tutor didn't come, and I helped you out."

"Oh," she was easily caught in his trap, "Okay!"

His face lit up and he took her waist once again, dancing to the waltz music in the distance. He could clearly see she was breathing heavily again. Her cheeks were claret, and she didn't look at him while dancing. After a while, he started a conversation again, "Rose?"

"Yes?"

There was a pause, "I want you to meet my parents."

"Okay," she replied, and then after a minute, as if she had thought about it just now, she asked, "But why?"

A smile appeared on his face. His feet stopped moving and he stared at the cherry girl in front of him, "Because," he paused, "I'm going to marry you."

Rose's face remained stoic. No smile, no frown, just a murmur, "Okay."

Henry took her face in his hands, forgetting he had to dance. He seemed anxious now as it appeared Rose wasn't happy with this. Leaning close, he asked her gently, "You don't want to marry me?"

Fixing his inscrutable eyes on hers, his heart started pounding. He couldn't afford a negative answer. She was the only one he would marry.

As he caressed her cheeks with his thumbs, Rose replied innocently, "Henry, I don't know what marry means."

First, he stared at her, then laughed with his closed mouth and embraced her in his arms, kissing her on her cheek.

Rose was puzzled, he could sense it as soon as they broke apart. Holding her hands in his, he explained, "To marry someone means... to live with that person forever, to love and take care of each other."

"You'll come and live with me?"

"No," he silently laughed again, "it means you'll come and live with me in my home. So, I'll ask you again, would you please marry me, Rose?"

There was silence. It seemed as if her words were stuck in her throat, choking her.

"Huh?' Henry encouraged. He felt his hands being squeezed, turning pale, but he didn't cringe. Finally, she looked down on her hands and replied apologetically, "I can't live without Mama."

"Of course," Henry swallowed, "Okay your mama can live with us too, now?"

Rose smiled, "Okay I'll ask my mama for permission."

"So that means a yes from you?" he said impatiently.

Rose had barely nodded when he lifter her up and twirled her around as she laughed. As soon as she touched her feet on the grass, he embraced her again, her head against his warm chest, listening to every beat.

"I love you. God knows I love you," he whispered.

This time, Rose didn't ask him love's meaning. Holding her hand, he led her inside once again. the light music was still there, some fancy looking couples on the dance floor. Eyes turned towards the cherry red girl, but Henry ignored them. His eyes were searching for his parents and he easily found them drinking champagne with friends and some important foreign diplomats.

Daniel was also participating, while Paulo stood silently by and Alex twirled around the dance floor.

"Hi, Rose! You're here?" Daniel gasped, surprised to see her.

"Hello," Rose greeted reluctantly, without shaking the hand he proffered. Daniel didn't mind and took it back.

"I've to talk to dad right now," Henry excused himself and Rose, "I'll see you later, Daniel."

"Okay."

Mr. Cavills was talking to the President of Sweden whom he had invited, along with two important ministers and his wife.

"Dad?" Henry waited for him to notice him, but when he didn't, Henry called him.

He turned to face his son.

"This is Rose," Henry told him confidently.

146

"Ah, the girl you were waiting for?" Mr. Cavills seemed friendly. All the people there were charmed by her beauty.

He held out a glass of champagne to Rose. She didn't know what it was, but accepted it anyway, exchanging a look with Henry.

"Are you enjoying the party, dear?" Mr. Cavills asked sweetly.

Rose nodded, took a sip and grimaced. The taste was weird, she almost puked, but controlled herself. Henry took the glass from her hand quickly.

"She is feeling unwell today," he covered up and took a sip from her glass.

The trouble had already begun but nobody noticed it.

"So… Miss Rose, where do you live? I've never seen you with Henry before," his father asked.

"I live in my home."

Mr. Cavills and the others chuckled, thinking it was a jest, "A good sense of humor, I see!" She stared at him but didn't corroborate her answer.

"And with whom do you live?"

"With Mama and roses," she was being candid. Henry's jaw clenched, sensing what a blunder he had made.

"Aha, your father?"

"No father."

"What do you mean?"

"I never had a father. It's just me and Mama."

There was silence. Henry tried to take charge and said immediately, "Like I said, she is feeling…"

Mr. Cavills cast his admonishing eyes at Henry for a second, which was enough to quiet him.

"Miss Rose," he continued the investigation, "What's your mother's name?"

Rose frowned, for a second it seemed she had no answer, "No, her name is Mama."

It was getting worse with every question.

"And your father's name?"

"I said I don't have a father," Rose seemed fed up now. One of the men in the circle laughed slowly and said in an undertone, "What do you mean? Your mother is somewhat like the Virgin Mary?"

Rose was puzzled, she exchanged a look with Henry, but he was already looking down. He couldn't help her, she had to defend herself. She answered, even if she didn't know it's meaning, "Yes."

Mr. Cavills gasped. She looked like an utter sociopath in the human world.

"Maybe she was adopted…"

And many whispers. The only person who was silent among them was
Henry. Rose was extremely confused, beads of sweat forming on her
forehead.

"How old is your mother?" Mr. Cavills asked.

"Twenty-six," Rose said, thinking hard.

"And how old are you?"

"Twenty."

More murmurs and whispers. All must have thought she was mad.
There was no further inquisition, but Henry was talking now. He was arguing
with his father in Portuguese and Rose couldn't understand. She stared at them.

Then Henry grabbed her elbow and began to lead her away. The meeting
had been a disaster and Henry seemed angry.

Entering the room, he released her and locked the door. turning around
fiercely, he almost yelled, "You ruined everything!"

Her mouth was dry, she was panting, and her eyes were welling up, still
she stayed silent.

"Rose. This is *not* possible. Why did you say that? Are you mental?"
She still didn't answer, watching Henry pace and sweep his fingers through his
hair. It was possible, wasn't it? She had it all and lived the life no one else did.

He didn't calm down.

"You know what? Nobody is born without a father. Not a single soul."

Rose dropped in the chair and Henry stomped toward her like a police
officer.

"And everybody has a name!"

It was advantageous that the music was still playing or everybody else
would have heard him.

Two slivery streaks dewed her rosy cheeks. She didn't dare look at him.

"And your mother can't be twenty-six, alright? It means she was six years
old when you were born." he said through gritted teeth.

"But it's true." Rose whimpered.

Henry knelt and looked in her eyes. Inhaling a deep breath, he closed his
eyes and opened them again, trying to calm himself.

Deep inside, he knew she wasn't a liar.

"Tell me the truth," he said gently, placing his hands on his knees and
uncurling his fists.

"The truth is," she looked in his eyes, "I don't have a father. My
mother has no name and she has been twenty-six ever since I can remember."

The frown deepened on his face, his fingers curled into fists again and
he said in a serious tone, "It's time to meet your mother." I hid myself.

Chapter 13

Henry and Rose were back in the forest and I was experiencing one of the weakest human emotions: fear.

Fearful of the questions that had made Rose silent since the ball. Questions that were lurking in her mind, making her reticent as she had never been before. A wealth of questions that weren't allowing any other words to cross her lips.

Henry was back in his usual attire, knee-length, brown leather boots, black jeans, navy blue shirt unbuttoned from the top, the bow and quiver on his shoulder.

He was walking behind Rose as they scrambled through the thorny bushes I had set in the way to the castle. Rose was back but not mentally. She wasn't the same as she used to be.

For the first time, both were silent, and their silence was growing uncomfortable for me.

I wanted her to talk, but I couldn't read her emotional state. They walked at a turtle's pace because of the difficult terrain and because it was getting darker with every step.

Darker and deeper.

They entered the land of the dead. The graveyard was dark, ghost quiet and so Henry couldn't see that they were passing through a graveyard. He couldn't see that there were graves on both sides of the aisle-like path. I was there, in the graveyard, a shadow in the spooky mist.

Rose's eyes were on the path as she was used to it, but Henry was wide awake. Even a person like Henry could get the shudders in that cold environment, what humans call a 'death-like place.'

He was looking around, staring into the dark as if he could spot something... me.

"I've never been to this part of the forest before," he whispered, as if any sound would wake the dead.

Rose, lost in a trance, interpreted it after a moment, "Huh?"

As she looked up to see him, her eyes went to my silhouette and I hid again. She didn't stop walking, unable to decide if she had seen something.

"What?" Henry looked at her.

She walked to the edge of the path and narrowed her eyes, "There... is something..."

Drawing his arrow and setting it in the bow, Henry walked to her and glowered into the darkness, ready to shoot anytime.

Even the sound of their breathing stopped.

Dauntlessly, he stepped in the part I had forbidden Rose to go. The graveyard. He walked in carefully and soundlessly, still prepared to shoot, without looking where his steps were leading him. Rose stayed in her place.

After a long pause, and he was sure nothing dangerous was around, Henry finally looked where he was, piercing the thick fog, which made him lower his bow unintentionally.

His eyes went on the endless stones. Kneeling, he cleaned one with his hand.

As soon as he looked at the carving in the stone, a frown appeared on his face. He quickly turned to the next one, cleared the dust and after that, he checked three more.

Finally, he let out his breath that he was holding when Rose called him, "Henry?"

He stood up and looked around. The tall, dead trees were hardly visible in the moonlight, their branches reaching out as if trying to grab him.

As he walked back, the dead leaves crunched beneath his boots, and the webs tangled his legs.

Rose was there, waiting for him. Standing face to face, he asked, "Aren't you scared?"

"Of what?"

Henry didn't reply at first, then he held her wrist and moved. She didn't. He looked back at her, "Come on."

Rose refused, "Mama has forbidden me to go there."

Henry frowned, annoyed, "Do you have any idea what these are?"

Their disturbance in the silence was like a ray of sun peaking from the black clouds.

"Rocks."

This time, Henry didn't ask her anything. He held her wrist, pulled her toward the gravestones, not caring that she was forbidden to go there.

He stopped and pointed at the stones, "These," he looked at her sternly, "are graves."

Rose didn't know the meaning of the word. She gulped, staring at him.

"I don't understand."

Henry let out his breath, which came out as a puffy cloud. He had to elucidate. He held out his bow and arrow, pointing at Rose, ready to shoot. Rose stared at him in horror.

"If I shoot, this arrow will pierce your heart, and just like that toucan, you'll die. Then I'll dig a hole in the ground, put you inside, and bury you. It'll be called a grave. Your grave."

They stared at each other.

Rose was breathing fast now as his story had scared her. Henry lowered his weapon as he looked around at the thousands of graves.

"These are…" she couldn't complete her sentence.

"Yes," Henry said, "They have dead humans in them." She was horror struck.

"Mama didn't tell me," it was a whisper to herself and nothing after that.

The rest of the journey was in silence. Henry had a tight grip on his bow, alert. Rose was in a trance, completely lost. No wonder with what was going on in her mind.

As the castle became visible, Henry stopped in his tracks. With his neck twisted to one side, he stared up at it, perhaps wondering who build it.

Rose never looked back at him until she heard his incredulous voice, "You live *here?*"

She turned around, watching his shocked face, "Yes."

The castle itself seemed haunted. There was some force illuminating it, but still, the darkness was overwhelming. As a gust of wind snaked through the branches, some of the leaves danced down towards them.

Rose walked in with Henry following.

Roses.

The wind carried their aroma to him, and he looked around. It seemed that he was in a rose garden. Who expected roses in such a haunted place?

"What's with the roses?" he asked, standing still again. Even the roses seemed spooky in the dead castle. Some deadly beauty.

Rose didn't bother to reply, she kept walking and Henry, sensing she wouldn't answer, followed her.

Ignoring him completely, Rose began to call aloud, "Mama! Mama!"

The echoes lasted in the castle for a couple of seconds but there was no answer. Rose licked her lips, letting them glow in the faint light and looked at Henry.

"She isn't home."

Biting the inside of his cheek, he meditated, "I can wait." Rose nodded. She wasn't like before.

151

After the first ray of light trespassed the castle through the window, Rose rolled over on her side. She hadn't slept all night. She couldn't. Henry's eyes were closed and the bow still in a tight grip. Rose sighed.

Her mother hadn't come home.

Perhaps she thought I was off to work or maybe I didn't know about her arrival. She didn't know when Henry had fallen asleep, but they hadn't talked. Even if they spoke in whispers, it was like waking the dead from the graveyard and welcoming danger.

Rose was only used to hearing my voice in the castle at night.

The dawn and early morning chirping woke Henry. He blinked, recognizing the place. When his eyes fell on Rose, sitting against the wall, staring at him, he sat upright immediately.

"You okay?" he asked abruptly.

It seemed Rose minded his questions, she seemed unhappy about it, "It's my home. Why wouldn't I be okay?"

"I mean..." Henry cleared his throat, "your mother sounds... unnatural. And you live in such a haunted place."

Rose was even more offended and frowned.

"This is my mother you're talking about."

"Of course! But you see... the way you talk about your mother... and this place... Rose, there is something..."

"Leave."

Henry stared at her, "What?"

Hurt by his comments, her eyes were welling up, she clutched the gown she was wearing, "Go away!"

"But..."

"Leave!" Tears were forming drops on her lashes and she was upset, "Leave me alone!"

He didn't waste time. He felt insulted and got up, leaving in a rage, never looking back.

Rose sat still for a moment, then she buried her fingers in her hair and breathed heavily in confusion and frustration. Hiding her face behind her knees, she wept.

***

Henry didn't come back. I did. And
what a mistake it was.

I came back after three days of patience, a thing humans lack. But it
feels so good to have something back after years, or days or even minutes.

I had prepared a speech on the question I knew she would ask me first.
"Who is my father?"

I couldn't practice it in front of the mirror like humans do when they
lack the confidence to say the words they want to say.

It is strange that the word 'confidence' seems so unfamiliar to me. I
don't know what it is, it seems I'll never know what it is.

Why?

I wanted to, but my reflection... I can never see myself in the mirror.
Hence, I practiced it, pacing among the weeds. How many times?

Six, ten, twenty, fifty... I lost count.

I don't know if she cried or not because I never went to see her again.
Why?

A lack of confidence, I suppose.

I walked through my home, the graveyard and reached her home, the
castle. I halted the moment my eyes fell on her. She was sitting by the stone
wall and my soulless steps woke her from her thoughts.

She looked at me with eyes that hadn't tasted sleep for three nights. I knew
it, I could sense it.

"Rose, I need to..."

"Hey, Mama," she got up, curling her lips, which seemed like a forced
smile, "I'm back."

As she got up, I stared at her. There was no sarcasm, no scorn or
question in her tone, and this bothered me. I didn't reply.

As she moved forward and gave me a hug, I couldn't even hug her back.

"How are you?"

Her first question made me forget my speech that I had prepared for her
assumed first question.

Holding my hands, she smiled again, "What happened? Why are you
staring at me like this?"

Something told me to act like a human and pretend to know nothing.

"Maybe," I swallowed, "It's because I haven't seen you since you left
home."

She chuckled, "Who left home? I'm back and you are here!"

Every word her tongue was delivering, sounded as if it was saying the same
thing to me: don't pretend that you don't know anything.

"Yeah."

153

"So, let's have a nice lunch first." She said as she went inside the castle.

First? Did it mean there was second thing too?

Rose never spoke during lunch and I also kept my mouth shut. The first long silence between us was making me uncomfortable.

A part of me wanted her to ask me all the questions written on her face. A part of me didn't.

Maybe she was trying to find some appropriate question to begin with.

Would she hate me?

Or would she love me even more?

That night, everything was silent, even the forest. The owls never hooted as she fell asleep.

***

The sky was beautiful as the sunrays filled it with colors.

There was something wrong with Rose. As I stared at the morning sky, I knew it at once. Rose was also beautiful but now she had no color. I couldn't face her anymore. Leaving a rose by her, I left.

It was afternoon when I returned with shame visible on my face. We didn't talk again, neither looked at each other.

At night, as she lay down to sleep and stared at the cosmos, I dared and asked her.

"Rose… I need to…"

"You didn't ask me," her unblinking eyes were still on the stars. I stared at her in disbelief. Rather than asking me, she was telling me to ask her questions?

Extraordinary.

And the Lord knows what she was talking about.

Locking her fingers together on her chest, she sighed when I didn't reply. She continued, "You didn't ask me how the world was."

I had never thought about it. I had forgotten that she had seen the world for the first time. I cleared my throat to avoid squealing the answer, "Yes. Of course. How was the world?"

Rose frowned at the stars, "Interesting."

OBSERVATION No. 26

The most difficult business for humans is to mind their own business.

I stayed silent as silence is the best answer sometimes.

"And you didn't ask me how the ball was?"

"How was it?"

154

Again, she frowned at the stars. What was their fault in it? why was she scowling at the poor stars?

Then she shrugged.

I knew that it had turned bad for her. I waited for the next question, but it never came. Soon, she closed her eyes. At least she slept when I was around.

***

"Mama, Henry asked me to marry him."

The bucket of water dropped from my hands. It was a totally unexpected assault of words. Rose, as if she was expecting it, stayed calm after giving me an anxiety attack.

It wasn't a question. I had no answer. It was nothing, just a piece of information.

"Did he?" I uttered in disappointment. I never imagined she would tell me that.

"Yes."

"And... what did you say to him?"

"Nothing."

There was silence. I picked up the bucket and walked to the door to hide myself inside the castle. But she followed me for reasons that escaped me.

OBSERVATION No. 27

Disappointment brings fear and fear brings failure.

It seemed Rose didn't want to fail. Escape from failure is to quit the thing but she didn't quit. She tried another way to victory, an unknown companion in mind, war.

"You have to come with me to have a look at the world. You'll love it, Mama." "No, Rose, I have to go to work," it was a polite refusal.

"But you have to!"

"No, please, not now."

"When?"

"Pardon?"

"I said when? When will you come?" her tone was changing slowly.

"Why do you want me to come anyway?"

I tried to change the topic and failed disastrously.

"Henry won't marry me unless you meet his family."

I turned to face my little girl who had grown to face me with crossed arms. That is the weird thing about children, eventually they stand up against the ones who raise them.

Correction, *human* children.

"It means you want to marry him," I knew it. Deep inside, I knew it.

"Probably, Mama, I mean," she paused, and her eyes looked coldly into mine, "You also married my father."

For a moment, I couldn't even recognize the person standing in front of me. Marrying Henry was fine. *This*. This wasn't.

Pulling my brows together, I tried to construct a flow of words, "Rose... what... I don't... what do you mean?"

The change of topic scenario never worked for me.

Without getting an answer, I dropped the bucket again, making my way out of the castle, silver robes waving behind me.

"Who is my father?"

The words, honed with distrust, hit me in the back like a traitor friend's dagger.

I stopped.

"I have to go to work," the same old excuse.

This wasn't Rose. Not my Rose.

"Where?" another knife.

I had never imagined she would ask me where or I would have had an answer for that. I was walking fast now, as if I would reach some place and she wouldn't be able to find me.

"*Where,* Mama?" I could hear her steps behind me.

"Where I normally go," I told her evasively.

"And exactly where is that?" she snapped back at me.

It was as if she were my mother and I was her child. I faced her sharply, annoyed now. I wanted to yell back, *"I am Death, I have authority here."*

But I must admit the only one who has authority is the Lord. No one else.

"Come off it, Rose."

"No!" she raised her voice, "Just tell me about my father! I want to meet him!"

"You can't!" I stopped near the willow tree. "WHY?"

her voice was angrier than mine.

"SHUT IT!" there was no way I was going to look at her. Rose held my shoulder and turned me around harshly.

"I have a right to know!"

Humans always are hysterical, by birth, by nature.

"And it's not my obligation to tell you," I said, jerking my shoulder away, making my way to the willow.

156

"It is! *It is*! You're my mother. You have to tell me!"

I remained quiet, no answer. But… I had answer.

"What is your name? At least you can tell me that!" she wasn't going to give up.

I was exhausted by her questions so I turned to face her, sighing, "What will make you stop?" Nothing.

Not a sound. But somehow, her eyes managed to deliver the message. And when her lips moved, it made me something only humans are. A liar.

"Truth," the word haunted me for days, "Truth, Mama."

Aren't humans supposed to lie? It sounded like an allegation, a slur. How can I lie? But to my daughter, I was a liar. I realized how cheap I was in her eyes, a worthless soul.

Life beats you down. Even mine, Death's life, beat me down to my knees. Humans know how to get up, they always do, they have no choice other than inviting me. I didn't know how to get up.

I figured out one of the best and worst things humans feel, the most glorious of human emotions, pain.

I was hurt and it felt unusual. To get hurt by the only person you think you own, the light of your life, the music to your ears, the song on your lips.

After a long pause, I replied shamefully, turning away again, "Then look somewhere else. I have none."

This made me cheaper in her eyes. as if a monster was crawling inside her, invading her, as her eyes turned crimson.

"What is your work?"

I stood in front of the willow, as if protecting it, expecting something miraculous to happen to satisfy her or make her forget everything.

I kicked the tree, "SHUT IT, ROSE!"

"I WON'T!"

For a moment, mother and daughter stood like foes. Disgrace for me, deception for her.

As the water streaked on the grass, Rose divulged the secrets her heart had concealed for a long time.

"I know your reflection doesn't appear in the mirror. But why doesn't it? Why not even in water?"

My mouth went dry as Rose looked at the river at her side. Two bodies standing on the grass. Only one body visible in the water. Even I became afraid as I saw it. And it hurt me even more.

I had no existence. I
was in a trap.

"Why aren't you…"

"Rose, why are you talking to yourself?"

At that moment of insanity, our faces turned toward the trespasser, Henry Cavills.

That son of a bitch was standing at a distance. Rose said nothing in her wrath.

"I… uh… I… came here to say sorry for everything."

Rose turned to me as if Henry wasn't there. as if nothing had interrupted her, "Why doesn't your reflection appear in the water?" I remained quiet.

"Tell me!"

There was bewilderment on Henry's face, as if she were mad.

"What the…" his voice was drowned in Rose's yelling.

"WHY?"

She was holding back her tears. I could see it. But I couldn't reveal myself.

"Rose! Who are you talking to?" again, Henry's voice was lost in her hysterical paroxysm of words.

"TELL ME!"

"ROSE!" This time, his voice was louder. Finally, he had gained her attention. Rose turned her face and looked at him.

"What? Can't you see, I'm talking with my mother?"

Henry stared at her. He opened his mouth to say something, but no words seemed appropriate.

"No… I can't see," he uttered with a frown.

With flared nostrils and a wide-eyed gaze, Rose said," Can't see? Look, here she is!"

She pointed toward me. No. Nothing. "Rose," he was trying his best to stay polite, "There is no one here except you and me."

"Stop lying to me! Why is everyone lying to me?" she almost screamed, "She is right here!"

She stomped toward me and held my arm, "See?"

Henry dilated his pupils and his jaw dropped, "I can't. There is no one here."

For a moment, there was silence. Then Rose turned her face toward me, forgetting her quarrel with me, she asked desperately, "Mama, why don't you tell him that you are here?"

I kept staring at Henry like a statue and didn't move an inch. Rose jerked my arm, "Mama! Speak to him! Tell him!"

No word escaped my lips. Death is supposed to trap humans. Not humans trap Death, it was unnatural.

158

The sun directed its rays on us, and Rose shifted her gaze to the ground. Out of the blue, her eyes widened, and I realized I didn't exist in their reality.

There was only one shadow. And

it didn't belong to me.

"Why don't you have a shadow?" it was a terrified whisper.

I couldn't look at her. I could feel her shaking hand still holding my arm.

"Why," she repeated as if among all the unnatural things, I was deaf as well, "you have no shadow?"

And in that petrified silence, there was only one human voice that wasn't getting her attention.

"What's going on?" Henry's words were futile in the forest.

"ANSWER ME! FOR GOD SAKE, ANSWER ME!" She cried, startling Henry.

"ROSE!" Henry gained her attention once again. She

directed her red-eyed gaze at him.

"There is no one here!" he corroborated.

Letting go of my arm, Rose went to him and held his arm instead.

"Don't you understand? Can't you see? She is there! Look!"

She pointed toward me, but Henry could only see her finger pointed at the tree's trunk.

"She isn't there!"

"SHE IS THERE! LOOK! MAMA IS THERE! I CAN SEE..." Arrows. Arrows. Arrows.

Arrows of her words were hitting me. And an arrow from Henry's bow.

With gritted teeth, he set an arrow, focusing it on me. A moment later, the arrow pierced my soul and dug itself into the tree trunk.

Rose watched in horror as the arrow went through me. No harm. No death. No blood. For a moment, she went breathless. Then holding Henry's hand, she broke into a run.

Away from me.

Chapter 14

That day, I learned another human aspect from her. Escape. How to escape from problems instead of facing them. And she left me alone to face the problems, something a human would do.

The first thing I remember is standing still by the tree behind me, which was physically damaged by Henry's arrow. And I was shot by Rose's arrow of words. We weren't bleeding. We weren't complaining. But both of us were in pain.

The black thought that Rose had left me wasn't sinking into my mind. It was hard to digest. I couldn't even cry.

How does it feel to have tears? How does it feel to shed tears?

I was… I was… what was that word? Ah

– shocked.

I was torn by her fear. She was afraid of me. I had seen it in her eyes. Her last look had told me she was afraid of me. The last thing I wanted was her to be afraid of me, afraid of her mother. I had raised her. *I had raised her!*

For a moment I stayed still, but then my legs gave away, and I fell against the tree trunk on my back. The only thing I can remember is the light from the sun falling on me.

The prayer I had sent to the Lord had hit the sky hard and fallen back on me. It was as if He was saying you're not meant to pray. You aren't meant to ask for anything. You aren't meant to question me because you aren't a human.

No matter how much you try, this flesh isn't real. Your existence isn't real. You aren't real.

And as the Lord blew the wind, the leaves from the trees fell on me, it felt like a rain of stones. Every one of them gave me pain.

The birds stayed happy, chirping and playing. The bees buzzed about, and the flowers danced with the wind.

Then why had only my world collapsed? Then why was everything okay but nothing was fine at all?

And as with the snow-covered grass, I could remember that day. Yes, the one when I had taken that child in my arms and rescued her from the cold world.

The past was repeating itself in the opposite direction. The way it should have been without me. She was going back in the cold world.

And as if I were watching a movie, I saw every single lovely moment with her. The day she started crawling. The day she started walking. And the day she started running.

Running away from me.

But again, isn't it obvious?

OBSERVATION No. 28

When humans are children, they fight and say *she is my mama*. When they grow up, they fight and say *she is your mama*.

Then they abandon her.

And the thought that Rose was just another human made me suck in air.

No.

I tried to suck in then let go of the air. I failed. I couldn't. I couldn't even breathe! I tried hard to breathe but couldn't. How unbearable.

As the gust of wind hit the trunk, it struck me as well. I couldn't feel it, but as it hit me, a pain inside me screamed.

It was as if my patience was on the verge of breaking. If I could die, I would have. If I could have committed suicide, I would. If there was another Death, I would ask her to kill me.

But alas, I was alone with darkness engulfing me. Rose was afraid of me. I knew she was, and I knew she would never come back.

For the first time in my life, I wanted to be a murderer. Yes, I wanted to kill that son of a bitch Henry Cavills.

He was a complete disappointment to mankind. He had stolen a daughter from her mother. It had happened because of him. If only he hadn't asked Rose to meet me.

And Rose… oh, my dear Rose… how marvelous.

She wasn't afraid of the man who had tried to kill her mother. She was afraid of the victim.

I couldn't even go and justify myself to her. the truth was unbelievable. It made me angry.

I couldn't force a tear out of my eye, I couldn't even scream from my heartache. I couldn't even complain to the Lord about it.

He had blessed me with a daughter and taken her away as if only humans should have that blessing. As if I were a prisoner bound to obey him.

161

For a long time, I kept sitting there. A very long time, maybe three days of a human calendar.

How was Rose? Where was she? What was going on in her mind? Had she eaten anything? What if she hadn't slept well?

Oh, Lord!

Rose never slept without me! How would she live without me? She must be so alone.

And I got up suddenly to go and meet her. But before I could take a step, I realized something.

Maybe it was different.

I never slept without Rose. I couldn't live without Rose.

And heavy sorrow began to fill my soul. How could my girl leave me?

OBSERVATION No. 29

Sometimes, life hurts you so much that it stops hurting.

And everything started coming back to me. Every word. Every hurt. Every second. How could she know my story?

She hadn't lived my life. She hadn't seen what I had seen. My past is my present and my future. She couldn't hear the answers I had screamed back at her.

I am Death.

I am your mother.

I am unheard.

I am unwanted. I

am unseen.

This is who I am, if I am anything. Sometimes, your eyes don't show tears. That's because they are shedding blood. Nobody notices. I wish there was somebody to tell me that it was okay. Everything will be all right.

But how could I forget the first time she smiled at me? If I had a heart, it would have stopped at her smile then.

And after that, nothing mattered, yet everything mattered. I did everything to make sure she smiled again.

So why would that person leave me?

Trapped in the sorrow of my life, I couldn't see the light. Couldn't see the sun. Couldn't see a dream. Couldn't be a human.

It seemed like a nightmare and the only question she had asked me a million times, echoed in my mind: why?

I was scared. Who will take care of her? So how can I see light?

The sun arrived every day, but it was hard to see the light or see the sun. It was hard to find peace. I kept moving around and days passed slower and slower. I wish I could say the seasons changed, but they didn't, and no bud of hope grew.

***

In a dream, I met her.

She turned her mother's life into a nightmare, and I could only envision of meeting her in a dream.

Lonely hours grew into pain. I ran fast, ran to take the souls. Take as many lives as I was asked to, maybe one of them would realize a human had taken Death's life too.

But no matter how fast I ran, I couldn't run away from the pain of memories. Isn't it a glorious feeling, pain?

Now I know why the Lord has made humans superior to other creatures, because they can feel. They can feel pain. And they can bear pain. I couldn't.

I had to tell my daughter. I had to see her. I knew she couldn't live without me. She had never stood against me. How could she not listen?

She had believed every single word I had told her. She had questioned me. Only I had the answers to her questions.

The castle was so alone without her laughter and it too was missing her.

A mother can forgive her child even if she kills her.

Then why wouldn't I forgive her? Even if... she never apologized.

Nobody could compare my love for my daughter. Not even all the mothers, dead or alive, or even future mothers.

She was the bloom of my spring. She was the song I used to sing. I would tell her that I was a prisoner, I couldn't escape. I would tell her to just have one thing in me that her biological mother had: faith.

So, leaving the castle, I went to find her. She had gone with Henry.

Again, I prepared the things I had to say to her: Rose, you have spent twenty years of your life with me. I gave you everything you wanted. Now I ask for only one thing in return: faith. I didn't want to have any signs of submission or sadness on my face. Peering in the stream, I smiled. But it vanished.

There was no me in the stream.

She was right, wasn't she? I had no reflection. Trying to hide my sadness, I traveled to the place I knew Rose would be. Near or far, where she went, her aura attracted me like a magnet.

There she was, I watched through the window, her side view. Fear was written on her face like a book, I couldn't move. Seeing her gave me such warmth that suddenly her happiness mattered most.

163

Not mine.

The first thing Rose learned after going to the human world was lying.

OBSERVATION No. 30

Every child learns to speak a lie before learning the truth about the Universe.

How strange that humans don't recognize the truth even if they see it every day?

Standing there, I stared at her, as the fear in her mind spoke to the person in the room.

"Henry, I was there. she was there with me. why don' you understand? My mother was also there!"

The tall man pacing in the room didn't look at her. Holding the arms of the chair, Rose fidgeted and continued, "I have lived with her for years! As long as I can remember!"

Oh, you can remember that you lived with me. Why can't you remember how we lived together?

As the cold wind blew my gown, her words gave me chills. "I remember everything. I remember she answered my every question. I remember… she always placed a rose by my side when I slept… so that when I woke up, I would remember her." For a moment, she was dazed, and I looked at her with hopeful eyes.

Please remember how it was when you made me laugh for the first time. You were six, we went to the riverside and you asked me what it was.

"That's called the beach, Rose. We are on a beach."

"Yayyyy, me and Mama are bitch!"

A smile tried to make its way to my lips but…

"I remember the beach, and I also remember she had no reflection there either."

I closed my eyes. She remembered, didn't she? Another gust of wind hit me hard like a cannon ball.

"And I remember when I ran away from my shadow."

And I had run after her, to tell her that it was okay. That the shadow was a part of her like…

"Rose! That's a part of you, as you are a part of me." She
had smiled and hugged me.

"And I remember she had no shadow then either. It was okay, it was okay for me. It was still okay…"

"NO!"

We froze, mother and daughter, staring at Henry's notorious expressions.

"No, Rose. This is *not* okay!" he had stopped and pulled his brows together.

OBSERVATION No. 31

Human beings are cruel when it comes to honesty. It is easier to trust a dishonest man than an honest one, because the honest one will always tell the truth about you. While the dishonest will secure your secrets.

"I swear…"

"Stop. Okay? Stop," he sounded desperate and angry at the same time with his fingers pressing against his temples.

I wanted to take Rose away from his resentment.

"Henry, please. Let me explain."

His gave her a devious glare to shut her up and she did. Her Bambi eyes had tears now and the chair seemed to be her refuge.

He walked to her gently, crouching in front of her. He looked up and said in a soft whisper, "Rose. You know this isn't possible. All humans have reflections and shadows. You must understand this."

"No, you have to understand. I lived with her," her voice was hysterical and loud.

"God dammit Rose!" his yelling made him stand up again, "I shot an arrow…"

"And it went straight through her!"

"No! It struck the trunk. It was to show you that there was nothing. Are you mental?"

Two streaks of tears were running down her face. She swallowed and whispered, "You think I lived all by myself in the forest?" There was silence.

"I don't know anything," his voice was low, but he wasn't yelling now, "I just know that you ran from there with me. And my parents are coming here tonight to see you. I'll send in the dressers."

"I've no answers to his questions," Rose said clearly when he turned to leave.

"Just tell him that you went home but your mother had already died from a heart attack. So, you know nothing."

Dumfounded, Rose stared at him with a frown.

"But… that's not… not…"

"True," Henry supplied, "Yes. But you can't tell them what you told me. Nobody will believe you."

Rose suddenly fired a question at him, "Do you?" Henry raised his eyebrow.

"Do you believe me?" she asked, and then there was silence from his side.

165

It seemed the earth would disappear from beneath her feet at his answer, "No."

She blinked and heavy tears fell, and wiping them away, she said, "Then I won't lie."

"Then I'll leave you where you belong," he grabbed her wrist like a cat claws a mouse, stomping to the door.

And this time, the earth disappeared from under my feet at her answer.

"I will lie! I don't want to go back!"

I blinked, but no heavy tears fell, there was no need to wipe away anything. The world became still. Rose... Rose didn't want to come back?

Cupping his hands on her cheeks, Henry kissed her forehead and wrapped his arms around her, "This is for us, Rose. Get ready."

He left.

Rose dropped back on the chair. I sprawled on the hard rooftop. The words I had prepared to tell her started fading away... like someone had poured water on the newly written, inky words.

Oh, you cruel wind, stop hitting me, stop whistling at me, stop mocking me.

I can't feel you.

I can just hear the flowers, the birds, the wind, the leaves, all laughing at me.

Desperation made me take my head in my hands.

Don't. Please don't lie.

I remained sitting there for what seemed like thousands of years. More than I have lived.

I will lie! I don't want to go back. Don't want to go back... don't want to go back...

She didn't want to go back to the person who was the pulse beneath her skin? How could she?

That flower. That poor flower given birth by an unwanted plant was isolated among the leaves. There was no sun, no water, and the plant had begun to turn dry.

The wind rescued the flower, blew it away from the dead plant to sow it somewhere in a forest, among other flowers like her.

And... one day... when the wind returned, the flower turned its face away towards the sun.

Was it resentful of the wind that had brought moisture and light rays to it?

I closed my eyes.

The moment I got up I saw her again as if my eyes were hooked on her.

She was still like a rose, when there is no wind around to make it dance. And her cheeks were still wet as if there was no sun around to dry the dew on the flower.

Without blinking, I stared at her as if she were the only human left on earth.

When the dressers came in, they styled her hair and did her make-up, and brought her a blue gown. But nothing mattered to either of us.

The last member was Henry. No praising, no cajoling, no beguiling. Just a hand to guide her to the new world she had chosen for herself.

Once, she had held my hand to guide her to the path of light.

The dining room was dark, and Henry's parents were already seated there.

"Sorry for the delay, Dad," Henry said offering a chair to Rose. She sat there without looking at any of them.

Candles were everywhere. She stared at one of them. And she knew very well that candles set things on fire. I had taught her that.

Standing there in the darkest corner of the room so that even Rose couldn't see me, I gazed at her lost face.

When Henry had also settled, hiding his eyes, Mr. Cavills cleared his throat after a minute.

"Shall we begin?"

Henry said without looking at him, "Sure."

"But I thought her mother would be joining us tonight?"

"Uh…" there was a heavy silence. As he stared at Henry for an answer, Rose sat there like a tailor's dummy.

"Uh… well… umm," Henry stammered as if lying was a new experience for him, "she… she couldn't come."

"Why?" Mrs. Fernando exchanged a look with her husband.

"Because… because," Henry was gulping repeatedly. It was so hard for him to lie to his parents, "Because… D-dad…"

"Because she is dead."

A long silence followed her clear announcement. It seemed she had no trouble lying, as if she had been practicing it, as if her whole life had been a lie. Except she didn't raise her eyes.

This was the first sin and I could see no shame on her face. Isn't it miraculous how the world changes humans?

Everyone, including me, stared at the girl in blue.

"Oh dear," Mrs. Cavills murmured, "I'm so sorry to hear that."

167

And she put her hand on Rose's for a moment, but Rose flinched at the touch. Just for a second, she opened her eyes, but the veil of lashes quickly hid them again.

Funny, Death is dead.

As they ate their dinner Mr. Cavills bombarded her with questions that sounded like accusations again.

"So. When did she die?"

Rose didn't answer, Henry did, "Three days ago."

"That surprises me. I mean, Miss Rose came here only three days after her mother's death."

"Dad!" Henry clenched his teeth and gripped the fork in his hand tightly.

"How did she die?" he ignored his son.

Rose remained silent. She knew only of one way that killed living things; Henry's arrows.

"Heart attack," Henry blurted out, "we found her in the kitchen, but before we could take her to the hospital, she was dead."

There was still no sympathy on Mr. Cavills' face, and he simply carried on as if he were an investigator.

"What about your father, Miss Rose? I'm sure you asked your mother about him?"

Rose looked at Henry for help again.

"He also died when she was little…" "I'm asking *her*. Stop answering for her."

There was a moment of expectation of an answer from her, but she said nothing. Henry tried again, "Dad, she is already upset."

"Henry, let her answer."

"You're bothering her."

"I'm just asking a question."

"But Dad…" "He disappeared."

Again, everyone stared at her. it was the second lie. She licked her lips, "He… umm… Mama said one day she came home, and he wasn't there… so she assumed he had died."

"And what was his name?" Mr. Cavills dropped his fork on his plate.

"Daniel."

Even I could hear her heart pounding in every part of her body. I remembered it was Henry's friend's name. Maybe his father sensed something suspicious was going on. He frowned.

"Miss Rose," he paused, "please give me your address."

168

Henry's jaw clenched again. Perhaps he knew that Rose wouldn't be able to answer the question. She had no idea what 'address' meant.

She opened her mouth but closed it again. She was ashamed of herself and couldn't construct a lie this time.

Mr. Cavills' stern voice made everyone speechless. He said something in Portuguese, I was unable to understand. Henry's eyes followed his parents as they left the room.

Rose was utterly confused, and Henry seemed disappointed. "Henry," she dared, "what did he say?"

Finally, Henry drew his brows together and closed his mouth.

"He… he said…" Henry looked at her with pity in his eyes, "Send her home."

The candles made her eyes flicker and she held his hand in trepidation. "I don't have a home. Where will I go?" and she burst into tears. Henry cupped his hands on her cheeks and calmed her.

"Hey. Hey, Rose," he wiped the tears from her face, "I'm not sending you home, okay? I love you. I'll talk to him. I'm sure he will listen to me." Rose nodded as Henry kissed her forehead.

"Now, go to your room. Everything will be alright, get some sleep."

Again, she gave a nod and got up to leave. As she reached the door, Henry called her again.

"Rose?"

She looked back, her face clear of tears now.

"Look, I'm sorry I was hard on you." She smiled, accepting his apology and left.

I left too.

***

"Dad, I need to talk to you."

Mr. Cavills looked up, he didn't drop his pen and continued scrutinizing the documents.

"If it's about the girl, I think I told you earlier…" "No. I told you clearly that I'll only marry her!"

"Then don't marry anyone, Son."

Henry stared at his father. Could it be that his father showed no concern and seemed more interested in the documents than his own son?

I waited for an answer, sitting on the gable. I could see everything from the small window there.

169

"Alright, I don't need your blessing then." Like father, like son. He was going to elope.

He finally looked up from his documents, "You are going to marry a girl," he paused, and his voice grew louder with every word he spoke, "who has no idea who her father is. Who says her mother is her own age and who doesn't know her address!"

"Yes."

There was a long pause.

Chapter 15

OBSERVATION No. 32

One type of ignorance is to indulge yourself in an argument knowing that you'll be neither convinced nor convincing.

"Tell me about her religion."

"What does that have to do with marriage?"

"You are the only son of the president of Brazil. It has everything to do with it."

"Dad!" his voice was louder, "Stop treating me like that. It's not politics, it's my life that we're discussing." Things were heating up.

"Tell me about her education."

Henry sighed, "She is more educated then you at least."

The satire was turning into hate now. I thought the tussle would never end, but it did. Quite unexpectedly.

"Henry Cavills! I will disown you if you marry that girl!"

After the loud and clear words, the silence seemed eerie. I frowned when the answer came, as it made his father shudder. It seemed that Henry would do whatever it took to marry Rose.

"I wish you had done this years ago."

***

Rose had lost her mother, now she was losing her honesty.

I had to stop her. No matter how heavy the grief was, I had to stop her. So, I tried.

While Henry was preparing to leave his father's mansion, I decided to convince Rose to come home. She could marry anyone, just come back.

Henry hadn't told her anything. She was alone in her room. I dared myself to enter. The door creaked open and I stepped in.

"Rose."

How hard it was to say her name, only I knew that. I had promised Aisha all those years ago that I would take care of her. I had to keep my promise.

171

Alerted by the sound of her name, she looked at me and terror appeared on her face again.

I had a vague hope that she would hug me. How unacceptable that was to me.

Now I think what a terrible mistake it was to meet her.

"What are you doing here?" her whisper was barely audible, "I saw you were… dead. Henry killed you. I saw…"

"And you are going to marry a killer," I answered, "A man who killed your mother."

Out of nowhere, Rose burst into vociferous crying and I was puzzled.

"You're not there," she whispered to herself, "I'm mad! This is impossible!"

"Rose," I tried, "Come back home. *Please.*"

"I HAVE NO HOME!" She wept and dropped on the carpet.

"You are my daughter," it hurt me, as if another Death was taking my life, "You have a home… where you planted your roses. They miss you. I miss you, Rose."

"LEAVE ME ALONE!" She sobbed.

I went to her and tried to place my hand on her shoulder, but she flinched away.

"Your roses are turning yellow."

"I DON'T CARE!"

She started screaming.

I was speechless by her reaction. I had never expected she would behave like this. Hearing her yelling, the sound of footsteps began to come toward the room.

I got up quickly. With one last look at her, I left. I was wrong.

My Rose was turning yellow.

How odd it is, humans sow a seed, watch it grow, and when the right time comes for the seed to return the favor, it betrays them. It begins to turn yellow.

"Rose! Rose? Are you okay?" Henry held her in his arms.

"My mother…" Rose was shivering with fright, "She was here."

Henry stared at her. Then he looked back at his parents who were staring at Rose.

"What did she want?" he asked.

"For me to come back home," she sniffed in his jacket, an inexplicable feeling in her heart.

"Huh," a sarcastic remark came from Mr. Cavills, "I thought her mother was dead. This girl is mental."

Angrily, Henry got up and faced his father like a foe, "She is," I knew he would say mental, but his words were different, "mental. So what?"

His parents exchanged looks, shocked. Rose, still crying, looked at Henry with hurt filled eyes. He also thought she was mental.

Rose was mental. But... his next words were...

"She is mental, Dad. She is. I know it. You know it. But nothing will ever," he said through gritted teeth, "*ever* stop me from marrying her. Because this mental girl isn't a human, she is an angel. And I love her more than I could ever love anyone else. She taught me things you can't imagine. She is my life, and I am going to live my life with her."

For a moment, the father and son fixed each other with searing glares.

Then Henry held Rose's wrist and left the mansion. Forever.

***

They took refuge in Daniel's house. He was a great host and arranged everything for their marriage.

While Rose decided not to think about me, I decided not to appear in front of her again, and Henry decided not to invite his parents to his wedding.

Whatever the grief was, I was still happy. My daughter was getting married to a person who loved her. This was a huge satisfaction for me as a mother.

I couldn't refrain from seeing her on her wedding day and secretly, I watched as she got ready.

The unusual thing was that she wasn't wearing a white gown. It was red, her favorite color. Her hair was pinned up with strands escaping on both sides of her face. She looked extremely beautiful.

There weren't many guests invited, just a few friends. I was hiding behind the fig tree, looking at her with a rose in my hand, how elegantly she walked with Henry's arm around hers. She looked extremely happy that day.

They were officially announced husband and wife. They had repeated their vows.

"I promise that I'll take care of Rose like a delicate rose in my garden."

"I promise that I'll be a faithful wife and make you happy forever."

How easy it is to say a few words to make someone happy.

OBSERVATION No. 33

There are three kinds of people in the world:

1.Those who know but don't think.

2.Those who think but don't know.

3.Those who know and think, but don't understand.

The last one is the worst kind.

Humans never understand what it means to make promises, remaining optimistic about the future.

I sighed.

As Rose turned to face the guests, her eyes fell on me and her smile vanished. Loud cheering didn't matter anymore. She was stunned in her place.

I tried to smile and placed the rose on the table, with the intention that she would know her mother was there to bless her.

The bouquet fell from her hands, and dropped to her feet, the rose petals lying there.

Henry looked at her and then in direction her eyes were fixed.

"Rose, what's going on?"

I could hear him. I could even hear Rose breathing. She didn't reply, just stared at me and I thought it was time to go. So, I hid again.

"Mother," I heard her whisper.

Henry closed his eyes and said, "Wait till the ceremony is over."

When it finished, I saw Henry looking for me everywhere, although, I knew that Rose was just she had no mother. But for her satisfaction, he searched everywhere. "Rose, no one is here, trust me," he walked toward her.

Standing where I had been before, I saw her holding Henry's hands looking worried.

"Henry, I swear I saw her. she had a rose," she stopped, as if talking to herself, and looked around finding it on the table, "See! This rose, Henry! She placed it here!"

This was no authentic proof of my appearance, but Henry distracted her.

"Mrs. Henry Cavills, did you know how beautiful you're looking today?" he smiled in his usual captivating way.

"No, I'm serious." "Are you
coming inside?" "I know she will
come back soon."

"Are you coming or?

"What was she doing here?"

Henry scooped her up in his arms without warning, "Okay, I'll carry you."

He started walking inside, and she laughed at his actions. The rose dropped from her hand and he stepped on it. I could hear her laughter as I watched the stomped rose for a very long time.

***

I decided not to ever give her a hint again that I was always watching her. She didn't want her mother in her life, she wanted to pretend that she had no mother.

Henry and Rose were living with Daniel in his house with what seemed like eternal happiness. Henry's parents never called him, and it seemed he was an orphan, like her.

Henry had money in his bank account and didn't need to work. He kept his promise, taking care of Rose like a delicate flower in his garden and never once did a tear appear in her eyes.

He showed her the world, humans, parties. She became so lost in it all that she began to forget where she had come from. She was forgetting me. She had no repentance about anything.

The materialistic world is fascinating. People forget many things under its spell.

Like religion.

She was forgetting her religion. She often missed her prayers, never reading her holy book, and it began to gather dust on the shelf.

Everything was changing about her. The way she dressed changed. Now she didn't wear the royal gowns, she wore modern clothes. The way Henry liked.

OBSERVATION No. 34

Sometimes, humans begin to worship the one they love.

Even if they are praying, they only have their loved one in mind. In worship they see only loved one's face. And when they ask the Lord from something, they ask for their loved one.

They eat, walk, talk, stand, sit, sleep, the way the one they love wants them to. They think about that person all the time and unconsciously, Rose was doing that.

This is the reason the Lord doesn't give humans the one they love, because they start worshipping them unconsciously. What a sad feeling it was to see her idolizing a human and being unable to help her.

It gave me agony to see her turn into a human again. I had tried to make her an angel, but she hadn't respected the things she deserved. And now it was useless to try anything.

OBSERVATION No. 35

A change in personality is inevitable and natural when a person enters the materialistic world.

And as if a rose could turn into a thorn, my Rose was changing.

Hope is a bitch.

That is one great observation I have always made in every century. When humans become helpless, they don't succumb to time. They don't want

175

to be vanquished. So, they find support in a thing they call hope, like an old, stooped man takes the support of a cane to walk.

What an odd thing, I also took support from hope, as if I couldn't surrender to time.

Yes, the roses in the castle were turning yellow, thorns were growing fast, because there was no Rose to look after them. And likewise, there was no mother to take care of Rose.

When the grief became unbearable, I returned to the castle. But its loneliness was even more excruciating.

Dark the sun and dark the light,

Twinkling stars in shadowy night,

Tell the moon to hide behind clouds, I

lost my daughter in the world.

I sang like a dead man singing. And every single moment I had spent with her came into my mind like a storm. Her voice echoed in my ears in that deafening silence as I watched the moon.

"Oh, Rose, you are adorable."

Opening the book to write its meaning, the cute little child asked me, *"Mama, what's adorable?"*

And my own laughter pierced my ears.

Red, the roses are bleeding,

All of them are grieving,

Tell the butterflies to feed on their blood, Will

they come when she is gone?

Chasing butterflies was her new hobby then. She ran as fast as her little legs would carry her. There I was standing to one side and listening to her cackle, *"Mama! I'm chasing flutterbies!"*

I smiled. Her laughter was gone. Everything was silent.

Silent the night, no whispers in the air,

Flowing the wind in a burning glare,

Tell the mockingbirds to hold back their song, Who

will sing when she is gone?

It seemed that the clouds were dry, like my eyes. and every ocean, every river was dry too. because no matter how hard I tried, I had no tears.

How unfair, the sky cries and the earth rejoices.

It began to rain, and I stood still in it to feel every drop on my skin. But no matter how harsh the downpour was, I could feel nothing.

The pebbles and stones were standing within the flowing water. To them, standing firm is all that matters. But how long can the stones stand against the water?

Dropping to my knees, I stared at the raindrops on the grass.

Oh, dear dew stay on the leaves,
Be my tears that she might see, Tell
the angels to take my soul,
Gone my daughter, where are you?

"Rose, what becomes of your teardrops? They are a waste, honey, don't
cry."

She had stumbled and fallen, but there was no scratch.

"Beauty. They are not a waste, Mama." "How
so?" I smiled.

She looked at me thinking hard. How would an eight-year-old girl know
anything about squandering tears?

But she smiled, *"My teardrops become stars."*

I looked at the sky. There were no stars in the sky that night,

***

After several months, I couldn't take it anymore. I had to see Rose.
The main reason was that it was her birthday.

I didn't like the way she was changing. I had to do something to save
the innocence left in her. And the best help I could give her was advice. The
same advice Aisha had tried to give to the cold world.

So, I bought a red dress for her. I always gave her a dress on her
birthday, this time as well.

It had been months since I had seen her. I didn't know how she would
feel seeing me on her doorstep.

This time, I didn't prepare a speech, preferring to improvise. Preparing
a lecture was futile as she never listened.

I picked a rose for her and wrote my advice on a piece of paper.

The streets were the same, everything was the same as when I left her
the last time. I couldn't help smiling with happiness. I was going to see my
daughter!

Daniel's home hadn't changed either. I walked to the door and it took
me a while to decide. Moving away from it, I walked to the window to see her
first.

There she was, setting plates on the dining table.

But my smile vanished.

Rose had changed, and her appearance was different. She had cut her
hair and it was straight and tied back in a ponytail. She had pierced her ears
and had studs in them. The one who never wore shoes in the house was
wearing heels now.

And red.

177

Not a red gown that would touch her ankles, and wrists, but the dress was revealing her white legs and naked arms.

And I didn't have the courage to go inside.

OBSERVATION No. 36

No matter how hard they try to avoid it, humans adapt to different situations whether they're right or wrong. Humans always have an excuse for their sins.

She had forgotten her education.

And Henry wasn't there. She was alone. Optimism faded in the golden evening, and I left the gift on her doorstep.

No, she wouldn't recognize me. I hid myself from her, so she wouldn't see me, but I had to hear her voice.

Henry came home. He also looked different and it appeared that he had been to work. As he rang the bell, I saw no sign of quiver or bow, or the hunter whom I remembered.

His eyes fell on the things on the doorstep, and he picked them up before going in. Eavesdropping is my hobby.

"You bought these?" her tone was normal.

"No, I just found them on the doorstep... must be from Daniel. But the dress is a bit old-fashioned, reminds me of you in the forest.

"Henry!" she sounded annoyed, "I thought we agreed we wouldn't talk about it!"

"Of course," now he was teasing her, "Happy birthday, stupid girl." There was a pause. Then the sound of footsteps.

"Rose, look, there is a note too." More
footsteps and silence. Wait.

"It says you are going to die," Henry's voice was low as he read it, "What does this mean?"

Silence. I wondered what her expression was. It seemed she had taken it as a threat. There were quick steps, then the front door opened, and I saw her face as her eyes fell on the rose lying there, which Henry accidently left behind.

I can still picture the terror on her face. She was still terrified of her mother. How cruel. And ignorant.

"This isn't from Daniel," she whispered as Henry reached there, "This is from my mother."

Henry stared at her, "How do you know?"

Rose gulped, "Mama left a rose every night I slept. She left this one here too. She used to give me a dress on my birthday." She looked at Henry. He burst out laughing. "Come on, Rose! Don't be stupid! Your mother is..."

"SHE ISN'T DEAD! HOW MANY TIMES DO I HAVE TO TELL YOU?"

"So, why would she kill you? Us?" he began to lose his temper.

With a glare, he stomped inside, and Rose marched behind him.

"Henry," she tried politely, "we have to leave this city."

"Are you mad? You know how hard it was for me to get a job. And now you want to leave the city? You are illiterate. Who will give us a job?"

"What is wrong with you?" she was crying now.

"Look," he paused, "I'm sick of this bullshit! Nothing is going to happen! You have no mother, okay? You lived in the forest for so long that you imagined you had a mother! Maybe you are an amnesia patient or something!"

Rose sniffed and hiccupped.

"I know... I know... she'll kill us... I was rebellious. We eloped. I shouldn't..."

"What? Shouldn't have married me?" his yell was full of wrath.

"No, I shouldn't have left her alone!"

"Shut up, Rose. I left everything for you. My family. My life. I was living like a prince and now the president's son is living in a slum like a destitute. Just for you!"

"Don't say that, I left my life too."

"What life? Huh? That life living in a forest? You call that a life? I have given you everything. What have you given me? *Nothing!*"

"I love you, Henry. I do. And that's why I'm telling you she'll kill..."

"SHUT UP!"

With a slam of the door, I watched Henry march off down the street. And Rose wept, making me feel guilty as if I was responsible for their fight. She wasn't being domineering, she was trying to protect her husband.

But it seemed Henry doubted her sanity, and it also seemed that he regretted marrying her.

And Rose was unhappy in the human world.

***

They didn't talk to each other for a couple of days. It felt as if I was playing the role of villain in their life now. I wished I could do something for them, for Rose, but I had already done the damage. Now even my presence was ominous for her.

179

One night, I heard footsteps and saw her through the window. Henry was sitting in the rocking chair, reading a book. She walked to him and squatted on the floor by his side.

After a long silence, when Henry didn't show interest in her, Rose dared to speak.

"Henry?"

"Hmm." He didn't look at her.

"I'm sorry."

"Hmm."

It was clear her apology wasn't accepted. Maybe she also knew that, so she kept sitting there, staring at his face. I could see their marriage was also turning yellow.

"How was your day?" Rose asked tentatively. "Good."

His eyes were on the book.

"Umm… let's go out for dinner."

"No." "Why

not?

"I'm reading, go to bed."

He was so serious, and he didn't look at her even once. But Rose put her head on his thigh, which made him look at her. "I said, go to bed."

"Henry, I am sorry!" this time it was hysterical, "I ruined your life. I'm so sorry. I didn't want this to happen. I thought we would live happily and mother…"

"Do you want me to get a psychiatrist for you?" his voice was cold.

"What's that?"

"A person who treats mental people," he said sternly, "like you."

Rose lifted her head at his words and stared at him in astonishment. His eyes were on the book again as if he hadn't said anything to hurt her.

"But,' she began quietly, "I'm alright."

"Then stop talking about your mother." He never looked at her.

"If," she said reluctantly, "if I stop, will you be happy again?" He seemed indifferent and just turned the page of his book, "Maybe."

Rose bit her lip, got up, and left him alone.

The subject of her mother never came up again.

***

Things began to go back to normal between them again. I assumed Rose never thought about me again.

When Daniel got married, Henry and Rose moved into a small apartment. It was difficult for him to adjust in such situations because he had lived like a prince in his father's house, but now, he had to work hard, live in a small apartment, and worry about earning enough money to pay the bills.

As time passed, he began to get frustrated with the little things, and often yelled at Rose, but his love was also passionate. He always knew how to apologize and make his wife happy.

Sadness grew on Rose's face. No matter how happy she was with Henry, she wasn't satisfied in her heart.

Something seemed to be missing from her life, making it incomplete. Like a hollow life.

Henry gave her less of his time due to work and most of the time, she was alone.

I didn't give up on her. how could I? Secretly I often saw her, following her to the market but she never saw me.

Whenever I saw that oblivion in her eyes about who she was and what she had become, down to earth I fell. And it never stopped.

I kept falling, a million miles an hour, hitting hard but hurting no one. No matter how close I got, the farther she went into darkness.

The sparkle in her eyes vanished, replaced by a flicker, and a flicker doesn't come unless there is something burning inside. That was the flicker of unshed tears she always had.

Henry's love had brought tears to her eyes and I hated Henry. He forgot his vows. It was becoming complicated. Sometimes, I felt it wasn't his fault either, after all, he had tried his best.

One thing that happened, after my last visit was that Rose started hating roses.

And worse, she never wore red again.

Chapter 16

OBSERVATION No 34:

Man finds sin in freedom and the Lord in loneliness.

Humans want to be liberal, but they forget too much of a good thing becomes a bad thing. Rose had found the Lord in loneliness, and now she was finding sin in the freedom of the human world.

Lying was just the beginning. Backbiting came next, envy entered her heart and many other sins. It was like the contamination of pure water.

And what was more, she didn't realize. One day in the bedroom, Henry was looking for his shoes, while Rose was in the kitchen. He searched the closet, then the drawers and under the bed.

When he stood, there was a magnificently carved wooden box in his hand. Neither large nor small, but he was certain he had never seen it before. Sitting on the bed, he began to open it. But before he could, Rose came in. When she saw the box in his hands, she rushed over to him and took it from him.

"Rose, what is this?" "Err... my box," she said evasively.

"What's inside?" he sounded curious.

"Well... some old stuff."

"Useless things? Throw it away then."

"No, no," she put the box under the bed again, "forget it, Henry."

She was about to leave but then she turned back hesitantly, "Henry?"

"Yeah?" he was only wearing his socks.

"I was... thinking... where is your bow?"

He halted, then pulled up his sock and eyed her suspiciously.

"Why do you ask?"

"You... err... I thought... umm. I thought we should g-go sometime to the forest and camp... or something."

He smiled then went to her and held her shoulders.

"You miss Henry, the old Henry, right?"

"What do you mean?" she looked alarmed.

"You know, the one with the quiver on his back, a bow in hand, kneehigh boots, dirty clothes, messed-up hair. That Henry. You miss him, I can see it in your eyes and they tell the truth."

"Oh," she licked her lips, relieved, "yes, I do. I do miss that Henry."

He embraced her in his arms and rubbed her back, "I miss him too, Rose. But he can't come back now. Not here. The time has changed."

Breaking apart, he held her upper arms, "Look at you. You have also changed. We should move on and never look back." Kissing her forehead, he left.

I could clearly see by the expression on her face the reason for her going back into the forest. It wasn't him. It was me.

***

After decades and decades and decades, I felt useless. No purpose, no goal.

Wrong.

Many purposes, many goals. But

just failure.

And I screamed in the darkness. Wasn't it eating me up? Was the darkness outside or was it inside?

Why didn't the Lord listen to me? What had I done to deserve this? Why didn't he answer my prayer?

I can get it that humans ask the Lord for many things. That's why He listens to some and grants them what they ask for. But I had asked Him for only one thing, and he hadn't granted it to me. I could doubt Him. All his creations.

Everything from the beginning to the end, but I didn't. I believe in miracles and they aren't explained by the laws of nature.

A miracle is defined as a happening of a remarkable event. Miracles are not explicable by natural or scientific laws and therefore attributed to a divine agency

Beginning from the bitch... hope.

***

I was following Henry on the road.

He seemed unwell, the way he was walking listlessly. He was going to work, early one winter morning, wearing a long overcoat because of the chilling effect from the wind and low temperature.

I didn't know why I was following him, but I was. I was surprised.

183

He coughed as a gust of cold wind slapped his cheeks, making his scarf loosen from his around his neck. Following his footsteps on snow, I looked back; I had no footsteps. I smiled, sometimes it pleases me to see such things. Marks of nonexistence.

For a moment, he stopped, and drew in heavy breaths. Then he put on his mittens quickly, as the snow began to fall again, puffy and soft.

I wore the hood of my white velvet robe, focusing my glacial blue eyes on him. He was walking again but fast this time.

This part of the road was lonely, and I wondered where all the humans were. Sleeping early morning or off to work.

After some wailing, Henry stopped again. He didn't move this time. I didn't know why because his back was toward me.

A sudden fear crawled in my mind, was he feeling my presence?

I halted, expecting him to turn around at any moment. But instead, I heard a moan, and he dropped his bag, clutching his abdomen.

I stared at him with a frown. Then he started coughing, harder with every second.

Must be the cold, I thought. Many humans caught cold in the winter. He would be okay in a minute. But he never became okay, he kept coughing, and was crouched now.

Slowly, I stepped toward him with a crease between eyebrows. Walking carefully, as if he would hear my footsteps.

The sound of him coughing echoed in my ears. A part of me didn't want to walk towards him or look him in his face, but curiosity destroys everything.

He was so close, I wanted to put my hand on his shoulder and turn him around. I stepped in front of him.

He had closed his eyes and was coughing without... without knowing... that... the snow... The snow... had turned red.

***

No, no, no... it couldn't be possible.

I continued to deny the state Henry was in. If there was one thing in the world I didn't want to believe, it was that Henry Cavills was dying.

I followed him again, this time, he was staggering toward the hospital. His eyes stern and panic on his face.

I watched as he stopped and coughed on his palm. Drops of blood again. he wiped them on the tissue paper quickly and continued his gait.

The hospital wasn't crowded. I had been to the hospital countless times, to take lives. I just hoped it wouldn't be Henry's here. I remember how he had rushed to the hospital and explained his suffering to the doctor.

I won't mention the details, but the doctor prescribed medicine for him and said they needed to run some tests. He had to wait several days for the test results.

He went home.

I went home too.

I don't know if he told Rose about it or not, but I didn't want to see him anymore. A part of me wanted him to die, but the other part wanted him to stay alive. I guess the first part had to do with motherhood. Maybe if he died, Rose would come back.

Of course! If he died, Rose would come back to me. I was so convinced about my theory that I almost began to feel happy and prayed for his death.

In fact, I wanted to go and take his soul, but that would make me a killer and it was also against my rules.

I wasn't depressed for him anymore. But it was possible if his test results were positive. I could hardly wait for the sun to sleep and rise again.

The next day, I followed Henry again. He collected his reports from the laboratory and without opening the envelope, he went to the doctor. My joy was enormous as the doctor gave him a terrible news.

"I'm sorry, Mr. Cavills," he told Henry, scratching his bald head. Then he put on his glasses, "You are sick, you have cancer." Henry sat still like a statue, hardly breathing.

"Don't worry, I'll give you medications…."

I went home, but I didn't follow him this time. I didn't want to see him giving this news to Rose or see her mourning. I just thought about the soon coming family reunion.

***

I spent my days staying busy with my job or fantasizing about Rose in the castle again. The roses will bloom. My Rose would also blossom once again. It would be like before and everything would be normal between us. It would be as if Henry had never come into her life and she had never married him.

I knew he would die, but I didn't know when. It could take years, or maybe just days, but I needed to be prepared for it.

No, better not to be prepared.

I smiled, whenever I got ready to say something, as it had always turned against me. But this time, I would be shrewd.

I just needed patience.

***

Eighteen days.

After eighteen days, I was standing in the street that led to Henry's home. I was happy, but not now, as nervousness had overwhelmed my happiness. I couldn't feel the aloofness of the winter as a gale made the leaves dance at my arrival.

On 30th December 1963, I marched toward the dark brown door, my shoes crushing the snow, my robes floating on it, making it smooth.

My eyes were fixed on the door, I strutted toward it, trying to stay calm. Facing the door, I blinked without knocking. I knew my face wasn't revealed as it was in the shadow of the hood, but this was the moment Henry would see me.

I came before his time, just for a talk. It was rather a royal way, and quite mannered as well, in which I was coming to take his life.

I had never knocked on a door to take someone's life before, so I was nervous.

Bad news... Henry was going to die.

Good news... Rose would come back to me. I couldn't stand outside forever, my white knuckles knocked on the door three times. No answer.

They were preparing for the New Year celebration. I couldn't even knock again. I lost my courage, but before I could hide, the door opened, and I was face to face with my daughter. She recognized me.

I didn't.

The dress she wore was revealing her arms and legs, but it appeared that she didn't care. Not anymore. Her hair was plaited, and her eyes had lost what little gleam they had.

For a moment, we looked at each other. It seemed as if even the wind had gone silent. Not even a breeze was there to disturb us. It seemed as if all the sounds had disappeared from the world, even from my throat.

Before she could slam the door in my face, I heard a voice, one that was soon going to vanish from the world. Henry's voice.

"Rose, who is at the door?"

Without unlocking her eyes from mine, I heard a cold tone coming from her mouth, "No one. Some child probably rang the bell and ran away."

Lies.

OBSERVATION No. 35

186

The best weapon a human uses to protect himself is a lie.

Even though she told him a lie, she just couldn't slam the door in her mother's face. The most surprising thing was, there was no fear in her eyes, and that encouraged me to stand there and face her.

"Rose? Rose?"

She didn't respond. It seemed as if only two people were on this small planet, Rose and me. One alive, one dead.

"Rose!"

Perhaps she was keeping the door open because she knew Henry couldn't see me and assumed he wouldn't be able to see me now either. How unfortunate.

"Rose! Rose… who is it?"

Finally, I turned my gaze toward Henry. I presumed Rose still believed he couldn't see me because she didn't reply. I asked humbly, "May I come in?"

The question was directed at Henry. Rose didn't move aside from the door.

"Rose, who is it?" He walked towards her and looked at her expression, "Do you know her?"

Henry looked tired and fatigued. His complexion had changed, and he wasn't handsome anymore. Dying makes a human look pathetic.

The snow was falling heavily now, and I knew it would be deep on the road after a while. But I didn't force my way inside. Sooner or later, I would be in the house.

"Do you know her, Rose?" Henry repeated.

Finally, when he shook her, she awoke from her thoughts and blinked. "You can… see her?"

Henry frowned, probably doubting his wife's state of mind.

"Of course, why shouldn't I be able to see her?"

Still staring at the uninvited guest, Rose said in a haunted whisper, "She is my mother."

Silence reigned the world.

"She is your… mother?" Henry looked at me.

What an awkward moment it was to be introduced like this to a person when I was the Grim Reaper.

I guessed Rose would let me in, and Henry was so stunned, I suppose he didn't know what to do.

I drew my hood back. I was looking young and beautiful. He hadn't expected me to be that young. He opened his mouth to say something, but

187

nothing came out. Rose was still staring at me, and I looked the same to her. There was a gust of wind and I spoke, "It's cold."

"Oh," Henry raised his eyebrows and moved away from the door, "please... uh... come in."

I knew Rose wouldn't take her gaze off me, it was better to converse with Henry,

I stepped inside, smiling kindly, "Thank you, Mr. Cavills."

I suppose it astonished him more that I knew his name too. I heard the click of the door. I knew Rose had many questions, but I needed her to compose herself.

"Have a seat, Miss..."

No name. I took a chair at the table and sat down without taking off my robe.

"Lovely house," I said without even giving it a look.

"Thank you," he replied, still standing, "Umm... it's just for the New Year celebrations."

Hesitation and confusion, I could almost feel the two things inside me. I waited for questions, but nothing came. Just uncomfortable staring and then silence.

I smiled at Rose, "What a beautiful young woman you have become." "I didn't expect Rose's mother to be so... young."

I smiled, turning my gaze to Henry. I knew my reply had a tinge of sarcasm in it, but I said it anyway, "I suppose you didn't even expect that Rose *had* a mother." "Well..." Nothing.

"Well..."

Nothing still.

"Well... I err..." a pause, "you never visited us before."

I had the confidence to answer every question. I didn't know where it came from, but I could feel it.

"Oh, no, Mr. Cavills," I said boldly, "I'm afraid you're wrong." He looked puzzled. I tapped my fingertips on the table rhythmically.

"What do you mean?"

"I mean, this isn't my first visit here," I was enjoying the look on his face, "I was even generous enough to bring flowers."

I could have laughed as his eyes widened. He must be remembering the roses I had left by the doorstep.

"I'm sure Rose knows I came here often, don't you, Rose?"

I cast my eyes at her. she was still standing by the door, looking at me with fury in her eyes. Resistance. I didn't say anything. I wanted her to speak now.

188

"She did tell…"

"Shush," I silenced Henry with a gesture of my finger. He was already intimidated by me. I looked at Rose. He didn't speak, knowing how intense the moment was.

"Yes, Mama," I didn't like the way she called me Mama now. It was so empty of everything, "and I remember your last letter very well. You are going to die."

"Ah… but you don't remember it *very well* dear," I told her and paused, "It was only a piece of *advice.*" "Does that even matter?" she snapped.

I leaned back in the chair, remembering how Aisha was and how different her daughter was.

"Of course, it does. It's just about the way you perceive words."

She folded her arms across her chest, "Well, I perceived them as a threat."

"Good Lord!" I laughed slightly, "Why would a mother threaten her child?"

She didn't move, "Exactly. Why would you, Mama?"

I sighed. There was no time to convince her. I would tell her everything when she came back and that would be when Henry died.

"Would you mind making dinner?" I asked her, changing the topic.

"I asked you a question."

"I'm staying here for a while. You can ask me afterwards."

"But…"

"Rose," Henry interrupted, "I think you should go and make dinner. Your mother will be staying for the night, I assume."

I don't know why he was so desperate for her to leave and happy to see me. I hadn't even expected him to allow me inside the house.

Without saying anything, Rose left us. It was good for her to go. I had to take Henry's life and it wouldn't be appropriate to take it in front of her.

'Have a seat, Mr. Cavills."

Henry sat on the chair in front of me. I knew he would start asking me questions, and I was ready to answer all of them now. But what he said confused me.

"I'm so glad you are here."

Whoa! I was so surprised that I couldn't answer, and my jaw dropped for a second. My eyes focused on him. Regaining my confidence, I crossed my legs, "Well, I know you have many questions. I want you to ask me as many as you wish. And I'll answer because you won't see me again."

"Oh, no, no, no!" he leaned forward in his chair, "But you have to stay!"

Poor man. How could I tell him it wasn't me who was leaving, it was him?

"Why should I?" I put my forefinger on my lips, thumb under my chin, attempting to control my smile.

"Because," he hesitated and continued in a low voice, "I have cancer. I'll die soon and I don't want Rose to be alone. She has often told me about you, and she has a great bond with you. I haven't told her about cancer. She said you are a great mother… a great friend, a great woman…"

He stopped because the smile of amusement on my face had been replaced by a frown of wrath. He hadn't told Rose! Screw you, Henry.

"And you, my dear Henry," I flared my nostrils, "are a great big bastard."

Henry stared at me as my words and tone had changed, and also, I had called him by his first name. And, of course, a bastard too.

"Pardon?"

"You didn't tell your wife! Why?" I controlled the anger bubbling inside me like a witch's potion.

"Because I didn't want to upset her. I wanted to spend my days with her in happiness as I'll die soon."

He glanced toward the kitchen to check if Rose was there, and then back at me. It was hard for me to control the urge to strangle him right there.

"Wrong," the words came from between clenched teeth, "You will die *now.*"

He was alarmed, fidgeting in his chair, "Are you threatening me?"

"Oh, no, I'm just *informing* you," I lowered my hand in my lap, "And here's another piece of information: I'll be the one taking your life."

He couldn't move, he was too absorbed in the conversation and also because my face was changing. There was no beauty now.

I was becoming a hideous figure, an old woman, with wrinkles on my skin and creases on my face. Henry's eyes widened in horror as he saw my road-mapped hands, and blue eyes turning grey.

I got up from the chair, it was the best time to seek vengeance from an old friend. My toothless grin was enough to make him shout.

"ROSE! WHO ARE YOU? WHERE IS ROSE?"

I stood in front of him, looking at the puny human, "She can't hear you."

White strands of hair escaped from the pins, a big mole appeared on my crooked nose, and my back became very stooped.

"WHY?" he began to get up, but snakes appeared form thin air on his chair, wrapping around his arms and legs, securing him to the chair.

Breathing heavily, he stared at the snakes in utter horror.

"ROSE!" he yelled with as much energy as he had. A dozen snakes were creeping toward him across the floor, he was shivering. "WHAT DID YOU DO TO HER?" he cried.

"No," I said airily, standing there like an old witch who could conjure snakes out of thin air, "No, Henry. I didn't do anything to her. She is fine."

"WHAT'S GOING ON?"

Now a snake was hissing by his ear, as if about to bite it. I bent forward, the mole on my nose almost touching him, "Don't you realize?" I grinned, "You are already dead!"

He was fearful of an old woman. Looking at the snake creeping on his neck, as if he were a magnet that attracted snakes, he yelped, "Why are you standing there? Take them off, help me!"

I smiled again. Poor man he was, "But I won't... because I'm the one doing it."

Henry looked at me suddenly. He had nothing to say. Perhaps he assumed I knew witchcraft.

"You see," I was pacing in front of him, very slowly, "I have to remind you of certain things –"

"STOP THIS!"

"Ahem," I didn't stop pacing but the snake slithered onto his lips, shutting them for me, "Bad manners to interrupt an old lady. I never thought my son-in-law would be so... *ill-mannered*. So, where was I? Ah... telling you certain things."

I looked at him thoughtfully, narrowing my eyes, "First, let me introduce myself to you... I am Death, Rose's mother and your mother-inlaw."

His eyes widened and I could hear his muffled sounds from behind the snake on his lips, "You are in nothingness. Henry Cavills is dead and I'm taking his life. Storytime."

I sat on the rocking chair like a grandma preparing to tell her grandchildren a story.

"Once upon a time, Death was wondering what the best definition of Death would be. She found a girl, whose name was Aisha," I paused, like a grandma pauses to catch her breath. He was turning blue now, "That girl called Death a belief. Death liked her definition, so when the girl died, she gave Death her daughter."

I looked at Henry who was listening, the snake still holding his mouth shut.

"Death named her Rose. She grew up to be a wonderful girl and Death grew with her as her mother."

The back and forth motion of the rocking chair stopped as I got up slowly and went to him.

191

"But one day, she met a bastard and fell in love with him."

My voice was turning angry and rising. I drew in a deep breath, purely for effect. A snake crept on my grey robes and stayed on my shoulder, facing Henry, "And that bastard proposed to her."

I wanted the snakes to bite him, eat him, go inside his mouth and pierce his body, but I resisted.

"They wanted to run away. When Rose told that man about her mother and showed her to him, you know what he did?" I crouched, face to face with him, "He shot an arrow at her." the nail of my forefinger touched his chest, "and it passed through her, right here."

He was shivering as if he was lying on ice, but there was sweat on his face.

"And it killed Death," I hissed like the snake on my shoulder, "not the arrow. But it killed her to see that he was a thief who had stolen her daughter." I drew back. A snake began to slide around his neck, "It is because of that bastard she became a sinner. And guess what?"

I turned around fiercely, "He never told her that he had cancer. Now she will never know how he died."

The snake was strangling him. His eyes grew wide, looking as if they would pop out of their sockets. I looked at the man for whom I had immense prejudice.

My victory.

The chair fell back from his struggling, and his head hit the floor hard. He couldn't even choke as the snake had shut his mouth tightly. I watched him as he closed his eyes and the snakes gradually drew back from his expired body.

"*The end,*" I whispered.

End of the story of Henry Cavills. I left because I didn't want to be seen beside a dead body or to see Rose crying.

Chapter 17

When the humans were celebrating the New Year, Rose was mourning over her husband's death. When everyone else was preparing for parties, she was preparing for a funeral.

Although I had hatred for him, I also felt sad for him, and it was because of that sadness, I decided to attend his funeral.

I didn't want Rose to see me even then. Wearing a black hood, I was the last person in the last row in the graveyard. That was only the second funeral I had attended. Everyone was wearing black, contrasting with the white snow, which was still falling steadily.

Poor Henry.

Sometimes I think it was all Rose's fault, not his. She decided to leave me. She decided to tell lies. She chose her life. But I couldn't blame my daughter for everything. Maybe I had more hatred for him than he deserved. He had given some of the best memories to my daughter, made her happy. Loved her.

I was going to leave when the eulogies caught my attention, especially when the priest invited Rose to speak. I couldn't see her from where I was, but I wanted to hear her voice to see if she was okay.

In that silence, I heard her clearing her throat, "Henry," her voice was slow and tragic, as if she had some weight on her chest, "I can still picture him with a bow… tall boots… and a dirty shirt… His messy hair and… and…"

She was crying, I could hear her sniffs, "I… love you. And I promise you, I will find the person who killed you… and kidnapped my mother…." She broke into sobs.

It came as a shock to me. She assumed I had been kidnapped! Oh, no. Won't she come back to me? To the forest? Oh, no. I didn't know what to do.

As I stood there, thinking of a solution, the humans began to evacuate the place. I was so lost in my thoughts that I didn't realize that only I was left there. Oh… Rose had walked past me… she hadn't seen me…

It was okay. Maybe she was so lost in melancholy that she had ignored everything. I didn't want her to see me anyway.

What to do now?

It wasn't right to stand there in the graveyard, a hooded figure only Rose could see. So, I walked towards the grave.

I crouched by it, looking at the gravestone.

Henry Cavills.

This would be the first and last time I visited his grave. I had been so cruel to him in his last moments, lost my temper and a part of me felt guilty about how I had frightened him, more than I had frightened Jason.

"Henry Cavills," I read the name again. There was nothing on his grave, no grass or flowers. Just snow. White snow.

And I remembered the first time I had followed him and seen red on white. I had thought it looked beautiful, what an evil thought I had.

Another guilt entered me. He had saved Rose's life many times in the forest.

I touched the snow.

"I'm sorry," I whispered. I knew very well that he couldn't hear me, but I had to say it. Then I brought out a bunch of red roses from under my cloak. I had played the role of an evil human.

I placed the roses on his grave, red on white.

A final act of kindness.

***

OBSERVATION No. 36

Humans have become so unholy because they love a human more than they love the Lord. So why do they mourn when the Lord steals that person? After all, they also stole the Lord's right and gave it to a person. It's only the Lord's right to be loved to the exclusion of all others.

Rose cried day and night for Henry. I could feel it, sitting by the tree in the forest.

I knew it because I could see the countless stars in the sky. She had said once her tears turned into stars.

It killed me to see her in pain. She didn't have patience.

As I scrutinized the different figures the stars were making in the sky, I thought about what Rose's next step would be. Would she go to Brasilia to see his parents? Would she report to the police that her mother was missing? Would she remain silent and live with it?

It was disturbing. The questions were disturbing.

I needed to keep myself busy and forget about it.

Maybe she wouldn't find me, then she would give up and carry on with her life. Maybe she would marry someone else.

194

Still, I anticipated her arrival at the castle. The nasty castle. It had turned dirty, the vines were creeping on the walls, the roses were dead, bushes had grown where plants used to be, and thorns were reaching out.

The worst thing was I didn't care. I didn't care to clean it. I didn't have any desire to clean it. Because somehow, I knew she wasn't coming back. She would never come back and see if I was here or not.

She feared this place now.

So, there was no point in cleaning it. What was the point of cutting down weeds?

OBSERVATION No. 37

Depression is a universal disease.

When I say universal, it includes me as well. It is just the amount of depression that matters. Some have it to a point that it kills them, some turn into the walking dead because of it, and some live with it, trying their best to be happy.

OBSERVATION No. 38

Just like the quiet ones have the loudest minds, the funniest ones have the most depressed heart.

In every century, I have encountered these kinds of people and I feel pity for them.

As a shooting star passed by, it gave me a flash through the eyes of a child.

"Mama, why was the star running?"

"Umm... I think it's in a hurry."

"Why? Where is it going, Mama?"

"I think it is out of shine so it's going to the sun to borrow some."

"And where is the sun?"

"At home. Okay, Rose, you have to make a wish whenever you see a running star."

"Okay."

"Quick!"

"I wish that Mama and I could stay together forever and ever and ever and ever and ever and..."

"Okay, okay! I think the star carried your wish with it and will drop it to the Lord."

"Really?"

"Yes."

The flashback ended.

The night was silent. There was no laughter. And in that night, I sang an old lullaby in a low voice, "Twinkle, twinkle... little star..."

***

OBSERVATION No. 39
Expect less to gain more.

I had always done it the other way around. I had always expected more and gained less.

I was roaming in the castle, the light was dim, and I was watching the walls on which Rose had written so many words in her childhood. I touched where she had written 'mama.'

Did she miss me the way I did her?

It wasn't fair. She could cry and I couldn't. She could talk to people, share her grief, but I couldn't.

It felt good to touch that word… Rose.

And it also felt good walking by the wall, I traced my fingers on them smoothly. Hundreds of words, it felt as if I was touching hundreds of books and hundreds of memories.

I didn't want to stop, but the snapping of twigs made me stop in my place. No animal had trespassed the graveyard so how had an animal come here?

I hurried out to see what it was, expecting a wolf.

But I saw… I saw… Rose.

She was walking boldly with a serious expression on her face. I was so happy to see her back. I hurried toward her to greet her.

"Rose."

Her face turned toward me, her feet halted and there was a twinkle in her eyes. As I approached her, my happiness grew steadily, reaching its zenith when I embraced her.

"You came back." I said, closing my eyes as I hugged her, "I missed you so much."

As I broke apart, I looked her indifferent face. I realized the sparkle in her eyes was because of tears. Holding her hands tightly in mine, it was hard to stop talking, "I was just thinking about you. I think about you all the time. Remember, you used to write on the walls? And when I asked you…" The excitement stopped when I heard the rustling of leaves.

Several voices. I looked behind her shoulder, and then back at her. Tears were dripping from her eyes now.

"Rose?"

Again, I looked behind her shoulder. There were humans coming that way.

"Go and hide, someone is coming," I tried to walk but was held back. Rose hadn't moved, her hand still in mine, but she was standing still.

196

And the sudden revelation made me pause. I frowned at her, "What's going on?"

She was about to break down. I waited for an explanation. And then came a whisper, full of indictment, *"You killed him."*

"Wha'?" I was taken aback and released her hand.

"You killed Henry," she whispered again, through gritted teeth.

The allegation made me stand for a moment, and I saw the men, several of them stopping behind Rose, looking at her.

"You are a murderer!" she whispered hatefully. I was so dumbfounded that I didn't know what to say or how to prove it wasn't true.

She had called me a murderer. Now I knew what people would call me if they saw me. Murderer.

And I felt an overwhelming hurt, "I... I didn't kill him."

"You did!" She snapped back, "and you'll pay for this!"

Turning towards the policemen, she said, "This is the woman who killed my husband. Arrest her, officers."

The men stared at her. Eyes of a dozen men were on her. I had no idea how to defend myself. When the men didn't move, Rose repeated, "What are you waiting for? Arrest her!"

I was too shocked to say anything. Perhaps she thought the officers could see me, just like Henry had been able to see me. How wrong she was.

"Sorry, ma'am, arrest whom?"

Rose pointed at me, "This woman, my so-called mother, she killed Henry!"

Silence ruled.

Her words were insulting as well as hurting. I stared at her, was this Rose? Was this the same person whom I had thought was kidnapped and was desperate to find me? How could she even think I killed her husband?

"I'm sorry, lady, there's no one here!"

As if the breath had been taken from her soul, Rose turned back toward me, held my arms and virtually yelled at the men.

"Can't you see her? She killed Henry!"

"Ma'am, I can't see anyone," then he looked at the policemen and asked them, "Can you?"

They all shook their heads, exchanging looks. Rose looked at me. The tears had stopped, replaced by horror. She looked back at the men, "Are you mad? Why can't you see her? I'm holding her arm, even Henry could see her!"

The final rays of sunshine were fading. Soon, delicious darkness would fall on the forest, but she was adamant to get me to jail.

"Why can't they see you?" she asked me instead.

197

I didn't answer. She asked again, this time, more forcefully, "Why can't they see you?"

"I can't tell you," I replied.

She locked her eyes on mine, "What are you? Who are you?"

Silence. I freed my arm from her grip and turned my back to her, walking away.

"TELL ME!"

"Miss Rose," the officer said, "Who are you talking to? There is nobody here."

"YOU MONSTER!" She cried. I didn't want to turn back now, and kept walking, "YOU RUINED MY LIFE!"

Different emotions were fighting for dominance in my mind; hurt, anger, guilt, confusion, regret.

Curling my hands into fist, I marched back to the castle.

"Miss Rose!" the officer seemed irritated, "There is no one here. You seem disturbed, let's go back."

"No!" Rose turned to him, "I was brought up here. Look at the castle, you must believe me!"

"I can't believe you because of some ancient castle. My men searched it, there is no one inside."

My assumption about Rose neglecting me had now been proven wrong.

"COME BACK, YOU COWARD!" She shrieked.

Coming to a halt, I looked back sharply, "Go home, Rose." The battle of emotions was still going on inside me.

"YOU KILLED MY HOME! YOU KILLED HIM!"

"Miss Rose." the officer walked to her with a gun in his hand, infuriated now, "You have no proof that someone murdered him."

"I have!" she was so hysterical and wild at the moment, no less than a wolf, "She wrote *you are going to die,* and she left roses on his grave. Only she leaves roses whenever she comes!"

"That isn't proof. I'm afraid we have to go back now."

The roses on the grave. My final act of kindness had turned against me. How unfortunate.

Raising her finger, as if she were admonishing him, she said, "I won't go anywhere without her. I'll avenge my husband's murder."

Anger was dominating all her feelings now. Typical human being. Yes, she was one of them. "Go, Rose."

"NO!"

The sun had set, and it was dangerous for them to be there now. Wasting time and provoking my anger. I knew she would never leave just like that.

"GO!" I shouted this time, the anger controlling me.

Black birds gathered in the sky, crows, bats, vultures, and ravens. The noise was remarkable. I had summoned them to scare away the humans. The men looked above, frightened, but Rose didn't.

I raised my head proudly. If she thought I was evil, then let it be evil.

She kept her expressions intransigent, glaring at me.

The ground trembled with an earthquake, the winds howled, and black clouds covered the face of the moon. The men were looking around in panic while Rose and I were too absorbed in each other's eyes, malice in hers and anger in mine.

The noise of the black birds grew louder, as they circled in the sky and the earth rattled again. The officer grabbed Rose's arm to move her away, but she wouldn't budge.

In the spur of the moment, she snatched the gun from his hand, pointing it at me, gripping it with both hands.

"You'll pay for this," her whisper was hardly audible in the noise of the birds and the howling of the gale, "Now, come with me!"

Ordering Death, it angered me to the peak. I glowered at her, *"NO!"*

The officer looked at the girl pointing the gun at nothing, her hair flying in every direction.

"We have to go, sir. A storm is coming."

"Miss Rose," the officer tried again, loudly over the noise, "Come on!"

"MOVE!" she ordered me again.

"I SAID," I thundered, "NO!"

The earth shook for the third time, sprawling men on the floor of my realm. The castle tumbled down like a house of cards. The men helped each other, fleeing now.

But only one soul held her ground like a warrior, Rose.

And then, in the noise of black birds and thunder, screaming men, screeching wind, and the roaring sound of the falling castle, only one sound was audible. The sound of a gunshot.

I never noticed the bullet passing through my chest, causing me no harm.

But it killed me.

Rose had shot her mother. Rose had killed her mother. I trembled with anger. Breathing heavily, the gun dropped from her hand and she stared at me in shock.

No blood.

Didn't she know I couldn't die? I could *not* die! Her husband's arrow hadn't killed me!

And the moment a daughter shot her mother, the black birds scattered, the sky became clear, the wind remained silent, and the earth remained still. Only a whisper rang in my ears before the officer took her.

"You are dead to me."

***

Sitting on the heap of obliterated castle, staring at the full moon, I was lost in thought.

OBSERVATION No. 40

Nature seeks vengeance.

I had sought vengeance from Henry for stealing my daughter, and Rose had sought vengeance from me for stealing her husband.

The scene kept rewinding in my mind, over and over, Rose was shooting me.

How can a daughter shoot her mother? And her final words kept echoing in the forest. You are dead to me.

No tears came this time, but the words were piercing me, deeper than a knife.

I had brought her up, I had taught her everything, I had taken care of her, then how could she not believe me?

I was wounded. I needed stitches. I needed someone to breathe life into me so that I could go to her, and everyone could see me, which would satisfy her. But no one could breathe life into me. And I couldn't go to her. *You are dead to me.*

Once again, a battalion of emotions began in my mind. This time, it was just two: anger and hurt.

Even when the wound hurt like hell, I got up and started walking beneath the weight of tons of memories. And the battle stopped, anger won.

I had never felt such anger in my life before, not even when I had taken the life of the greatest sinner.

Not even when I had taken the life of Jason or Henry.

This time, Rose had played the part I was meant to play, the role of Death. And she had taken life out of me, her very own mother.

The black birds sensed my anger and came to me again, crows, ravens, bats, and vultures.

Her presence still lingered in the forest even when she was gone, and I wanted it to remove it from my realm. Because of her, the castle was destroyed and there was no place to call *home* now.

Among the noise of the black birds, I could hear wailing and mourning of all the souls I had taken, and the howling wolves. Because someone had died, and Rose was responsible for that. A daughter had killed her mother.

The sound of gunshot pierced my ears again.

The black cloak swept the forest floor as I walked toward the place destined to be her mother's final home, the graveyard.

I knew she wouldn't ever leave me alone. Even when she was gone, I knew she wouldn't ever leave me alone.

After all these years with her, I wanted to be alone now. I was never meant to be her mother.

My pleasant life had gone.

As I walked, all the memories came back, one by one from the beginning, hitting every part of my body like pebbles. It was hard to stand. It was hard to even think.

There she was wrapped in Aisha's headdress. In the next moment she was in my lap and I was her mother. I had never slept, watching over her.

I had always known that humans couldn't harm me, but no one had ever hurt me like this.

I was chasing her, a little girl in the forest.

At once, I broke into a run. I couldn't cry so I ran, trying to escape from her memories. And the black birds followed me, and I just ran.

It felt as if I were falling from the sky and hitting the cold, hard earth again and again.

She stumbled, but I caught her, and didn't let her fall. At every stage I caught her when she was about to fall.

And then I stumbled, hitting the ground hard, my cheek rubbing against the soil. I clenched the earth with both hands, several pebbles in my fist. Getting up, I let it slip through my fingers and left only the pebbles in my hand.

With the stones in both hands, I ran faster this time, all the way to graveyard.

There it was, Aisha's grave with the words 'You are going to die' on the gravestone. I stared at the words in anger.

It was all her fault. If only she hadn't given me her baby that day. The vulture landed on her gravestone. The air was still and silent like a tomb.

"You ruined my life," I whispered in anger.

Dropping the stones, I started digging beside her grave. My hands shook, alone on my own. I had made mistakes and it wasn't possible to start over.

I dug more, kneeling, I dug with my bare hands. And even then, her memories were haunting me.

I was getting the result of my mistake as I wasted away. And as I dug, the black birds came with pebbles in their beaks, circling everywhere.

I dug deeper. Her words were echoing in my ears; you are dead to me. Dead… dead… dead… dead…

How I wished I was dead from her gunshot. I was done with digging the grave. I had dug my own grave.

I stood up as the pebbles began to rain down on me. I crouched, picked up one, twisting it in my fingers, watching the scene clearly as it had first hit my eyes.

"Where were you, Rose?"

"I was out, making something for you."

"Let me guess, a drawing?"

"No. I made you a crown of flowers, Mama."

I shot the pebble in the grave with as much force as the bullet had passed through my heart. I picked up another stone.

"I was looking for you."

"I was sitting on the tree, Mama."

"Don't you leave me like that!"

"We are always together!"

And the stone landed in the grave.

And another memory. Another stone.

Another memory. Another stone.

Soon, the grave was full of stones. I watched all the memories in the grave. They had turned hard and cold like stones.

I could never be whole again. She had killed her mother and it was her mother's funeral, only black birds were invited. I was the only one at my funeral.

I was the only one to say the eulogy for my death. No flowers, no tears, no life. I was only a crack in a human's life. All memories were dead. "Goodbye," I said to myself like a dead man singing. I lay down in the grave, saying farewell to everything.

Now I was only Death, no feelings, no life. Rose's mother closed her eyes.

Chapter 18

SIX YEARS LATER

The wind was different, so pleasant, making my hair fly, granting freedom. The grass swayed with the wind. The grey clouds invaded the sky, announcing the arrival of rain. The sun, as if afraid of the rain, sneaked behind the clouds, trying to pour some rays of light before vanishing.

The wind tried to move everything, trying to make everything notice it.

Nature was communicating. Wind with grass. Grass with butterflies. Butterflies with flowers. And flowers with trees. I communicated with nature now, not humans anymore.

I communicated with the stars and took long, lonely walks in the moonlight. It felt good to talk with nature.

I walked in the meadow, my hand passing smoothly over the golden grass. The distance had to be covered between the meadow and the cottage.

It had been years and I never went before time now. I went to take life when the person was dead, no more palaver or observations.

My golden eyes passed on the grass as it slipped beneath my palm. I cast my eyes once on the cottage as the screaming started because of the fire there. How did the fire light up? I didn't want to know.

I kept ambling in the grass that was reaching my waist, and the shrieks kept disturbing my serene time.

It would be over soon.

The cottage was the only one of its kind in the area, no houses anywhere. A lone place. The fire reached up to the sky, I watched it trying to touch the sun.

It ate up the wooden cottage like a mite eats wood. Even the wind was unable to extinguish it.

The flares were hitting the ground from every direction, like drops of splashing water. After some time, the screams stopped but the fire didn't.

Drawing near, I stared at the fire, the ashes falling like snow now. Without wasting time, I stepped inside.

The fire caught my clothes, lighting them up like a candle's wick, but nothing could burn my skin. My golden eyes searched for the dead human.

The wood from ceiling fell and the fire roared, sending up tongues of flames.

I turned right, there was a door. maybe the human was trapped inside and couldn't get out in time.

My searing hand opened the door, and yes, there was a young man, dead on the floor, half burned. My golden eyes stayed at him for some minutes, as if I were the one responsible for the fire.

He opened his eyes and looked startled, sitting upright, moving back from me.

"You are on fire!" he cried, warning me.

I didn't reply and just kept staring at him.

"Let's get out of here!" he was in utter panic.

He got up and began to run out of the door, but the beam from the ceiling fell, blocking his way.

"How am I going to get out?" he was talking to himself now.

The only thing that mattered to him was his life. Not even a burning woman caught his attention, only the wish to live somehow.

He turned toward the window, grabbed a chair, and hit it on the glass, shattering it. but the fire covered the window, blocking his way. He ran back, coughing and panting, but couldn't find a way out.

Finally, he gave up, slumping in one corner. Then he realized I was also there, he stared at me in horror.

"You are burning!" he told me in terrified voice. I didn't answer, just stared at him.

"You – are – going – to – die!" he stressed every word as if I was deaf.

His eyes widened. I was burning but my skin was all right. It frightened him even more.

"What are you?" he cried.

I had no interest in conversation now. I widened my golden eyes, it frightened him, and he grimaced as pain hit him.

In a moment, the man was twitching on the floor like a moth lured toward a flame.

He was gone.

For a second of two, I stared at the dead human, then I remembered I had other business as well, other lives to take.

The schedule was busy. I walked out of the cottage, and the wind blew, extinguishing the fire on me.

Once again, I moved on, in the meadow.

***

Beautiful lies.

The world is full of beautiful lies, most of which humans create themselves.

Standing in the center of the city, among the tall buildings, I recalled the schedule in my mind.

There were thirteen murders, twelve suicides, seventeen executions, nine death penalties, thirty accidents, six hundred and seventy-eight deaths in hospitals, fifty-six natural deaths and nineteen extras.

Very busy, no time to think about anything, no time to waste. I walked among humans, crossed the road and went to the building. Took three lives. Went to Cuba, then Japan, Mexico… in fact, I traveled the world. The last country was Norway.

The streets of Oslo were packed with snow. No one in their right state of mind would come out that day. I was alone, leaving no footprints in the snow as I walked toward the hotel.

Inside it was warm like summer. Some humans were there too, reading newspapers or eating and talking. I had to go to room number 394.

The elevator was packed, so I took the stairs. The room was on the third floor of the hotel. That part wasn't crowded, every now and then, an attendant would pass.

Looking at the doors, I stopped outside room number 394. I was early and had to wait. Standing outside, I could hear voices.

"What would you like for dinner, honey?" it was an old woman's voice.

"I'm not hungry today," the answer was of a weak old man.

I frowned. His voice seemed familiar. I stopped pacing, moving my ear closer to the door. I tried to hear more. "Very well, I'm also not hungry," there was a pause.

"Give me that book." Yes.

The male voice was definitely familiar. I wondered who it was, I could hardly see. I had never heard any familiar voice for the past six years. I had never gone back in the forest or to the castle.

I had never even seen someone familiar.

"I wish we had never come on this trip," the female spoke again," it's all snow for a week. I guess I should go and call the airport."

"Yes."

When the door opened, the woman came out, and I slipped inside the room.

Oh, this man. I stopped.

And the words 'Take this girl home' fresh in my mind. It was him, Henry's father: Fernando Cavills. I kept looking at him, he was old and weak. He looked torn by his illness, no longer a president.

He was reading a book. After a minute, he put it down, took off his glasses, and got up slowly. He paced to the shelf and it was clear from his expressions that he wasn't feeling well. He rubbed his left arm, then stopped, holding his jaw and frowning.

Before he could go to the door, his hand moved to his heart and he flinched, holding the wall.

The heart attack seemed severe.

He dropped to his knees, clasping the front of his shirt, trying to speak but no words came out.

Eyes closed, he sprawled on the carpet. It was the time to take his life. When he opened his eyes, he looked around, dumbfounded.

We were out, in the snow, he was barefoot, wearing short sleeves and yet not cold. Getting up, he looked around and saw me.

"Mr. Cavills." I wanted to hear something, to ask something, but didn't know what.

"How do you know my name?" he asked in surprise," Why am I outside? Why can't I feel the cold?"

"I am Death," I answered the question he never asked. This was the first time I had spoken to a human for six years, "And you are dead."

Before he could show his disbelief, I continued after a short pause.

"Only one question: why didn't you attend Henry's funeral?"

I could see, standing on the snow, the red roses that I had placed on his grave. And his parents weren't there.

"Do you also attend funerals?" "No.

Answer my question."

Folding his arms as if he were feeling cold, while in reality, in that nothingness, he wasn't. He hesitated to give an answer, "Because I didn't know that my son had died. Not until his wife came and told me."

"His wife? Who?" I asked forcefully.

"Of course, you don't know her, his wife, Rose."

"She came to you? When?" I frowned.

"Why are you surprised? Why are you interested?"

"Just answer the question," I said sternly, "When did she visit you?"
"About five years ago. She came with a baby, claiming it to be Henry's child and asked for his rights to the property."

I stared at him. Was it true? Rose with a child?

"She told me Henry was dead."

I hesitated. There was a pause. Perhaps he was waiting for me to ask more.

"Did..." I asked reluctantly, "did she... tell you how he died?"

"No," he frowned as if he had never thought about it. Then he asked me a question, "But if you are Death, you would know how he died. How did my son die?"

I didn't answer. It didn't matter now, "Why didn't you ask her?"

"I was angry with her and my son for eloping. I had disowned him. He wasn't my son anymore."

I was lost in thought again when he broke my reverie.

"How did he die?"

A flashback, red on white, then snakes on Henry. The reports in his hands.

"You have no right to know, you disowned him." He
opened his mouth to argue but nothing came out.

"But he is my son, I want to know before dying!"

"He *was* your son, and you are *already* dead."

It shut him up. It seemed hard for him to believe he was dead.

"So," I walked on the snow, "What happened to the girl?"

"Who?"

"His wife."

"Oh, well... I turned her away."

"WHAT?"

"I..." he seemed frightened at the sudden change of my tone, "I had disowned him."

"What did she say to you?"

"She wanted money."

I couldn't believe Rose would be so greedy.

"She used her child as a weapon against us, asked us for a share in the property. We didn't know if it was Henry's child. We had no proof."

"So?"

"So, we turned her out of house."

"You did what?"

"Asked her to go away, never come back. Never show her face again."
There was silence. How odd... humans even lied after dying. He couldn't say

he threatened her to make her leave... I stared at the man, wanting to say something. I didn't know when the words shaped themselves and came out.

"Where is she now?"

"Don't know," he shrugged, "Never saw her again."

Damn. Why did I want to see her? I shouldn't. Why? After she had killed her mother? There was no point.

"Why are you asking me about..." A

flinch and he was gone.

***

Wherever in the world I went to take a life, my eyes searched for a person, Rose. I found many roses in spring, not the one I was seeking though.

My thoughts were entangled in the man's words even now.

She had gone there for money. he said it as if she was the greediest person. It was strange she had a child. Was it a girl or a boy? But most importantly, was it Henry's child?

I couldn't imagine Rose betraying Henry.

Six years is a long time, I had no clue where she would be. I went to see her apartment where she and Henry lived, but it was inhabited by other humans now. I went to see all of Henry's friends' houses; Daniel, Alex, Paulo. No, they were living happily with their families.

The seasons changed and it was summer when I started wondering if I'd ever see her again. But she wouldn't live forever. Maybe I would have to wait twenty years, or even more to finally see her.

That was a long time.

I needed to see her now. Just once, for the last time. It was a fear of how much she had changed. Was she good and pious? Was she a balanced soul? Or had she changed like a rose in autumn.

The leaves began to fall. A year had passed since I took that old man's soul. I resisted my urge to see the forest. I knew if I would go there, a thousand memories would hit me like the stones I had cast in the grave. Pebbles of memories.

It was December 1970, when I saw her after seven long years.

Wearing a red cloak, with red eyes, I walked on the snow. It had already started in that season and it would end in that season too. It was Brazil and she was living in a village there.

I couldn't wait to see her, and at that same moment, I didn't want to see her. It had come as a shock to me. I hadn't expected this day would come so soon in her life.

I had expected her to live a long life.

The village was small, the snow was falling slowly and soon it would cover the streets in piles. The people were moving their things inside.

I had come before time again. Way too early just because… I don't know why.

There was a fountain in the middle of the village, a beautiful fountain with two figures of young girls, standing arm in arm. The water coming out of it was freezing cold, but I stepped on the circular marble of the fountain that was five feet above the ground.

Having courage, I began to walk on the stone-hard marble, my arms stretched out like a bird's wings to keep balance.

The side of my red cloak dipped in the water as I walked gracefully. No human could see me. From there, I could look around and see many faces. My eyes searched for the soul I had to take the next day.

But I couldn't see her.

So many people, would she ever come out that day? Would she pass by the fountain? Would she see me from a distance and run away? Or would she run to me again to kill me? Did she hate me that much even now?

I couldn't do anything but wait and watch. Circling the two figures, I couldn't help but imagine that one figure was her and the other was me. It gave me hope.

OBSERVATION No. 41

Helplessness and desperation in hope always gives pain.

A woman caught my attention. Her hair was covered with a scarf, her blue dress was covered in stains and dirt, her eyes had shadows under them, her shoulders hunched, her eyes down on the path, and several cracks on her red lips. She had no grace as she walked along the path.

She was a wilted rose, unworthy and unnoticeable.

My steps on the marble stopped as I stared at a once so familiar face.

OBSERVATION No. 42

Humans say time can heal everything. Sometimes, past leaves such deep scars that even time can't erase them.

And those scars were quite visible in her stroll, in her expression, in her appearance. She didn't even look up at me as she passed by. And it was then that I noticed a little boy holding her hand, skipping steps.

That boy appeared to be about six years old, very cheerful and full of life, reminding me of Rose in her childhood. He was just like Rose, her son. Had she remarried?

But I was more concerned about her state than marriage. She hadn't seen me, so I didn't call her. I watched as she turned a corner and vanished. My eyes remained on the place she had changed her path. Changed her path…

209

When she had chosen the human world, instead of the world I had created for her. If I had known it would make her *this,* I wouldn't have let her go and locked her up.

After several minutes standing still, I began to walk on the marble again, around the statues.

There was nothing to do be done. The sun had long set in and soon it would be dark. My legs didn't get tired from circling.

The stars illuminated the sky and I lay down on the marble, the street having emptied long ago.

My hand was in the water and the other on my chest, my knee arched and the other leg dangling down. Eyes glowed red as I looked at the stars. It was fear that kept me lying there all night.

OBSERVATION No. 43

Man was born to betray the Lord. Life is a game that humans play with Him. if they play fair, they win. If they cheat, they lose.

I didn't know how much she had cheated. In which category she was. How would I scare her and give her pain while taking her soul? I couldn't do that, and it scared me.

Rolling over on my side, I slipped my hands behind my head but kept my eyes on the stars. Why were there so many that night?

I watched the twilight, then the false dawn hiding the stars from me… Rose would hide too, disappear from the earth and then there would be no stars because she wouldn't cry.

Then came the beautiful dawn. I hadn't watched it for ages. It was the most charming moment earth had. I could hear chirping, and the windows opened.

I also got up, sat on the marble, my crimson eyes fixed on the narrow alley Rose had gone into last night.

Many people came out and the square was crowded again. The snow had stopped falling long ago and it was a pleasant, sunny day.

There she came, wearing a hand-knitted cardigan, her hair in a bun, but no boy by her side. She was going to work, with a bicycle. She passed by me without looking, and I followed her.

After walking for some time, Rose mounted her bicycle and rode it slowly because there were people there. it was a good speed for me to follow her.

Should I stop her and talk to her? Should I take her life without explaining anything, without a word?

But it seemed unfair. She hated me. Was it fair for her to die in that hate?

But what was the point of explanation? She would die and there would be no need for it. It had been half an hour and Rose wasn't stopping anywhere.

Where was she going? The village was left behind. In fact, the city wasn't far away. She was in a populated area, riding with a straight face.

She took a turn, I followed. What if she noticed me? I pushed away the thought, it was out of the question.

She was going toward an industrial area, no people just cargo trucks. And it occurred to me that she worked there.

Why did she work so far away? Where did she leave her child? With whom? A honk.

A truck moving at speed came out from the left, and Rose was lost in her thoughts.

"NO!" I screamed.

She looked back at me, recognition passing across her face.

"ROSE!" A

honk.

She looked sideways. A scream.

I closed my eyes. Silence.

I didn't want to open my eyes. I couldn't see her. Noise, many steps, many voices.

Claret eyes saw three men there, looking at the woman lying in the middle of the road in a pool of blood. I walked toward the scene.

It was too bad to even look at her, redder than the cloak I was wearing. Her skull had broken, her limbs lay there as if she had no bones. I can't describe it. it horrified me to see her like that.

I wanted it to change, go away, so I changed it all into her nothingness.

When she opened her eyes, she was on the soft, green forest floor, a once known place. She blinked, confused at what had just happened.

Then her eyes settled on me and she stared. I had expected nothing, except hate from her, but what she said made me speechless.

"I had… a very strange dream…"

I wished I could tell her it wasn't a dream. But feeling no pain and all right, she must have assumed it was a dream.

"How did I get here?"

I didn't reply. Wasn't she supposed to berate me? Why was her tone so soft?

She remained silent after that. sitting on the heap of castle stones, I couldn't guess her intentions.

Slowly, she got up and went to the bushes where once roses used to blossom. She scrutinized the wild bushes for some time. I didn't want to disturb her.

After some minutes, she knelt, touching the weeds where once refined grass used to be. It was now a garden full of weeds. Her eyes moved to the heap of webbed rocks and she went to them, touching them.

Tears began to fill her eyes. She must have been encountering the memories of her childhood. Her castle, her home, her garden, her birds, her animals. It had gone, all of it.

Then she sat down on the rock beside me without saying anything. I never looked at her. I knew she would burst into anger any time. It would all be malice again.

But she never said anything, and I never looked at her. After several silent minutes, I heard a sniff, which made me look at her. The silvery streaks of tears were rolling down her cheeks.

"Why are you crying?" I asked kindly.

"Because," she sniffed, "I'm so ashamed of myself." Oh, no.

Fear again, no, please don't be a sinner. I couldn't handle that.

"Why? What did you do?"

I frowned. She wasn't answering me. She must have done some great sin.

"I did something terrible."

"Which sin?" I had nothing to say to comfort her.

"I am so... so... so..." she emphasized the word, "so... sorry, Mama."

How strange it was to hear the word Mama again. It had lost its meaning to me, that part of me was long gone, dead.

But I was more concerned about the great sin.

"Why?"

We never looked at each other.

"I – I – I," she struggled to overcome her reluctance, "I accused my mother. And it's a great sin. I... I found his medical reports and he had cancer." I relaxed. That didn't count as a sin. She continued as if she were accepting everything standing before a judge in a court.

"I blamed you that day. I was so horrible to you... I'm so sorry!" she looked at me with pleading eyes.

I swallowed and licked my lips. How mature she was now. It was hard to believe.

Silence existed. I didn't know why there was hesitation between us. How could I ever tell her she was...?

"I'm so glad you made time to see me," she said slowly, "How is your life?"

I cleared my throat, "Busy."

"What are you doing?" her voice was humble.

"Work, like always."

At this, I heard her laughing slowly and sadly, "I remember you used to go to your work and I never asked you what your work was. What is your job?"

I shrugged one shoulder, "You'll know soon."

"I hope it's better than mine. I feed the pigs."

I didn't reply. It seemed she had led her life in poverty.

"So, how's your life?"

"I really… don't know. Work, home, my son, Jim."

"And your husband?"

She looked at me and smiled, "He *died* seven years ago, from cancer."

I frowned, "You didn't remarry?"

"No… I couldn't…. I was pregnant. I went to his parents when I couldn't pay my bills. But they didn't let me come in. I told them it was Henry's child, but they didn't believe me. And when they heard Henry was dead, they were even angrier with me. They threatened that they would take Jim away from me, so I left."

That diplomatic man, he had said Rose was greedy. He should have told me how helpless she was. I didn't sympathize with her. I was feeling guilty at what would come next. Would her hate increase for me?

"I can't remember how I happened to be here. There was a weird dream and…"

"What happened next?" I diverted her attention.

"Oh. I had nowhere to go and I was so ashamed of myself but… I came here, in the forest. I had no other home. But you weren't here." She paused, her fingers on the rock.

"My home was gone, no home here either. I couldn't face you, so I left. I met an old and kind woman who gave me shelter and helped me find work. She lived alone, so I stayed with her at her house. I go to work, and she takes care of Jim."

I was curious; why wasn't she afraid of me? The bullet had passed through me, the arrow as well and they hadn't killed me. she was afraid of me then, why not now?

She wasn't even asking the questions she was once so desperate to know the answers to.

"I came here again, two years ago."

"Why?"

"I wanted to see you and ask for forgiveness before I died."

213

And the scene played in front of my eyes again; the bicycle, the loud honk, the truck, the scream, the bang.

I clenched my red cloak in my fists, closing my eyes. I couldn't see that again.

"But you are already *dead*."

Her eyes looked at me in disbelief, questioning and complaining. I had my eyes fixed on hers now.

"It wasn't a dream. The truck hit you and you're dead."

Tears began to well up in her eyes. there was nothing I could do to comfort her. "You're lying," she whispered.

"I'm not."

"Stop! Mama, stop."

My jaw clenched, "And I'm not your mother."

Another bombshell fell on her head. It was worse than the first one. It seemed she wasn't as shocked by it this one.

It seemed all the sanity in me was fading away, there was too much that time couldn't erase.

She turned her face away from me, "Leave me alone!" I didn't. I couldn't. *I wouldn't.*

Impulsively, I held her wrist and started strutting. She didn't protest, following me. I couldn't look at her doleful face.

Walking fast, we reached the graveyard and I didn't know if she had seen where we were going or not. It was her presence, the old Rose that still lingered there, pointing at the gravestones and asking me what they were.

I stopped, dragging her forward with a jerk.

Pointing at the gravestone, the dusty words were still there. I didn't know what I was feeling, but I was sure all my sanity had been chased away.

Aisha Jason
1915 – 1940
You are going to die

"Your mother."

She remained still, staring at the words. Without wasting time, I held her upper arm and led her to the next grave.

Her mouth slightly open as if she were having flashbacks of things she was ashamed of. For which she had wanted forgiveness. And she closed her eyes, the tears fell from her cheek onto the grave's soil. I stood beside her, staring at my own grave.

Mama
Beginning to end
You are dead to me

Then I held her shoulders and turned her to face me.

"Look at me!" the order was like that of a feral monster. She didn't open her eyes, shaking her head.

"LOOK AT ME!" I asked loudly, insanely.

With a startle, she opened her eyes and looked at me. My chin trembled.

"I am Death," without pausing, I continued, "Jason forced Aisha to marry him. She was his slave. When your pathetic father was going to sell you, the drunkard fell down the stairs and died. Aisha ran away but she soon died and asked me to take her baby, *you*. I agreed because she had a strong belief in me and because it would give me a chance to be a human." I shut my mouth, and Rose was crying harder now.

I said without regret, without hesitation, letting it all out, "I wish I hadn't!"

She looked at me suddenly. No tears were covering my face like hers, but those eyes... those red eyes, they were shedding invisible tears that only I could feel.

I gulped and confessed, softly this time, "I loved you, Rose. I loved you... and look..."

I cast my eyes on my own grave, "And look what you did to me."

There was nothing left. I had told her everything. Slumping on the ground, I was lost. I didn't look at her, it was difficult.

"History is strange. It repeats itself but differently," I said in a trance, "Aisha was forced to leave her home, and you left your home willingly." I swallowed my pain, "For her, the words 'you are going to die' were the best advice, yet for you, they were a threat."

I paused. How different she was from her mother. "She was forced to marry Jason, and you married Henry willingly. Jason forced her to change her religion, and Henry asked you once and you changed it. Aisha had a daughter. You have a son. How different you are from your mother, Rose."

I fell silent.

The raven sitting on the skull stared at me as if I were the cruelest person on earth. Unblinking, unmoving.

As Rose sobbed, the silence of the graveyard grew deeper. I knew it was time to leave now. It was killing me, even the thought of taking her life. History repeats itself... but differently.

"You took your mother's life," I whispered, "Now your mother is here to take your life."

She continued her sobs. It was as if my bones groaned as the harsh reality hit me once, twice, thrice... I didn't want to do that.

I just wished there was another companion who could take her life, instead of me.

If she had to leave, I wished she would just leave because I knew she would never leave me alone. Even if the memories were in the grave, they still haunted my mind.

"I'm so sorry! I'm so sorry!" she sobbed.

"Me too," I whispered.

Everything was my fault too. The blame couldn't be placed on her alone, "Time for you to go."

"No! Wait." she controlled her crying, "Can I... can I see my son for the last time?"

"Yes, you may. But he won't be able to see you, nobody will." She nodded.

"Close your eyes, let me take you home."

She closed her eyes, I held her hand and she closed mine too. I didn't want to open my eyes the moment she touched my hand. But soon, she slipped her hand out of my grip.

My eyes remained closed for a long time, it was a very strange feeling and all I knew was, as the moment grew close, I didn't want to feel anything anymore.

Upon hearing a sniff, I gulped but didn't open my eyes. I could still see her childhood in those closed eyes. Her teenage years, her past with me.

I didn't want to see *anything*, but I opened my eyes.

Her home. It was a lot like Jason's, cardboard patches on the windows, clothes lying waiting to be attended to, empty water bottles on the floor, everything out of order.

It seemed I was back in Jason's house. I had always thought she was Aisha's daughter, and had forgotten Jason was her father too. How could I think she would be entirely like Aisha?

I walked around, staring at everything while Rose looked at her son who was playing with his toys.

There was a bed, a rocking chair, some old, torn books. It represented a clear image of destitution.

She had lived in a paradise and now *this* was her home.

I held the book, nothing special. I held the pen, twisted it in my fingers, dropped it on the floor, rolling away. It stopped, a box the obstacle in its way.

The box. It was the same old box I had seen years ago under the bed, and Henry had asked what was in it. She hadn't told him.

I crouched, touched the box, frowned, glanced at Rose. She was too busy looking at her son.

Kneeling, the red cloak spreading on the floor, I held the wooden box, slowly opening it. *Red.*

There was nothing left in me. I couldn't even touch it as if it would burn my fingers. I was nothing, was I?

My trembling hand reached out and held the rose lying on the top of a red gown. I had left this last rose with a note, 'you are going to die'.

The red dress.

Picking it up in both hands, I laid it down on the floor beside the rose. There were some drawings, the ones she had made in the forest.

Slowly, I looked at them one by one, my red lips slightly apart. Animals... birds... plants... scenery... and me.

The last one was of me. She drew it when she heard I couldn't see myself in the mirror.

I looked at her, her back was toward me.

Back at the picture.

OBSERVATION No. 44

Every picture tells a story.

I left the pictures and looked in the box again. There it was; Henry's bow and quiver. Then there was a crown of flowers, roses. There was a teddy bear too.

She had treasured these things, the things from her past. Were they a memory or punishment?

Slowly, I stood up, it was time, slipping my sketch in my cloak, hiding it from her.

"Rose."

After years, it felt strange to say her name again. She turned around, her face wet with tears as if she had never cried that much in her life.

"Please forgive me, even if I'm not worth your forgiveness," she wept, whispering in desperation, "You hate me. I know. I also know that you won't cry for my absence because no rose showed up in my house. I waited seven years for just a single rose... nothing. You forgot me, Mama."

I swallowed, trying not to lose my sanity again. She waited for an answer but there was none. The time had come when I could be alone again. No one to talk to, there would be no one at home. There would be no home. If only I could lose my memory.

"Can you do something for me?"

I nodded. I knew it would be like Aisha's request: put these words on my gravestone.

She walked closer.

217

"Take my son away in the forest. Make him your own son, please!"

As if someone had breathed life in me, I raised my chest, a crease appeared between my eyebrows.

OBSERVATION No. 45

History repeats itself. *But differently.*

Her hopeful eyes were begging, my red eyes were bleeding.

"Once, a mistake," I paused, "twice, a fool."

I grimaced as her tears fell on the floor, I could hear their splash. Her eyes were still pleading. The fingers around the rose tightened and I held it up. Then fear and pain.

I shot the rose toward her, the pointed end in her chest. Her eyes popped as the it hit her, dropping her on the floor, with the rose in her chest.

I closed my eyes.

When I opened them, I was back in the industrial area, standing on top of the highest building, looking down at her cadaver with an eagle's eye view. The red rose had disappeared, but she was bleeding from where it entered her chest.

Standing there, my jaw trembled as the wind blew, waving my cloak like a flag.

I had lied to myself. I could never forget my daughter as the memories were still alive. And this pain would stay with me forever.

Moving forward, I jumped.

Hitting my feet hard on the road, my fingers on it, I stood straight up. Blinking once, I then walked toward the dead body.

It hadn't hurt, jumping from the highest building. Then why did it hurt as if I was being punished in hell for killing my daughter?

OBSERVATION No. 46

Man learns from experience. Finally, when he has learned everything, his life ends.

I took a step, but something caught my eye.

A book.

I crouched to pick up the familiar, old book that I hadn't found in her box. Sticking out of her pocket, the color was stained with blood.

***

It was her funeral, and I was sitting in the forest, leaning against a huge rock of what was once a castle.

Staring blankly in the air with the book lying in my lap, I had no courage to open the Pandora of memories. Her presence still lingered there. It was just too much, even when I was going to live forever, it couldn't be erased. With trembling hands, I opened the book and read silently.

Rose: me
Mother: mama
Butterfly: beauty
Sun: life
Imagine: to think unexpected

Every word brought back a memory. There she was, writing wrong spellings of beauty, telling me about her dream when she was flying on a butterfly, trying to look directly into the sun without blinking, holding the injured toucan.

Every word in her book had a meaning except one: death.

Turning the page, wearing the same red cloak, wearing a smile on my red lips, I didn't notice as I reached the last page.

There was the word death without any meaning.

When I saw the last word, I knew I would never be able to forget it.
She had asked that question when she met Henry, but I hadn't answered because I had no experience of that word.

How ignorant I was. All these years, it was all the emotion I was feeling. Sometimes, the brightness in the eyes is not the reflection of stars, it's something burning inside that ignites the soul.

Rose was wrong when she said I wouldn't cry.

Red streaks of tears escaped my red eyes, the fire inside sent flames to the sky, turning to ashes what was left inside.

Living a long life is a curse.

Love: Mother.

THE END

From the Author

Thank you for reading my first novel, *Death's Life*. I hope that you enjoyed reading my story as much as I enjoyed writing it. As a selfpublished author, I rely on reviews and hearing your feedback, so please take a few moments and post a review on Amazon.

Thank you again, and I hope this will be the first of many novels. You might like to read my anthology of poems, Death's Lament, which is currently available on Amazon: https://books2read.com/u/3JVJzQ

For more information and the latest news about forthcoming novels and events, please contact me at b.latifauthor@gmail.com or visit my website www.blatifauthor.com or my Amazon Author Page: https://www.amazon.com/author/blatif

Best wishes

B. Latif

Made in the USA
Monee, IL
01 May 2020